TARGET HUDSON

Imperial Germany
Strikes New York Harbor

A NOVEL

RICHARD SACKERMAN

HELLGATE PRESS   ASHLAND, OREGON

TARGET HUDSON

Published by Hellgate Press
(An imprint of L&R Publishing, LLC)

Published by Hellgate Press
(An imprint of L&R Publishing, LLC)
2350 Ashland St., #104-176
Ashland, OR 97520
email: admin@hellgatepress.com

Cover & Interior Design: L. Redding
ISBN: 978-1-954163-87-4

Printed and Bound in the USA
10 9 8 7 6 5 4 3 2 1

To my wife Patty, who played Jill to my Jack
and went up the hill with me.

1

The Docks 7/26/16

I DOZED OFF IN POP'S favorite chair by the open window. It was hot and humid, and I was exhausted from my shift at the docks. Summertime in Jersey must be experienced to be appreciated, and I don't mean liked. Think of trying to breathe through a few layers of burlap while your shirt is soaked with sweat and your shorts keep riding up under your breeches, chafing you between the legs. That's July in Jersey City. Nestled between the Hudson and the Hackensack, Newark Bay and the Kearny swamps, we've got more humidity here than Borneo and more mosquitoes than Panama – at least, that's what I imagine. We baked in the sun all last week, too, with a heat that rivaled the Sahara itself. Folks keep to the shade in the daytime and hover about their stoops late into the night. Not saying much, not doing much, just sittin' out front trying not to sweat. I've had a rash for over a month down below and only petroleum jelly gives some relief (I hope to be over that before my girlfriend Molly makes it back from the Poconos). If she gets a look at me scratching, she'd wonder if I picked something up from one of the saloon gals on Grand Street. Well, the truth is, I don't much go to those places, and if I do, I'm with my buddies. I've been through a lot with them and we all steer clear of the harlots these days. Sort of a mutual protection pact, if you will.

Molly showed up on an unusually cool day about a month ago at the Hudson River, when I was caught up with a crew loading a few tons of wire for the Brits over in Belgium or France. I saw her looking down at the water in frock coat and beret and wondered what it would be like to talk to her. She'd lean on a piling for a few minutes, gazing out at the harbor or Lady Liberty, and then she'd up and move to the next piling or a bench. Her coat was unbuttoned and as she moved, a flash of red would flicker from beneath it. Long, blond curls trailed out from under her hat. This was the last week of June and a nicer day for working hard you couldn't pick. We were hours from finishing, and I had to keep my eye on the bales of wire or I'd cut my hands on the barbs while guiding it. Lenny was up on the derrick and he had a rhythm going that was hard to catch up with if you missed a beat. He'd pick up a load off the dock, swing it slowly landward, and then bring it back to the ship for the stevedores to guide into the hatchway. He said the load gained momentum that way and sped things up. I think he's nuts, but he's got the steam-crane certificate, not me. We were half done loading the pallets and she was still there, staring down into the waves or looking across at Manhattan. By the time we had the 500 rolls aboard she was gone.

Two days later it rained, and she showed up again. She had the same frock coat but a blue peaked cap hiding that explosion of wind-blown curls. There was a shipment of medical supplies to deal with and I was working a hoist with Nick while Lenny attended to huge crates of bully beef and biscuits on his coal-burner. I'd peek over at her occasionally but lost track of her before lunch. "What's a gal doing by herself walking the docks in this weather?" I wondered, but like I said, there was lots to do and I lost sight of her. The wind kept playing tricks, too, and you had to keep an eye on the swaying cargo nets or you'd get whacked. Lenny finished up first and went up to chat with Foreman Schuyler while Nick and I wrestled up our last few bundles of bandages and boxed cotton. Ten minutes later Len was back telling us the boss said shipments were picking up over the next few months and wanted to know if we had any friends looking for work. I remember it rained all day but seemed to stop a minute or two before quitting time. I left my slicker on a nail in the shack, picked up my lunch pail and joined Nick and Lenny for the walk home.

We stopped for a shot and a beer at Sully's, like most Friday nights, and talked about this or that. Nobody mentioned seeing the woman, and I wasn't about to bring it up either, as I thought of her as my personal challenge. John Sullivan himself was behind the bar and after our first round refilled our mugs for free out of the new Pabst tap. "Try this Blue Ribbon and let me know what cha think," he said, sliding the mugs downstream to us. Well, he got three glasses raised in unison and an old Gaelic *Slainte* for his trouble. And a fine beer it was, that lager, and we hoisted a few more after that.

We might order it again next time, too, but more likely we'd be back with our usual Ballantine. Old habits die hard, and the Sullivans had not carried Pabst in all the years I'd been going there. As Newark breweries go, Ballantine's seemed to have the best water-source, and you saw their delivery wagons all over the area. For Pabst to make a comeback in Jersey City they'd have to beat the price at the tavern or beat some heads on the delivery routes. Maybe a little bit of both?

"And why are you suddenly tapping Blue Ribbon in this foine establishment?" asked Lenny. Now, just so you know, Lenny's a six-foot Polack, but could pass for an Irishman with his red hair and green eyes. He always has a ready smile and is good for a laugh. A hard worker at the docks, he often has a few more irons in the fire than I can track. Sometimes it's a team of horses for sale, or a few crates of scotch he picked up and needs to dump cheap. Other times he's collecting for some church function or Saint Theresa's Orphanage. But here he was on his stool at Sullivan's, affecting his Irish brogue. After the first three or four he could pass for County Cork.

"And why would I not?" replied Sully. "When I could pick up a discount from my relations? My new brother-in-law just so happens to be a brewer at their Raymond Boulevard plant." Well, we had heard of this marriage between Mary Sullivan and Tommy something-or-other but knew little of its benevolence on us until now.

"Right, and pour us another one then," chimed Lenny, "and here's to the lovely couple!" Nick then stood up suddenly, raised his glass, and in a fine tenor, began the strains of George M. Cohan's ditty:

For it was Mary, Mary, plain as any name can be.
But with propriety, society will say, Marie.
But it was Mary, Mary, long before the fashions came.
And there is something there that sounds so fair,
It's a grand, old, name!

• • •

Nicky O'Halleran is a native of Galway, a dark-haired sort who fancies the cards and dice. To look at him, you wouldn't think he could sing like a choir boy, but he sure could carry a tune. He plays a fiddle Saturday nights at the Hibernian Hall on Bergen Avenue, and the snare drum while marching with their Pipe Band. A nicer fellow you couldn't meet, but woe to the sport who tries to scam him. With his five feet height and 140-ish weight, he was quick on his feet and could hold his own in a sparring match. His face did show a few adjustments to his features made when he wasn't quick enough, but that didn't keep him from speaking his mind, or lessen his charm with the ladies. He's lately going on about starting a baseball team with some of us dockers, where we'd get together on weekends over in West Side Park in a league that's started up over there. It was a big deal last year, with a good group of teams formed up already. Up 'til now, the dock bosses wouldn't allow it, but things change. We've heard a lot about it on the job, here at Sully's, or anywhere folks get together to shoot the breeze. Lenny said he made some money on it but he didn't say how. Nick thinks we've got a good shot, as dock work gives you the shoulder muscles to knock the ball far. There's a whole set of rules to it that he's been explaining while we're loading the ships, as if we didn't know them already. We've thrown the ball around a bit and I can even hit it pretty far once in a while.

• • •

I was born in a small town in Westphalia, Prussia, in the Ruhr River Valley. Like my parents, I have the blond hair and blue eyes common to the region. Mother and Pop brought me through Ellis Island in '96 and together we picked up American quicker than most, what with Pop's job working at the produce market and dealing with the public. He'd educate us at supper with the phrases and local slang he picked up from the folks who stopped by for tomatoes or peaches that day. Pop had an ear for translating the European tongues spoken in our neighborhood with help from hand gestures, a small chalkboard, and his years at the customs house back in Elberfeld. His six days a week at Bengston's Market got him more than just nine dollars a day or a few free potatoes — he'd light his pipe in the parlor after dinner and share the new crop of words, news, or political views he'd learned over the vegetable scales that day. Night after night I'd pick up varied tidbits such as how to greet somebody in Lithuanian or French, the new way Manhattan folks serve green beans, or the scoop on getting favors at Tammany Hall. There were bits of wisdom on how to deal with noisy drunks, snobby ladies, or the clergy, who always sought a discount. Other times when Mother went off to the kitchen, he'd lower his tone, lean over toward me and say something like, "Augie, you won't believe who walked in today when I was choppin' onions," and he'd go on from there about how "This big, brute of a fellow come in and quietly asked me for ten pounds of butter, winked at me, and said he was having his boyfriends over that night." Then there was the time when a well-dressed lady looked him in the eye and whispered, "How about a quick roll out back?" He stood there with his mouth agape, hands covered with grease from chopping meat when, gratefully, in walked Mrs. McAllister from next door, asking, "And how's the Missus today, Herr Landesmann?" Well, that quelled the hussy's urge in a hurry, and out she went without further ado. Yes, I can see now why Pop would keep those cards close to his vest! Mother would have a fit if she heard him telling me those things, and not see the point behind his exposing me to the darker side of folks. Looking back on it, I can see there was always a reason behind the storytelling, sort of a moral lesson to impart to me, his only son.

Taking my eyes out of the beer mug I caught the reflection of Nick in the mirror, just wrapping up his melody, and nearly tripping over the Sullivans' cat as he approached me. "Damned cat," says he, "folks'll think I'm in my cups and me with but five pints under me belt." He draped his arm over me and quietly said, "That gal from the docks I seen ya eyin' this afternoon, what's up with that?" Well, he could have knocked me over, for I was certain I was the only one who noticed her. My shock must have shown, because he patted me on the back and said, "She's all yers, August, I was just wonderin' why you didn't take a smoke break and go have a word with her!" (Nick always called me by my given name, or worse, "Mister Landesmann," despite my younger years and protests. He'd say I looked like a leader and damned if he wouldn't treat me like one).

"She's been by a few times the past couple days," I told him. "I was sort of wondering what must be going on in that head of hers. Could be she's blue about something, or missing someone, or maybe she's thinking of jumping in and ending it all," I took a swig, and continued. "You hear of this sort of thing from time to time on the docks, and I figured, well, if she did something like that with this current, she'd be swept away before any of us even noticed it happening!"

He looked me in the eye and said, "August, yer a nice fellow, smart and all, but ya don't notice much, do ya?"

"Huh?" I replied, not having the foggiest notion where he was headed with this.

He tossed down a shot of Jameson's, belched, and continued with, "Well, in my vast experience with women, having been with a few myself, I've yet to see a gal down in the dumps who was whistlin' and tappin' her foot! Cheesh, August, yer imaginary dark thoughts are cloudin' yer perceptions! Had ya joined the pipers with me a few years back like I asked ya, perhaps the feel o' music would open yer eyes!" *What with all the keening and screeching sounds, the last thing I'd do would be to beat a bass drum in the Pipe Band like he suggested. I did like the uniforms, and thought I'd look impressive in those tartans, knobby knees or not. I told him I'd think about it, but a few years passed since that day!*

Nick always seemed to confuse me with his antics. Was he pulling my leg about her? Or worse, was I too dense to notice such a detail? I began to feel a bit warm around the neck and burst out with, "Tapping her foot? Whistling, too? You've got to be kidding, pal! She was blue as can be, staring down into the Hudson on a dreary day. How can anyone be musical on a dark, rainy day?"

He laughed out loud and said, "Maybe ya were right to skip the Pipe Band, August. If ya had but listened to me and picked up those drumsticks I'd a gotcha educated in all sorts of music — not jus' yer marches and jigs, but yer dirges and requiems, too. Even today's Ragtime or nee-gro spirituals share some of the basic rhythms and beats. It's all mathematical — ask yer Pop. A rainy day is perfect for thinkin' up new tunes, what with the sound of the wind and rain to help guide yer way."

Two more Blue Ribbons appeared. Sully grabbed off two nickels. Lenny came back from the john just then and said, "Hey, what about me?" Quick as a flash, the barman completed the third transaction, and plopped down a basket of peanuts to boot.

Nick continued, "What yer missin' about this gal was she was creatin' music on the spot, with her whistlin' and toe-tappin'. That can only come from the heart, and a sad-hearted creature don't see fit to create like that."

"Come on now, Nicky," said I, "you were standing right next to me while she was there; no way in hell could you have heard her at all – I sure didn't!"

"Laddie," he said to me, putting his brotherly arm on my shoulder again, "neither of us could hear her, that's for certain. But while you were lookin' at her legs in an impure way, I was detecting a fast, two-step ditty, judgin' by her toes. There was a sway in her hips, too, and I knew when she got to the Finale. God knows what you were thinkin'!"

That was Nick in spades.

2

The Ride: 7/1/16

T HE NEXT DAY WAS SATURDAY and a bunch of us normally pick up four or five hours at National Docks loading odds and ends before quitting for the weekend. I got there early and waited at the gate for Lenny and thought about my conversation with Nick about that girl. I wouldn't be seeing Nicky until Monday, as he normally helped his brother Clarence out at their old boardinghouse in Newark on weekends. They'd be re-building the front porch today with a bunch of scrap lumber we got together from some large packing crates. Next week they planned on painting it all to cover up the stenciled lettering on some of the boards or you would see some strange words on them like "10 Ox Tongues" or "Rio de Janeiro" or "High Explosives." You bet; they would have to paint those steps!

Maybe he was right about her, and then again, maybe he wasn't. I decided right then that I'd amble over to the dock-girl the next time she made her appearance at the water's edge. If she were blue as I thought, well, maybe I could cure what's ailing her. But if she was as happy as Nick was suggesting, maybe she could cure what was ailing *me*. I'd been too long moping around, feeling sorry for myself and not getting much fun out of life these days. I couldn't tell you why, either, but I had a feeling this gal could be just what I'd been waiting for. There was something interesting about her and I was going to find out what. I'd put on a clean set of overalls Monday and see if I could have a word with her. It may help if I whistled something on the way over; one of the Irish tunes would work. I'd have to think about that a bit and make sure I picked one I could handle.

"Where in the heck is Lenny, anyways?" I began to wonder. It wasn't like him to keep me waiting like this, and I was just about to consider going through the gate without him when a motorcar pulled up, Lenny at the wheel, and his pair of Sheltie dogs in the back. They started raising hell, too, when they seen me, because I spoil them every chance I get. I pulled out my ham sandwich and broke off some of the crust for them. Blackie sat on his hind legs and gave me that soulful begging look while Whitey sat perfectly still. They're both mostly brown, by the way. I began feeding them part of my lunch and looked at Len to explain his turning up in this machine.

"It's a Ford," he tells me. "Model T," he added, like I wouldn't know for crying out loud. What I didn't know was what he was doing with one. He'd drive a truck on the job from time to time, but I've only ever seen him outside the docks in his dray wagon. That's how we got the packing crate lumber over to Newark last week, with Lenny's draft team pulling the load. Since he had the dogs with him it didn't quite look like he'd be working the hoist with me today.

"Hop in," he says, "and let me fill you in on events." Well, I'd never had the pleasure, so I ran to the other side and climbed on in. He worked some pedals and turned the wheel a bit and we were off! The dogs sort of tumbled back there in the box but before you knew it they were running around, poking their heads through the stake sides and barking at some of the chaps coming in for their half-shift. I waved over at Dave Hinchcliffe, and he flipped me the one-finger salute we so often share. Most folks would look down on that, but we dockers take it as a compliment.

"Well, you're probably wondering where I got this here Tin-Lizzie," he said, smiling that big oafish grin of his. He had his cap on backwards and was working the gear shift, looking left and right and then going on thru past the trolley tracks on Johnston Ave. It looked like we were speeding up, too, so I held onto the metal bar above the windscreen. "I sort of cut a deal last night," he continued, as he turned west onto Communipaw Ave. I looked back to make sure we still had both dogs, but they seemed to be unfazed. "Cost me two cases of Black Label, but it's going to be worth it."

"What is this all about, Lenny? What Black Label? Why this Ford, this, what do they call 'em, 'Flivver'?" I closed my eyes for what looked like a sure impact with a mule cart. A blast of the *ah-oogah* horn and a quick dash to the left and by the time I looked, the mule was plodding away untouched.

"Scotch, Augie, the best I could find on such short notice, and it cost me dearly, let me tell you." He tootled the horn once again at some boys tossing a ball and they both started running after us, but they couldn't keep up for long. He went on through a large puddle along the curb, splashing a drunk who was out for the count on a bench. "Remember that Jersey cow we acquired from Old Man Dentz a month or two ago, for that load of grain? Well, she's gone to her maker, she has, and just when I was beginning to like my tea with milk." That load of grain had come from the docks late one night after the boss left Lenny in charge of the crew. While Mister Schuyler was off for a shot and a beer, Lenny had me drive a wagonload through the gates and park it in a shed a few blocks away, walking the horse back to the dock stables. "No way can they track missing grain," he had told me, "unless it's already bagged. But when we're loading from the hopper car right into the ship's hold who's to miss the odd half ton?" He was right about that, too, and we drove the wagon the next day over to Kearny where Gustav Dentz had a dairy farm. Afterwards Len dropped me at home and drove off with a milch-cow tied up in back. Where he kept her, he never said, but for the past month we had fresh milk on the job each day.

He pulled the gearshift as we climbed the hill headed toward the Lincoln Highway and the Hackensack River Bridge. They opened this highway a few years back and it was the quickest way over to the Kearny Freight Yards and from there over to Newark's Ironbound Section. He poked me in the ribs and said, "Wait 'til you see what this machine can do once we're out of the busy streets." About a mile later we climbed the bridge ramp, and I looked down at the "Hackey." I always liked seeing the sun glint off the ripples — made me think the eye of God was watching. He honked the horn just for the fun of it and said, "So, let me fill you in, now that we're free and clear of any obstructables." He then floored the pedal and off we went over the new road surface. As I held on more tightly and checked the dogs for the fifth time, he explained, "Augie, I got us a sweet deal. We won't be at the docks much the next couple months, not me, not you, nor Nicky. No sir, not one of us! We're gonna be switchin' gears, you might say." He looked at my skeptical reaction — so typical of me when he starts his planning, and continued, "Just listen, Augie, you're gonna love this. You know how old man Schuyler has an affection for the hard stuff, but his Missus keeps him tied down at the house? Then, don't forget his excursions to the tavern where he leaves us to our own devices — we know he ain't got a gal-pal, right? Well, I hinted I'd be moving some cases of scotch on the sly for my brother and his ears just perked right up. He'd really love to have his own private stash away from her prying eyes, see? He out and asked me what was up with that, so I told him about a shipment of Johnny Walker that got mislaid on a siding in Newark that my brother stumbled upon and, knowing my connections, was relying on me to help distribute."

"Dang, Lenny, how many cases did he come away with?" This sounded like happy days were coming, and soon!

He looked over at me and replied, "None, actually, that's why I needed to trade the cow."

I stared at him, speechless, as we bounced down the ramp onto Kearny Point. He turned off the macadam onto a cobblestone side-road that led to the Kearny Freight Yard, pulled over by the marsh reeds and began to tell me the scoop while the Ford's engine rattled.

"It's like this, lad, and I'll make it brief, 'cause we're expected in the Yards. You see, I was just sounding the old man out about the booze, figuring if he didn't bite it wouldn't matter at all. Once he opened his blue eyes wide, I merely spun a web as soon as I could, knowing it wouldn't be too hard to lay my hands on some hooch if I had something to bargain with. The milk cow was the quickest thing I had at the house, and it was down the street to the Red Rose Saloon we went."

Before I could express my befuddlement, he went on, "Come now, Augie, you know the 'Rose' adjoins that butcher shop — Carbonetti's — what better spot in the whole city to bring her? All I had to do was set up a deal between the two proprietors and be on my way with the goods. I stopped at the Red Rose after Sully's last night and was out of there in five minutes with a case of Black Label in my hot little hands."

"Aha!" says I. "Yer one case shy, by the sound of it. How'd you miss that, Lenny?"

"Oh, we're good, buddy; the going rate is about one case per cow, depending on size, age, type of liquor, and so on, but you wouldn't know that, not being in the private '*Marketing Business.*' No, we've yet to earn the other case, which Mister Schuyler expects next month. Tis not a problem at all, once we get rolling on the deal I was telling you about."

I nodded in understanding and added, "So, we've got to get another cow from Dentz? Do we have to fill the wagon with grain again?" I was beginning to catch on!

"Cow? Grain? What are you going on about, Augie?"

"Well, I just thought..." I stammered. Maybe I wasn't beginning to catch on after all?

Lenny lit a couple smokes, passed one over to me, and said, "Remember last night I told you shipments were about to increase, and Schuyler was asking did we have any pals looking for work?"

I nodded as I took a deep drag and started to think of a few possibilities. It was picking up lately and we were busy enough already.

"Well," he continued, "in the big picture, it's even more complicated than that, not just for our outfit, but for the boys loading artillery shells, too. What with more munitions trains coming into the area to support these spring offensives in France, the rail yards are full up with explosives. They've shunted fully loaded trains to the sidings and the backlog just keeps growing. The warehouses on Black Tom are all full to capacity and now there's that trolley factory up there in the meadows, what is that, North Arlington?"

"Kingsland," I said, having an aunt living there. Nice, quiet place.

"Yea, that's it, up by Rutherford. The Canadian Car factory up there just retooled the foundry to assemble shells and plan to ship over three million a month. Problem for us is they're getting priority access to the Hoboken Docks since a main rail line runs right past them. That's gonna reroute some of the other Hoboken-bound freight through Newark instead, which means even more of a backlog for us. On top of all that, these ships keep coming faster than we can load them!"

I chuckled, dumped ash, and added that our cranes and derricks weren't the best machinery in Jersey either, not like the docks down in Elizabeth.

"You're always going on about the equipment, August, just because you worked 'Lizabethport last summer. Sure, they got one on us for modernization at the water's edge, but the heart of Jersey railroads beats at the Hudson Docks!" To illustrate his point, he tossed his butt at a puddle on the road and missed. A gull dove toward the target and thought better of it.

I followed his missile with my own, hit the puddle, and lamented, "We do what we can with what we've got, Lenny. What more can we do?"

He gave a thumbs-up to my shot and said, "Oh, we'll get better machines soon; you can bet-cher life. Meantime, we'll have plenty of overtime if we want it, and we're looking to hire fifteen or twenty more men. That's where the deal comes in!"

"*Ach!*" I barked. "And just what is this deal you keep harping on?" Lenny could be tiresome at times.

"I was just getting to the heart of the matter. Gee, Augie, what's with you anyway? Like I was saying, we're looking to hire a new crew to handle the overflow and I get to assign their duties. This puts me in a position to pick and choose should anything special come our way. Now that summer's here, I thought it would be swank to pull some light duty during the hot days and put some extra hours loading in the evenings, when it cools off a little."

His logic was sound, as always, but there were still a lot of unanswered questions. Like, what kind of light duty would ever come down the rails? And what about those cases of scotch? I was just about to open my mouth to speak when he said:

"You'll see, just as soon as we get in the Yard."

At that, he put the Flivver in gear and we headed through the gates to the Kearny Point Yards. The dogs came back up to the front stakes and started barking again, at nothing. We made a sharp right turn around a caboose, rumbled over a crossing, pulled up to the northern sidings and I was amazed to see dozens of these Model T Fords! They were lined up on the grounds by the score, alongside two sidings worth of flatcars of two Fords on each, with large wooden crates stowed between them. Some "Ts" were black, some were olive green, and more than a few were camouflaged. Most were ambulances with a large red cross within a white circle. Others had stakes on the sides, some had just flat beds, and there were a few with water or fuel tanks built on them.

"Dang," I stammered. "Is this the light duty you're talking about?"

Lenny smiled.

I added, "Does this have to do with the deal?"

He smiled ear-to-ear this time.

"Yup," he said, his arms opened wide in an all-encompassing gesture. "We're goin' in the delivery business."

3

The Yards: 7/1/16

W ITH THAT, LENNY SHUT OFF the engine, hopped out, and began walking toward the Yard Shanty. Before I could even get out of my seat he turned and, in that barroom voice of his, blurted, "Augie, get those dogs out, will ya? I don't want 'em taking a leak on the floorboards."

I climbed down, adjusted my cap and pants, and sauntered to the rear of this remarkable machine. I took a moment to admire the pneumatic tires, the dark black wheel spokes and rims, the smooth metal fenders. *Yep*, I thought, *a marvelous contraption, this Tin Lizzie. Boy, what a ride that was!*

I bent over the rear bed of the T and was about to loosen the chains that held the tailgate up when a cold, wet tongue darted into my ear, and an even colder nose nuzzled my cheek. I jumped back, but not before a Sheltie paw knocked my cap right off my head onto the muddy ground. "Darnit, Blackie, that wasn't called for!" I whined as I bent to pick it up.

Lenny hollered back, laughing, "Oh, stop your bellyaching and get 'em down." He shook his head and added, "And that was Whitey, anyways!"

Well, I hate to say it, but all Shelties look alike to me, with their mottled colors and long noses. I swear their snouts are longer than any other breed of dog I know. They just look different, I guess, but it's kinda weird and takes some getting used to. I dropped the gate and gave both a hand down to the ground. They rambled off barking while I caught up to Lenny at the door to the shanty, a typical Pennsylvania Railroad structure from the last century. The clapboards were once painted brick red but had faded to a dull, softer tone with the wood grain bleeding through. Of the several windows down the front and sides, a few were missing a couple small panes. These were plugged with boards or oilcloth that complemented the chipped white paint of the sashes and frames. As we strode through the doorway into the darkness within, I noticed a heavy odor of pipe tobacco and heard the loud tick of a clock somewhere. I shot a glance around and was surprised to see Lenny's brother Peter sitting at a table, a pitcher of water in one hand and a glass in the other. He was in the process of pouring a glass for Yard Boss Charlie O'Reilly, who looked up at us and said, "What the hell kept you boys?"

Lenny, who was always quick to reply to most anyone about anything, was unusually respectful of Charlie and merely said, "Well, I had to make a few drop-offs of those samples we talked about last night."

Peter put down the pitcher, slapped his younger brother on the back, and extended his hand to me saying, "Ah, August, but it's good to see you again! Lenny speaks highly of your automotive abilities and we're going to need every good driver we can find!"

My "automotive abilities" being limited to the past half hour as a scared passenger, I was about to reply that there must be some mistake, when Lenny chimed in with, "Oh yeah, Augie is quite the driver indeed — makes the rest of us look like amateurs, he does. Makes deliveries across town for his Pop's market, in fact."

"Well, then," said Boss Charlie, "this calls for a drink." With that, he picked up the pitcher from the desk where Peter had placed it and poured two glasses from a nearby tray. He handed Lenny a tall, clear glass and me a shorter green one and said, "To good friends, good health, and good fortune. *Slainte!*"

I didn't know what was in that jug, but suddenly knew it wasn't water. As I tipped that glass, I had the quick thought that this meeting was going to change my life and, also, a hope that it would change it for the better. Funny how quickly our minds can race within just a few seconds! At the same time, I also considered that Lenny was lying for a reason and knew it was in my best interests to go along with him. When Lenny "puts the game on," as he says, it's best to hop on for the ride and admire it for the thing of beauty it always proves to be. I trust him like my own father, and here he was trusting me in front of Boss Charlie. My final thought before I tasted that liquid was, *If Lenny says I'm a good driver, then I'm a good driver.*

My next thought is not clear to me, even now as I look back on that day and the moment the liquor hit my tongue, for a very hard liquor it was. Nor was it your normal bar-served booze that I'd been swilling for the past few years, but something that either came down from heaven itself or up from "Down Below," what with the heat it had to it. As I tasted it, my mind exploded with something like "Holy God Almighty!" I do recall that as it went down, I nearly followed it to the floor! I swayed, I buckled, I hung on to the desk, but I kept to my feet after all. It felt cool, and then it felt hot. As it hit my stomach, I thought of shotgun blasts and how they always made me jump. I coughed a bit and tried to get my breath.

The other fellows eyed my reaction to this unexpected detonation and put their empty glasses on the desk. Boss Charlie puffed his pipe, pulled it out of his mouth, and burst out laughing.

"That was some booze," I whimpered, tears in my eyes.

"Now don't you worry about it, son," Peter said. "You'll get used to it. It burns a bit going down, it does. Haven't you ever had 'Shine' before?"

Charlie refilled their glasses. He motioned to me, but I just put mine down and covered it with my hand. "No," I managed to say, "but I can see why it's illegal."

Peter nodded, picked up his glass, and said, "Yes, and that being illegal is going to make us a ton of greenbacks!" The three of them all smiled at that, picked up their glasses and were about to toast again when Lenny said, "Hold on, fellows. I think Augie's ready for another belt — better make it a short one." I could have killed him.

Charlie hit me with about a third this time and I found the courage to hoist it up to about chest height while I waited the executioner's command. After all, you only live once. Yet, I thought I could buy some time with a question and said, "Just so I know what I'm toasting, would you mind filling me in on just how we're going to be making a ton of greenbacks?"

This seemed like a fair question, resulting in several nods of affirmation that would buy me the time I needed to recover. Unfortunately, it didn't help after all, because Peter raised his glass higher still and said, "To Moonshine!"

Charlie joined him and said, "To Hooch!"

Lenny added, "To White Lightning!"

I raised mine and said, "*Mein Gott!*"

And with that, we drank. I didn't cough this time, but the feeling going down was the same. I was worried if it was going to burn on the way out, too.

• • •

It felt good to get out into the fresh air after that liquid fire. The bright sunshine was a stark contrast to the dim, smoked filled chamber we just left, and the Yards seemed a lot bigger than when we first arrived. We left Boss Charlie at the large blackboard that showed the rolling stock and locomotives at Kearny Point at any given time. Before we left, he pointed at the tracks with a wooden stick and gave us the lowdown on the two sidings full of Model Ts that needed to be off-loaded from the flatcars by Monday night. Lenny assured him we'd take care of it, "*No problemo.*"

As he put down the pointer Charlie said, "Those two trains need to be sent west by Tuesday, as there is a huge backlog of shells up the line that need to be shipped to the docks. Shells have priority over all other freight, so management's big idea was to dump these Fords right here in the Yards and drive 'em right to the ships instead. This works out fine for the new booze delivering business of ours, so no surprises fellers. We can't afford to slip up with the schedule or someone might start snooping around."

"Oh, don't worry 'bout that, Boss," said Peter. "We're on the case."

Boss Charlie raised his eyebrows at that and said, "You'll find that Kearny Yards won't work the same way you guys run the Newark setup. We're compressed here between the two rivers and don't have the real estate to shunt trains off when we need to hide 'em. An odd boxcar or two won't raise any questions, of course." He yawned, then continued, "That reminds me — I've stuck a Lehigh Valley reefer car off on a short siding behind the tool shed. It's got a red Out-of-Service card on it because of a broken coupling. We can use that to store the hooch once it comes down the line."

He then dismissed us as he was expecting some freight through shortly and had to evacuate a train held up on the mainline as soon as another was done coaling on a siding. The rail yard is a busy place!

Just as I suspected, glints of Len's plan were beginning to shine through. Boss Charlie clearly spoke about the new booze delivering business and storing the hooch once it comes down the line. The only unanswered questions were who would be buying it and how much we would sell it for. I was sure Lenny had a list.

We walked toward the first group of Model Ts as I breathed in the fresh meadowlands air. The salt marsh and the Hackensack River have a unique smell that is altogether pleasant. The hot sun hitting the creosote RR ties gives off an odor that reminds me of the wharf. I was about to mention this to Lenny when Peter tapped me on the shoulder and said, "I'm ready to learn if you're ready to start teachin', Augie!"

I stared at him, looked at Lenny, then back at Peter and said, "I think I'll need to familiarize myself with these Fords first — these are sensitive machines, not like the beat-up ol' truck I've been driving for Pop."

This cracked the two of them up and Lenny chimed, "See, I told you — he's my pride and joy!"

Peter nodded and respectfully added, "And it's like he didn't even miss a beat; I'm impressed!"

I was once again playing catch-up with Lenny's antics but caught my stride and said, "Ok, so I'm not the only one who doesn't know his arse from his elbow when it comes to automobilin', is that right? Well, Len, don't cha think it's about time we get to work?"

"Oh yes, indeedy," he replied, "and if you gents would climb up front here, we'll get started immediately. Augie, you better take her out first because Pete hasn't even had a chance to ride in one yet. Now, you know what to do — you was watching me the whole time up from the docks."

"The whole time from the docks?" I blurted. "I was watching out for dogs, trees, people, wagons, any number of things I was sure you were going to hit! I had no clue what you were up to, and you were driving like the devil himself was after us!"

"Oh, give me a break, lad. It's a cakewalk, really, just sit on down there and let me crank her up. You'll hold on to the wheel with both your mitts, and keep your left foot there, and your right one there. I'll explain how those pedals work a bit later." At that, he stuck my two feet between three pedals sticking up out of the floorboards, hopped out and bent down on the front of the Flivver.

"Now," he said, as he opened the hood cover, "lookee down here at the engine and what I'm about to do. There's a fuel line petcock handle you gotta turn to get gas into the carburettor. It's shut right now, and you just turn it in-line, like this." He turned it, and went on. "It's gravity-fed, so once we get her going she'll get a steady supply of juice, but there can be problems going up steep hills when she's low on gas." At that he shut the hood, flicked a clasp shut, and walked over to me.

"Next," he continued, "push that there lever on the steering wheel all the way up to the top, like that. It's called the 'spark-advance.' You must always have it UP when the engine gets cranked, or it'll kick back and break someone's arm."

I did as he asked. Nothing happened. I was getting a little shaky and said, "Now what?"

Lenny smiled and replied, "We're getting there, we're getting there. Now we gotta give her some throttle. It's on the right side of the wheel and needs to go half-way up to start her. Go ahead, move it up there."

Still nothing happened. My nervousness increased and my hands were gripping the wheel. They were clamped on tight.

Lenny noticed my white knuckles, tapped them with his hand and said, "Lighten up, Augie, the good part's about to begin. You'll need to move the handbrake lever backwards like so," at that he moved a lever on the left side of the front seat and continued with, "that's gonna put her in neutral, the transmission, that is, so she won't move forward when I'm up there cranking!"

I nodded in affirmation (it was the least I could do), and said, "She sure runs quiet."

Peter offered, "That's because she ain't running yet, Augie. We didn't crank her up yet!"

"Well, that's for certain," said Lenny. "Fact is, we have to put the key in the coil box first — right here on the dash," he pointed to the "Magneto-Off-Battery" switch, handed me the key and in a voice worthy of oratory said, "I now present you with the Key to the City!"

I put the key in the designated hole, and nothing happened. I looked at Lenny and he said, "You'll have to turn it, Augie."

I did. Nothing happened. Maybe I broke it?

Lenny held up his finger and said, "Ooops, my mistake. Turn it back off. It's still a bit confusing and here I am trying to teach you two. Allow me." At that he walked to the front of the car, bent down to the crank handle, turned it a couple times and yelled, "OK, now… turn it to 'Battery.'"

I did. Something started buzzing in the coil box in front of me. I bent my head down to look when all hell broke loose under the hood. The gas must have caught the spark and the T started vibrating wildly, shaking me up, down, and sideways!

I had a good hold of the wheel and was worried we'd be gliding right over Lenny, but he just got up and came back around to my side of the T, hopped in back and said, "Now we have to trim the spark speed to the proper level. Push in that choke button on the right and now bring the spark advance down slowly until you hear and feel the engine begin to smooth out." I did as he said and was surprised to hear the cacophony blending down into the familiar, almost orchestral blend of machinery that I recalled from our ride up from the docks.

"Now all we've got to do is figure out where we're going, bring up the throttle speed, and set the advance-spark lever to half-way — and we're golden." As he said this, Lenny handed us each a cigar and said, "And now the hard part."

4

The Meadows: 7/1/16

THAT NIGHT I COULDN'T SLEEP well at all. It was nice and cool for a change, and I had the window open to let the breeze in, but I was too keyed-up from a day full of events that had shocked my system time and again. I finally started to doze, only to be awakened by a jolt from my right leg. I rolled over and bent the pillow over my head to try again, but a minute later my arm started shaking. I rolled over onto my back and tried to relax. Then my left foot started jumping every twenty-five seconds or so. What the hell?

I got up, grabbed my cigarettes, and went out back to take a leak. A mosquito buzzed my ear and I smacked it with my free hand. We always left the outhouse door open in summer to air it out, but as a result you either had to shoo flies out of it or just ignore 'em like I do. Mosquitoes are my number one enemy. I swell up from the welts like you wouldn't believe and have even taken to applying castor oil, which seems to work most of the time. Leaving the outhouse for the fresh air again, a smoke seemed like a good idea. I took a seat on the front porch rocker and lit up, sat back, and began rocking.

It had been a full day — full of fun, frightful near-misses, and learning all sorts of mechanical terms. I guess my brain was as overworked as my body felt. I had bruises on my legs, a cut from whacking my head on the windshield, and a sore lower back. Worse, was the difficulty I had concentrating on anything. Lenny's voice was rumbling around inside my skull, much like my body had been bouncing around the inside of the Fords I drove all around the meadows. We spent the whole day there without even a thought of going back to the docks.

I would never have thought it possible to learn to drive so quickly, for when I took the machine out with Peter on my right and Lenny leaning over my shoulder, I was nervous and scared. I kept screwing up. At first it was hard to steer, and my arms felt rubbery. At one point, I drove right over the railroad tracks and nearly got stuck on 'em, but all I had to do was goose the throttle and she just jumped right over the rails and continued on her way. Later I crashed into a bunch of fifty-gallon drums but all they did was clatter away and I kept on. Lenny made a face, and I learned a valuable lesson on paying better attention. An hour soon went by, and we stopped back by the shanty where he put me in my own machine and let me initiate the starting procedure. I did well with it, too; only getting mixed up with the spark gizmo (I think I have it now).

He gave me his blessing and told me to "Go wild" and to "be back when you feel like you got it nailed," thinking it would help me to be on my own driving around the Yards and the meadows just outside the fence. I took the T all over the Yards and got her up to full speed a few times alongside the mainline. The wind blew through my hair as I raced along, and I felt a kind of freedom that is hard to explain unless you've done something as exciting yourself. Let's just say I think the whole motorcar thing is going to really catch on here in America!

The pedals are easier to learn than I thought they'd be. The right one is the brake, but certain times you'll need to pull the hand lever instead (like on slippery roads). He said something about wearing the brakes out too quickly with the foot pedal that I need to ask him to explain over again. The middle one is for going backwards, and the leftmost one is for putting the car in low or high gear. The throttle lever controls how fast you can go. After driving by myself for that spell, I began to think I did have it nailed and went on back to find the two of them.

I came to a halt where I started out but didn't see any sign of them.

Blackie and Whitey were laying in the shade of that reefer car Charlie had mentioned. Everything seemed quiet, so I thought I'd take a circuit outside of the fence. I went through the gate and drove down the cobbled entrance, splashing through a couple of the big puddles on the way. The water whooshed through the wheel spokes and splashed a torrent outward, only slowing the machine slightly. It seemed to pull to the right. I was curious how she would handle deeper water and set about looking for some good possibilities on a dirt road that ran off to the right, toward the Town of Harrison. I had been on this route many times before with wagons of scrap wood for Nicky's place and remembered a lot of standing water, overflows from the swamp, big ruts full of mud, you name it.

Just as I was approaching a huge, dark brown standing pool and was about to turn into it at a good clip, I heard the roar of another engine and a loud *ah-ooo-gah* in my left ear. Out of the corner of my eye I saw Lenny at the wheel of a black flatbed racing by me on the left. I had to suddenly wrench the wheel to the right to avoid my intended target as Lenny hit it at full speed! An enormous wave of dirty, smelly water engulfed me and there was nothing I could do but curse him. As I headed toward the next puddle I had to slow down and compose myself, when suddenly, another roar and a repeat of an *ah-ooo-gah* had me look to the left again, only to see Peter racing by behind the wheel of a green ambulance with a giant red cross on its side. He hit the water with a huge splash and I was again drenched, this time with a foul, oily-smelling brew that got me gagging. I pulled off to the side, dripping wet, and recalled the words of my Pop, who always said when people messed with him: "Don't get mad – get even."

I wiped my face on my sleeve and thought, "If these two brothers think they can team up and make a swamp rat out of me, they've got another thing coming!"

I put the Ford back in gear and got going again, now at a full throttle and there may have been steam coming out of my ears. They had already gone around the curve and could be taking the fork to the Newark–Jersey City Turnpike, but I had an idea they were headed toward Frank's Creek instead. I also knew a narrow track through the swamp grass coming up that I could cut down to head them off. The creek is a tidal stream that winds through the meadowlands, draining out to the Passaic River. Some folks call it Bom Bom's Ditch, for some reason I can't fathom. There was no way these newly minted aqua-nuts were getting across that ditch, not at high tide, and they had to be pulled up there thinking about it, the morons. You could ford this stream without getting stuck in the mud in just one place I knew of — where gravel had been dumped for that purpose — but you had to time it with the tide being out. Years ago, the Swift Meat-Packing Company spread out several tons of crushed gray stone at this crossing, but there would be a good five or six feet of water over it right now. In fact, there used to be a wooden bridge at the very spot but it got wiped out by some hurricane or other, and never got rebuilt. Still, Swift sends a couple wagons across each day to this area to dump cow manure and chicken dung in this section of the meadows. Local farmers buy it up for fertilizer after it composts about a year or two and haul it away to their fields.

The short cut I was looking for lay partly hidden in tall green marsh grass and reeds, but I quickly spied it and took a fast right through some cattails, getting back onto the hard-packed earth of the trail. A plan was beginning to form in my mind and, since we had quite a bit of rain lately, it looked like a golden opportunity was about to present itself. Suddenly, a pair of pheasant darted right in front of me, startling me back to attention. The female nearly got clipped by the right fender as I raced past their path of ascent. Large pieces of marsh grass were getting caught on the bumper, fenders, horn, and windscreen so I checked my speed a bit until things cleared a little. I had just slowed down when the Ford ran over small, downed birch tree and got airborne, coming down with a crash and a splash. It's a good thing I wasn't going full tilt right then! These ambulance cars bounce around a lot and it's a good thing they have a nice steering wheel to hold on to with both your mitts, or you may be flung outwards after a heavy jolt on these dirt roads.

Even though I was in eight-foot-tall reeds, at this stage I could see the top of an old sumac tree next to the crossing where I expected to find the two muskrats who doused me. I opened the throttle to full again and raced down the path. Now, what was that sequence of events? Was it a roar and a splash and a horn blast, or did the horn come first? No matter, I'd improvise. As I emerged out of the swamp grass in my Flivver, I saw just what I expected up ahead. Nay, even better than I had hoped, for Lenny and Peter were indeed pulled up by the creek, perplexed by the high-tide, but I never thought they'd be dismounted, having a smoke. The black flatbed and ambulance were side by side, parked before the stream. The brothers were similarly side by side, looking across and chatting. Right behind them, directly behind them, lay Swift's fertilizer field, the edge of which was a morass of slime and ooze produced by heavy rains draining out of a ripe mixture of barnyard sludge. Yup, a golden opportunity is not to be wasted. I aimed the Ford at the edge of the dung field, blasted the horn, and skidded through the sludge at full tilt!

I was right. It was a roar. Then the *ah-ooo-gah.* Then the splash!

The boys turned at the sound of the engine, saw a maniac at the wheel, and started to say something when the torrent rose to meet their words.

Don't get mad — get even!

5

The Kitchen: 7/2/16

Pop was quick to give me permission to skip the Sunday morning service at Emmanuel Lutheran when I told him I could put in some overtime involving urgent war material for France (The British Royal Navy blockade started in 1915, putting an end to German shipments. Prior to that, American industries could sell to any buyer, including the Central Powers). I didn't go into the whole ambulance story, as it was bound to capture his interest and I really had no time to get hung up giving him all the details. He'd love to discuss the engines, for instance, and I only had a rudimentary knowledge of how they worked so far. In fact, he knew quite a bit about them himself, just from his overall inquisitiveness about such things and how they work. There would be a time and a place for that discussion, but today wasn't it.

Lenny said he'd pick me up at 7:00 a.m. and we'd go right to the Yards to begin unloading the ambulances from the flat cars. We'd have all day Sunday and Monday and, just like Mister "No problemo" had said, those trains were going to be empty for Boss Charlie come Tuesday. In railroad parlance, Tuesday would begin at one second after Monday's midnight, so we had less time than you could get away with say, in a factory.

It would be an early day for Nick, too, although he did not know it yet. Peter planned to drive over to Newark to get him out of bed and have him skip the apartment chores he was slated for. Instead, he'd be in for a full day of learning the Model T basics and running down cattails and critters in the meadowlands. Once he gets his own "Go wild" opportunity, Nick will be a natural at the wheel. With his musical talents and sense of rhythm, he was certain to master the levers and pedals the way I've seen him play the church pipe organ — hands and feet all over the place!

While I was having a cup of coffee and polishing off a few pieces of toast, Pop came into the kitchen, rinsed out a cup from the drain, and brought the coffee pot over to the table with him. "Son," he said, "do you want me to top it off?"

"No, Pop," I replied, "go ahead and finish it."

As he poured the rest of the coffee, he looked at me and said, "You know, I'm proud of the work you're doing at the docks for the war effort." He then pulled out his chair and settled into it, continuing, "When this all started two years ago, I naturally favored the Fatherland, thinking they'd beat the French quickly as in 1870, and it would be 'over by Christmas' as everybody was saying. But here we are two years later and with no end in sight!"

"I know, Pop. It's gotten way out of hand and the loss of lives is incredible."

"Good God, Augie, it's beyond incredible; the world has never seen anything like this! Who could imagine both sides becoming entrenched from the English Channel to Switzerland, the massive artillery bombardments, the carnage on the Somme that I was just reading about on the porch? Bombs dropping from the sky on England, merchant ships being torpedoed without being stopped and searched first – what about that *Lusitania* that was sunk a year ago? She was carrying 1,200 innocent civilians!"

I could only nod in agreement at these points Pop was making. I had heard on the docks that RMS *Lusitania* was carrying shells and several million rounds of rifle ammunition, which would make her a fair enough target in the zone where the U-boat found her. But, when Pop got on a roll it was best not to interrupt him. I took a gulp of coffee and shook my head at the loss of life. He looked pained as he said, "America cannot remain neutral for much longer and from what folks say, we're bound to join the British and French Alliance. Can you imagine going to war against our old homeland?"

I had not thought of that before, being only five or six when we left Elberfeld, but the old man seemed quite upset at the thought. It must have been eating him up, because I noticed a nervous tick he sometimes got by his eye had returned. I finished my coffee and looked at the clock on the mantle: 6:45. Lenny would be honking that horn out front any minute now.

"Augie, what are you going to do?"

"Huh? What, Pop?"

"Are you going to join up? Would you fight if America declares war on Germany?"

I did not expect things would get so far along as this and hoped Pop was jumping the gun, but felt I needed to make my own thoughts known to him, as he was quite upset. I stood up, took my empty cup to the sink, rinsed it out, put it in the drain, dried my hands on one of Mom's embroidered towels, turned to him and said,

"What would you do, Pop?"

He got up and went to the window, pulled the curtain back, looked out and said, "I've thought a lot about it, son, and it hurts because we still have family over there. Your cousin Max is your age, and I imagine he's at the front by now. Lots of my old friends from the Landwehr Reserves might already have been called up despite our age. Their own boys are in the thick of it for sure. When I think of that life we left behind, our family and friends, the old neighborhood, the comradeship in my regiment — and my oath to the Kaiser — I feel that old patriotism of ' *Vor Koenig und Vaterland.*' But we left that life a long time ago and we're Americans now." Pop turned around then, paused for a moment, and looked me in the eye before continuing. "More importantly, is there nothing more sacred to a man than keeping his word? When we became citizens of America, we took a pledge and must be true to it. We left the Empire for the freedom of this land and have made a good life here. We're part of some great thing that I am only beginning to understand, despite my supposedly being old and wise. Our neighbors open their doors for us and offer to share their food, my customers come to my store because they like dealing with me, even if I charge more for bread than Smolski across the street. You can talk politics openly here, without the police coming to haul you away or beating you with clubs. This is truly the land of the free and my loyalty is here now."

"So," I jumped in, "your mind is made up, and I agree with you about being Americans and that we must be true to our word. I would expect nothing less from you or myself. But even beyond that, I cannot believe some of the atrocities Germany is committing! From everything I read in the papers — the 'Rape of Belgium,' sinking the *Lusitania*, to that British nurse who was executed last year..."

"Edith Cavell," Pop interjected.

"Right, Cavell — a woman no less!"

"Yes, but that one was iffy. She was helping soldiers escape from a war zone. I could go either way on that one," he said as he sat back down.

I was surprised by his reaction to that, but he *is* older and wiser. I filed that tidbit for future thought.

"Of course," he added, "You can't believe everything you read in the papers."

"What?"

"Oh, you know — propaganda. The papers are naturally full of it, mostly because they'll print what the government tells them to print — or withhold. The *Freiburger Zeitung* will tell you the nurse was a spy, in touch with Britain via telegraph, hiding Tommies in the hospital, et cetera. The *London Times* will simply call her a frail woman, a mother, a compassionate healer. Which to believe, son? It can't be both ways!"

He had a good point there, and I added it to the now growing pile for future thought.

"But how do you know what to believe if it's all lies, Pop? I mean, how do you know what's really going on?"

"Augie, it's not all lies, but a lot of it is. It helps to read newspapers from both sides if you can, do not believe either of them 100 percent, and try to arrive at a compromise somewhere in between. If the *Berlin Post* blares out that 20,000 French were killed at Verdun last month but the *Paris Gazette* claims 7,000 dead, I tend to think there were maybe about 12,000 new French graves."

"A-huh," I nodded comprehendingly. If they put the true numbers in the news, the enemy would know how well they were doing. It made sense.

He added, "Or let's say a dozen ships were sunk last month by the U-boats. Neither side can lie about the number of ships sunk, as they're either here one day and *poof*, gone the next, or still afloat, which could prove embarrassing to a paper. Undoubtedly, the British Admiralty will lie about the tonnage, cargo, number of crew, destination, whatever, because that information has value. The *Kreigsmarine* will similarly hide the truth of the number of U-boats sunk because they cannot let the enemy know how successful their tactics are.

"Now," he went on "you can't read French very well, but I can. I noticed a weird thing about the French papers. While their headlines are much like the British or American papers as far as casualty figures, they almost always exaggerate where ground has been taken or minimize lost terrain. I think this is simply French pride — the war is being fought on their turf, after all, and they must keep up morale both at home and at the front, and the two are not really very far from each other!"

"Surely they can't get away with that!" I exclaimed.

"*Au contraire*, they can, and they do. That is, until the next action, when ground again changes hands. It's as if they rely on that happening to cover their arses should the truth come out. Then they'll simply shrug and say, '*C'est le guerre.*' The French are a strange people. If you go over there, you'll see what I mean. That brings me back to my original question, son. Have you thought about what you're going to do should America join the war against the Triple Alliance?"

At that moment, Lenny honked out front with that *ah-ooo-gah* of his. I stood up and said, "Pop, I've gotta get going — that's Lenny outside. We can talk more about this tonight when I get home, but I really don't think President Wilson is apt to join the fray. His campaign slogan is 'He kept us out of war.' I think he means it."

I grabbed my lunch pail and reached for the doorknob when I heard him ask, "Son, how do you know when a politician is lying?"

"Huh?" I turned and said, "Well, ah, I don't know. How?"

He shook open the newspaper, smiled at me and said, "His lips are moving."

6

The Sidings: 7/2/16

WE GOT TO THE YARDS in record time with Lenny swerving around things a bit faster than he did yesterday. It being so early had a lot to do with that, too, as there were a lot fewer folks crossing the cobblestones or horse-drawn traffic clip-clopping down the road. I was surprised to see him driving along one–handed, with a bottle of coffee in his right mitt. He simply stuck the bottle between his legs and made turns with both arms handling the wheel, as it can indeed be cumbersome. He caught my eye as I watched him grab the bottle again and said, "Learned a lesson yesterday myself — you can't drive one of these cars with a coffee mug in yer lap. It's a good thing it was cooled off before I went and soaked my crotch."

"Oh yea," I replied. "I noticed that right off yesterday but thought you had wet yourself from the vibrations. You're not a young man anymore, kiddo."

That got me the Lenny-look I've told you about, so I felt inclined to go on, and said, "Still, it must have been nice to have that warm feeling down below again after all these years. Do you miss it?"

He gaped at me and accelerated down the bridge ramp, shaking his head.

• • •

Boss Charlie was nowhere around when we pulled in, nor were Peter or Nick. The sun was arching upwards, and a mist was slowly rising out of the swamps. It was peaceful for a change but for the usual diving gulls and their squawking. We drove right up to the sidings where the Fords were paired up on the flatcars and shut the engine. Lenny hopped out and went over to a tool shed and rapped on the door.

"Yar?" came a voice from within. I didn't recognize the voice, nor did I know what "Yar" meant. To my surprise, I was soon to become a user of it myself.

"It's me, lad, Lenny, and I've brought young August with me to help unload the Lizzies."

The door swung open, and a massive blond-headed giant came out to greet us. He had to be six-foot eight and must be up in the high two-hundreds as far as weight goes, maybe even over three. He was clad in blue railroad overalls, covered with oil, and had various wrenches and screwdrivers sticking out of every conceivable place. There were rags in his back pockets, larger tools on his belt, a grease-gun in his left hand, and an oil wrench in his right. His hands were enormous with huge, brawny arms, and his legs were tree trunks. He wore a brand-new red bandana around his neck and an ancient but clean railroad cap on his head.

"Hello, August, I am delighted to meet you," he said, and stuck out the hand with the oil wrench in it. Not being adept at the social graces when confronted with such a puzzle, I grabbed the wrench with my left hand, squeezed his massive paw with my right, began shaking it up and down and said, "Yar."

He smiled at that and said, "I'm pleased to make your acquaintance, my good fellow. Ollie Olson, at your service."

Well, to hear actual words uttered by this behemoth was a good sign, but that an immigrant Swede could have such a turn of phrase and a British accent had me curious. Also, he didn't crush my hand the way Nick always did so there was possibly a level of sophistication to Mr. Ollie Olson. I looked quizzically at Lenny.

"Ollie's been with the Railroad for a few years now, Augie, but he comes with quite the pedigree. Back in Sweden he maintained the engines of Prince Gustav's Royal yacht and his touring car collection."

"Yar," said Ollie.

"Wait," said I. "How did he get from the prince's yacht to the Kearny Yards? Did he drown the Royal Family or something?"

"Ah, Augie, but that is a good question," Lenny replied, "yet, it merely had to do with a high stakes hand of poker that Gustav Adolf overplayed."

Ollie took over and said, "Quite right, Leonard, but it was not simply the result of one hand of card play. No, it was more like a series of humiliating strokes delivered by none other than Teddy Roosevelt to my poor dear Gustav. Tragic really. The prince was quite unsettled by that loss."

This posed more questions than it answered, and I was about to leave that for the nonce, when Lenny jumped in again with, "Of course, shooting at that lion didn't help matters."

I perked up at that, considering how T. R. had been on a world-renowned safari after his presidency. It was in all the papers, so I had to ask, "Was Ollie on safari with President Roosevelt?" If so, this was amazing.

"Oh goodness, no, August," Ollie answered. "That lion business happened in Oyster Bay, after he came back from Africa. I had become his personal auto mechanic as part of his poker winnings, along with five of the prince's automobiles. I truly miss Sweden, but the idea of traveling to America in the employ of Theodore Roosevelt was more than I could pass up. I was put up in the gate house to the mansion on Long Island, had money in my pocket, and excellent food and drink. I ate with the servants of course. Unfortunately, Colonel Roosevelt was more likely to ride one of his horses than get behind the wheel of the cars, and I found myself with a lot of spare time on my hands. I would go for hikes in the woods, became friends with the local farmers, and taught myself to play harmonica. One day I was playing along with a fiddler at the local grange when one of the farm boys came in all excited, claiming a large mountain lion had pillaged his henhouse and that it leapt right over the fence when he came upon the scene. He wondered if anyone else had a similar experience in the area, but it was news to all present.

"We armed ourselves with a few old rifles and decided to go with the boy on a safari of our own, to see if we could somehow follow the big cat to its den. I thought the size of its paw prints was formidable, and it was not difficult at all to track the animal in the sandy soil. To our surprise, it had made its lair beneath the Roosevelt barn, with clear evidence of its comings and goings beneath the southern wall. We heard a low growling sound coming from within the barnyard, left the boy to watch the rear, and went over carefully to look. We slowly raised our rifles. To our surprise, there was Teddy Roosevelt on a small stool milking a cow, unaware that a mountain lion was creeping up on him. Just as I was about to pull the trigger, the boy yelled 'He's back here!' and fired his gun. This distracted me and made my own shot go wide, hitting an oaken barrel with a loud ping. The big cat sprang into the barn. The cow mooed and kicked the pail out from under. The farmer held his fire and ran to the back of the building. Udder in hand, Teddy looked up at me and said 'Bully shot, that, Ollie. I've been meaning to bag me a barrel one day, too. Now, just what the San Juan Hill is going on here?'

"I told him we tracked a mountain lion right here and how there must have been two of them, one hiding right in his barn and the other underneath it. He then said I ought to leave the hunting to him and get back to my engines, that I was far safer with a wrench than a Winchester. He let me go the next day. Turns out the expedition mascot lived in the barn, was perfectly tame, and kept the coyotes from pestering the cows. The boy did bag the real mountain lion, which turned out to be a bobcat, and not that big."

Ollie put his head down at that point and it was clear the memory troubled him. Lenny didn't say a word, and it seemed a response from me would be appropriate.

I quickly weighed a few thoughts in my mind. His story, while interesting and incredible, still did not clear up the British accent thing. Yet, I felt that asking for that explanation would possibly be even wordier than this last and could wait. Instead, I said, "Well, you can always say you hunted with President Roosevelt and just leave off some of those particulars. And I'd guess you had the wooden barrel mounted over your mantle?"

At that, Mr. Ollie Olson smiled broadly, leaned back far with his belly out and his head back, and guffawed. He turned to Lenny, red in the face, and said, "You were right about the young chap, Leonard. I am certain we shall enjoy working together on the project!"

With that we went over to a large open-air work bench where were gathered the usual group of mechanic's tools, oil cans, wooden boxes, and various bottles. Ollie showed us a clipboard with two *Rail Master Lading* forms describing the freight contents of each of the two trains before us. Each train had a compliment of forty flat cars, five box cars, a tanker car loaded with gasoline, and a caboose. There were two Model T vehicles of various configurations to each flat car, with spare equipment stowed between them. The box cars contained medical supplies such as stretchers, bandages, medicine, splints, and boxes of plaster. Some genius back in Newark figured we could use the spare room in the meadows to not only unload the machines from the trains, but also to pack each Ford with the contents of the freight cars, according to a set of packing instructions.

This was beginning to look like we had bitten off more than we could chew. I stated as such, but Lenny merely shrugged and said, "We'll get it done, Augie. We've got a plan worked out and won't be doing any heavy lifting either."

"We'll just be driving, right?" I felt the need to clear that up.

"Oh, you bet," replied Lenny. "But for now, we'll just be lining them up in that grassy field until they're all unloaded. Then Pete's boys are going to stuff 'em with the supplies and, once they're packed, you'll be ferrying them over with Nicky and Pete to the docks. I'll bring a load too but always drive an empty car with you guys back with me. We can make about ten or twelve trips per day and the dockers will hoist the Fords aboard with other cargo. They're not all going on one ship, but in dribs and drabs for safety reasons."

"I would like to drive a few through the city streets to the Hudson myself," added Ollie, "except I have my hands full with topping off the oil, gapping the plugs, and a bunch of other little items to check. Even though these machines were built on Henry Ford's new assembly line, I am quite surprised at some of the inconsistencies I found. You may put it down to the human element, I expect. In any endeavor, once you add people to the mix, something is bound to go wrong."

"Spoken like a true optimist," said Lenny.

"Don't you mean pessimist?" I said. "I mean, it's a negative thing for things to go wrong."

"Oh, and right you may be, lad," he said, in Lenny-like fatherly fashion, "but he sounded awfully positive that things would go wrong, and to me that is pure optimism."

I sometimes wonder about Lenny. He's either got a screw loose or I am just slow. Sometimes I don't know if he's pulling my leg, serious about something, or just plain off-kilter with some of the things he says. I looked pensive, I guess, for he next patted me on the back and said, "Of course, that's just my opinion, you've got yours and I expect Ollie's got one of his own. Nonetheless, it's time we get to unloading these Lizzies!"

Opening his arms wide, as if embracing the rolling stock before us, he led us over to the siding and pointed out the concrete platform that ran for about a hundred feet between the two stationary trains. The platform had a ramp at the eastern end we could drive down, and someone had bridged the gap between the lead flatcars and the platform itself with a series of oak planks, laid side-by-side, at the front-most car of each train. Since we had no switching engine at the head of either train, they were stuck in place and we'd have to offload them, one Model T Ford at a time. There were thick planks laid from one flat car to the other, creating a sort of lengthy bridge, all the way to the freight cars at the rear. Were these guys serious? Could this work without incident?

"I know it looks clunky, fellows," Lenny explained, "but we've done something much like this before in the Yards here and Boss Charlie himself laid it out for us. Those planks are nailed solidly down, so don't worry about them shifting as we drive over them. All we need to do is get a good pace going and we can swing this. We'll all have our own tasks and function like one of those baseball teams. Nick will be no use driving until he gets some hours in behind the wheel himself, so I've got him turning the hand cranks and moving these boxes from between the Ts. Ollie will be up ahead making his final adjustments on the motors. Augie, I'll need you to drive these babies off the train with me. While one of us is walking back from the parking field, the other will be starting up the next vehicle."

"What about Peter?" I wanted to know about him and his boys who would be packing the ambulances with the supplies. Would he be using dock workers or some of the kids from the streets of Newark, as he was known to do? Those young fellows from the Ironbound Section were quite light-fingered. Then again, so were many of us dockers. Lenny handed Ollie the clipboard and replied, "Ah, yes, Pete. When he finally gets here from Nicky's house, he's off to South Jersey on a long ride to the Pine Barrens. That's where the hooch is coming from. The Pineys distill it out in the swamps down there and sell it by the jug. It's been quite the tradition in the Barrens for almost two hundred years. They say the Devil taught the recipe to the locals, way before the Revolution. You tried it yesterday. They call it 'Jersey Lightning.'"

7

The Tightrope: 7/2/16

WELL, LENNY HAD IT PART right; there was a Devil down in the Pine Barrens, but he had nothing to do with making booze. From what Peter said when he got back a few days later, around the same time the Barrens folk started making their hooch, stories about a strange creature began cropping up. You know, like the Loch Ness Monster, but in the woods. Livestock would go missing or be found half-eaten, inhuman screams would be heard at night, unusual hoof prints would be found in the barnyard, that sort of thing. He said they swore by this even today, that many of them had seen signs of it themselves. He said it was creepy walking the pine woods at night.

Pop knew all about it when I mentioned it after dinner one night. He had not heard of the monster at all until back in '09 when the papers carried a bunch of stories of folks seeing a strange creature with a horse's head, wings of an eagle, talons, and a long pointy tail. Some fellow shot at it but must have missed. Lots of people claimed to have seen it, even a few policemen and a minister, but it always flies away on those big dragon-like wings. Probably just a turkey buzzard I guess, but when you're walking through the woods at night and one of those big black bastards comes winging up at you from a thicket, I could see how someone's imagination might make them crap their drawers and run like the devil himself was chasing them. Hence, a Jersey Devil. Yup. Right. Maybe the Pineys made the whole thing up to keep people away from their stills, eh?

I have heard some strange things up here in the Kearny Meadows, now that I think of it, but the place is full of big rats, wild boars, and who knows what else? I'll keep an eye out just in case.

At any rate, that Sunday Peter had a long trip ahead of him in one of the Fords. It was conveniently fitted out as a water tanker and was the fifth car off the train. I rolled her off the flatcar myself. It felt a bit heavier than the ambulance type of T, but maybe I was mistaken, what with all the imagining of devils, eagles, buzzards, and the like, I had all sorts of things flying through my skull as I drove those vehicles down to the parking field.

"Ollie strapped on some extra spare tires and a few five-gallon cans of gas to her," Lenny told his brother, and added, "But try to save the cans for emergencies and fill up in those places on the map I gave you."

"How long a drive is it?" I asked. From the map, it looked over a hundred miles and who knew how long it was going to take him.

"Oh, he's just got the ride to Newark first where he'll load up on the train down to Philadelphia. The main driving is going to be from Philly over into the Barrens, and back of course. They've got PRR tracks laid down that way, but the trains are infrequent, so a bit of a trail blazer will be our Petey."

Well, it had not occurred to me that Peter would be riding the rails down south and back in the Hooch Wagon, but it made a lot of sense if you stopped and thought about it. Why not take advantage of all the tools available to us? It's the American way!

Peter was gone on his way by 11:00, leaving a ticked-off Nick behind. "Why do I get to do all this hand cranking when you guys are having all the fun?" he complained. Still, he busted his butt like only Nicky could, starting the cars, moving the crates, and only stopping occasionally to mop his brow or strip down to his tee shirt. He could sweat bullets, Nicky could. Hell, we all could.

I had the honor of taking the first ambulance off the lead flat car. Lenny guided me to the hard left turn off the "flat," over the collection of planks and onto the concrete platform. From there it was a glide down the ramp at the end and over the gravel path to the field he indicated. I shut her down, walked back for another, and saw Nick helping Len start the next one up. Ollie was up the train and out of sight doing whatever he needed to do, and I had a minute to look around at the sky and meadows. The Kearny Yards is just another railroad depot, to be sure, but it is surrounded by the most beautiful meadows and tall waving grasslands. The sky was a brilliant blue and the sun was doing its darndest to remind us of its great power. You could hear crows, seagulls, and blue jays overhead, along with the rumble of a locomotive approaching from the west. There was also the sound of hammer blows from up-train and I figured it had to be Ollie. The tidal pools gleamed with sunlit sparkles. I looked to the north and spotted Snake Hill, a large outcrop of rock that dominated the area, looking like an island in a sea of green cattails. I've never been up it, but they have a sort of sanatorium up there (Pop called it a nuthouse, actually). They also say it was a pirate camp back in the old days. Lenny's dug around up there, "…in the obvious spots," he said, but never found any treasure.

I climbed the ladder to the next flat car as Len trundled his T over the plank bridge. Nick was already waiting in front with the crank handle in position and we started her up lickety-split. Well, I knew what the plan was, but it was a bit scary, so I took my time at first. With very little throttle, I eased the Model T onto the wide oak boards bridging the space between the two flats. I looked down to the left, slowed down, looked to the right, slowed some more, and suddenly found myself on the empty flatcar ahead. With a bit more confidence I drove slowly over it and made that left turn onto the makeshift bridge again. Before you know it, I was down the concrete platform and parking my second vehicle next to Len's, in a nice, straight line. Well, maybe not that straight, but I figured I'd get the hang of lining them up better with practice, and we had a long day ahead of us.

Peter left us a few minutes later once I got that tanker off for him. Lenny gave him some last-minute instructions as I went back up for my next car. Before you know it, we had two dozen parked over there and I wasn't even aware of it until Nick pointed it out.

We all took a lunch break at 2:00 and after we ate, Ollie said he would spell Nick a bit so he could take a quick driving lesson from Lenny. We took five or six more cars off before the boys were back, Nick a bit green around the gills. I had to ask, "What happened, Nicky? Bang into something?"

"Wise ass, ain't you though," he replied. "As it so happens, I blew out two tires going over the tracks too fast."

"All part of God's plan, Nicky boy," chimed Lenny. "You had to learn how to fix a flat eventually, and what better place to learn but under Ollie Olson's tutelage? You can get to it later. For now, she can stay where we left her with her sagging tires. I plan to drive us all home later in style, in an officer's car. Meanwhile, you had better get back to cranking them up so we can finish one of these trains by quitting time."

"I'd best be starting on the other train myself," Ollie added, and off he went.

So it was that we all resumed our roles and began offloading these Fords in earnest. Some of the train cars were missing boards here and there, making it a bit dicey as you wouldn't want to get a tire stuck in a hole. Before long we were driving over twenty empty flatcars, as over a long bay bridge somewhere. Going the length of the train from one flatcar to the next reminded me of the circus act where a man on the high-wire carefully keeps his balance as he walks from one end to the other with the crowd watching for him to fall. I imagined myself in that role as I carefully drove over the boards from one flat to the next to the next and so on.

By nightfall Sunday we had almost one entire train unloaded and would have kept working at it but for our first mishap. It was just getting dark, and we had already off-loaded over sixty Ts, when a spike holding down one of the planks between two flatcars came loose, causing the ambulance I was driving to slip sideways just as I was over the gap. She landed with a jolt on the lip of the next flatcar, held up by the front frame-bar, with both front wheels off the planks. The rear ones held, thankfully, or it would have been a bigger mess yet.

Ollie was there immediately with a portable winch and cable, and we righted the car in under twenty minutes. We were sitting ducks for the mosquitoes and were constantly smacking as the buggers would buzz into our ears.

Lenny decided we had enough for the day, and we were all grateful to call it quits and ride together back in one of the autos set up like an officer's car, with seating for six. Lenny drove with Nick beside him, giving some appropriate verbal lessons as we went from the Yards back over the Hackensack River, promising to have him behind the wheel himself by mid-afternoon tomorrow. Lenny knew how to stoke a fellow's enthusiasm, he did.

We dropped Ollie Olson off at his tenement over by Lincoln Park and continued to my house. Len told me I did a great job today and not to worry about any more mishaps with the planks; that he would go over each one carefully at dawn tomorrow. When we got to my place, Pop was out front smoking his pipe and I just knew he would be interested in why I was pulling up in a big Ford staff car, complete with camouflage paint. I hopped out and told the boys I'd be ready, "Same time tomorrow, then." They both waved to us, then put the car in gear and sped off.

"Welcome home, son," Pop said. "How about a bottle of beer with your old man?"

8

Das Rheingold: 7/2/16

J UST AS I FIGURED, POP was very curious to know why we were suddenly riding around in military vehicles. Considering I had been walking the two miles to the docks and back the past few years — he had a point. Leaving out the part about the White Lightning, I told him about the easy duty Lenny pulled for us driving Model T Fords down to the docks over the next few weeks. How he had traded a cow for some booze and so on, giving us the chance to do something different.

"*Ach*, Lenny, did you say?"

"Yes, Pop. He's quite a guy."

"The same Lenny who was shipping Chinamen west on box cars for a buck each last year?"

"Yes, Pop, but only as far as Pittsburgh. He gave that money to the orphanage, though; most of it anyway. He had to pay off a few guys, too."

He pried open the cap on a bottle of Rheingold and handed it to me. Raising his own beer he said, "Prosit, August." I tapped his bottle with mine and replied, "*Zum wohl, Vater.*" I always said this to Pop — it means, "To your health" in the old tongue.

"Always remember son, if you have your health, you have everything."

"True enough, but these days it helps to have a bit of money socked away, too," I replied.

"And so, the overtime will come in handy for you, eh?" This was just like Pop; his next sentence was going to be about driving the automobiles, and the one after that would be about Lenny and what his latest deal was. He was always worried about me being in over my head with some of Len's schemes.

I took a swig, wiped my mouth on my sleeve, and said, "You know I'm saving as much as I can to get my own boat one day?"

"You've spoken of this boat since you were nine or ten, so I'm not surprised you'd still be chasing that dream of yours. How's that coming along?" He seemed delighted at the idea and taking that tack would be a distraction from the Lenny business, so I went with it.

"Well, Pop, I've got over $200 socked away, and have my eye on a Twenty-footer on the Raritan River," which was true. "But the owner wants $375 and won't go any lower. This summer I hope to top $300, and it won't be long before I can buy her."

He looked truly amazed at the massive sum I just quoted, raised his bottle once again to tap against mine, and said, "Good Lord, son, but you're well on your way indeed. And you think this extra work with the ambulances will give you enough hours this summer to meet that goal?"

"Sure hope so," I answered. "I think I can make it, at any rate."

He looked doubtful, and continued, "It seems to me like you'd still fall far short. That's a lot of money to make in just a few weeks. Unless, of course, your friend Lenny has something going on behind the scenes, as usual. That boy thinks in multiple layers, he does. He wouldn't be shipping anything on those Fords from the Yards on the way to the docks, would he?"

It was my turn to be amazed. *How did he do it? Is this what happens to a man once he raises kids? Was Pop a mind-reader? Did I let something slip?* It was time to come clean, so I said, "Well, sort of. I mean, we do have to drive them all to the docks anyway, and he figured it would be a great way to help make ends meet for all of us."

"Don't tell me it's stolen goods, August. I could not tolerate you dealing in stolen goods!"

I shook my head, saying, "No, Pop; not stolen goods."

"Is it livestock again?"

"No, Pop."

"Chinamen? It had better not be more Chinamen!" He was turning red.

"No, Pop, not Chinamen, not people of any sort at all."

"For the love of God, August, just what…wait! I've got it!" he was getting excited.

He turned around and went back inside for about half a minute. I couldn't imagine what he was up to. When he came back out, he had two more bottles of Rheingold in his hands, already opened, and handed one to me. Again, he tapped bottles with me, then took a sip of his beer. He looked me in the eye and said, "Traded the cow for some scotch, eh? Traded the cases of Johnny Walker for the easy duty, eh? Now don't tell me he's gone and acquired some ill-gotten booze and is delivering it to taverns between the Yards and the Docks, is he?"

My, Pop was good.

• • •

That night I thought I'd sleep like a log. I remember thinking that it had been an eventful day and tomorrow would bring more of the same. My bones were weary as I crawled into bed, and I more fell into it than lay down. Before long, I dreamt I was riding in a Model T over a high bridge, with a deep chasm below. Nicky was driving and Lenny was throwing bottles of hooch over the sides down into the gorge, shouting, "Take that, you scum!" The bridge was on fire and collapsing behind us as we crossed over. The T was slipping off the edge, it was leaning over, it was falling!

I awoke with a start, sitting bolt upright. I wondered what it all meant. I stood up, confused and muddled. I needed a cigarette.

Grabbing my pack of Camels, I stumbled out onto the porch again. These late-night smokes always helped clear my head. I lit up and took a quick drag, settling back into the wooden rocker. I looked up and down the street, but nothing stirred. The crickets were singing in the background and the full moon showed through the slow-moving clouds. It might rain tonight, from the looks of it. I wondered how that would affect offloading those machines in the morning. I mean, my car slipped off that loose board last night! We had no choice but to work on the Fords tomorrow, rain or shine. What could happen if the wood was soaking wet?

That dream seemed so real, the danger intense. Then I saw it clearly — the dream was just a replay of what happened to me last night. I remember thinking of the tightrope act while working — the high bridge was the long string of flat cars. And the falling — well, my Ford did fall between two of them! Lenny and the hooch bottles made sense, too. I mean, his throwing them off the T must represent making the deliveries he planned. Yes, that made a load of sense! As for the bridge being on fire and collapsing, well, I had no idea. I didn't want to think about that.

I noticed the empty Rheingold bottles Pop and I had placed in the wooden crate down in the corner of the porch after our discussion and smiled. True to form, Pop had it nailed. I told him all about the ambulances, the Pinelands, Peter's ride down south, White Lightning, Boss Charlie, delivering hooch to the bars, everything. I thought he would be upset, that he would have something to say about my being involved. I never expected him to say what he did, and I love him for it: he ordered two jugs.

9

The Rain: 7/3/16

It rained overnight. In fact, it was still coming down when I woke to the clanging alarm clock next to my bed. I whacked at it with a well-practiced swipe of my left hand and sat up drowsily. Damn, six o'clock already? Shoot. Ah, well, I'd better get up soon. There was something important to do at the docks today and, wait — not the docks — the Yards over in Kearny. That was it. We had to unload the other train and now it looked like we'd be out in the rain doing it after all.

It was pouring hard as nails out there. The two windowsills in my room were soaked and the screen on the front window was plastered with raindrops. I got up to close the windows and noticed a stiff, cold breeze coming in on the east side of the house. A torrent of water raged at the gutter, gushing downhill toward Grove Street. It ran a good six feet from the curb, easily overflowing the drains at the corner and continuing its urgent descent to the Hudson several blocks below. The sycamore trees were waving frantically, and the ground was strewn with leaves and small branches. What a day!

Lightning flashed. I looked out across the street to the McGregor's house and could see lights in their parlor. That's how dark it was. I don't recall ever seeing a morning like this in July but hey, a first time for everything. A sudden clap of thunder made me wince and then banged liked a kettle drum overhead. As its roll diminished, the intensity of the rain increased. It was one hell of a storm out there! I closed both windows while the lightning continued flickering. Next, I wiped the sills with some rags from the closet and tossed them on the wet floorboards to help soak up the drops. I'd hang them on the porch when I got home if Mom didn't pick them up first.

I needed coffee and knew Pop would be up already having a cup. He opens the store before 7:00 a.m. on weekdays to be there for his early birds. These old *Bobcis* and *Babushkas* will still come out in heavy rain for potatoes or onions, so he'd be leaving shortly. I put on my pants and boots, changed into a clean shirt and headed downstairs, grabbing my cap and slicker along the way. The thunder rolled as I opened the door to the kitchen and saw Pop looking up at something on the ceiling. Then I noticed the punchbowl on the table as it received its latest drips.

"Son," he said as he pushed a plate full of sliced banana toward me, "Do me a favor and empty the containers before you leave for work today. I had better be off now if I'm to get to the market without having to swim for it."

"Good morning, Pop," I said. "I can't believe how hard it's coming down right now. In fact, if you don't wait for it to let up some you're going to be drenched. The sewers are all overflowing, and Wayne Street looks like a river!"

"August," he replied. "I'll have all day to dry off. How would it look if a couple old women are standing in front of the store in the rain waiting for me to finally decide to show up and let them in?"

He had a point.

He finished his coffee, put the mug in the sink and said, "Just don't forget to empty the pails and this bowl before you leave. They're filling up today faster than usual — must be the way the wind's blowing. We'll have to get up there on the roof again before the winter."

He grabbed the doorknob and was about to walk out when I had an idea and exclaimed, "Wait, Pop! How'd you like to ride in a Model T to the store? Lenny will be here at 6:30 and we can have you at the shop in less than ten minutes. You won't get all soaked then."

He shook his head and said, "No thanks, Augie," as he grabbed his umbrella off the hook by the door. "I've walked this earth for fifty-two years in all kinds of weather; no sense in changing now."

"But, Pop," I contested.

"No buts, son. Have a great day!" And with that he was off.

Knowing that older folks are set in their ways I merely accepted his stance. I made one more mental note (Pop always gets me making these mental notes) not to be that way when I got old, too. I filled my mug with black coffee and watched a long stream of water cascade into the punch bowl. *Dang*, I thought, *that's some wicked rain out there.*

The clock on the cupboard bonged the half hour at about the same moment that Lenny tootled the Ford's horn out front. I almost dismissed it, as the *ah-ooo-gah* was muffled by the force of the downpour. I put the sou'wester on, dumped the punch bowl and pail both into the sink, crammed my mouth full of banana slices, grabbed my mug, and opened the door to a *whoosh* of wind and a spattering of rain.

I was pelted by sizable drops as I ran down the flagstones to the street. Pulling back on the side-flap I climbed in front next to Lenny, who was adorned with a pair of goggles. He had a stogie going despite the early hour, dumped the accumulated ash on the floor of the Flivver, and said, "Holy smokes, Augie, but wait til you see how she handles in this flooding!" He put her in gear and off we went, the heavy rain pounding on the canvas rooftop. I asked him why the windscreen was down, and he replied, "It gets blurry at times, hence the eyewear. Here, I got you a pair for your very own." I hastily put them on and found they were a big help. After a while they collected drops, but you merely had to wipe them off with your hand. We almost looked like aviators but lacked flying helmets and scarves. A scarf would be soaked through in no time, what with the rain coming straight at us sometimes.

It was a thrilling ride to the Yards in that thunderstorm. There was a constant flickering of lightning punctuated with long rolls of thunder and it even began to hail for a few minutes! Thank God, the streets were devoid of people, carts, and horsemen. Lenny was driving with an intensity like Lucifer himself was following us. He had her at a good pace but seemed to slow at the turns a bit more than he's usually done since I've begun noticing such things. I asked him why, and he splayed his fingers out over the wheel, steering with his palms, shook his head quickly and said, "Oh, you gotta slow down on the turns or she's gonna slide away on top of the water." His voice had an unusual high pitch to it when he said it so I thought I had better not follow up with a second question as is my usual wont. It didn't take long to find out what he meant, as he failed to slow down turning onto Grand Street and the Flivver skidded sideways, bounced a few times, and felt like it was going to tip over!

"God, there it went again!" he cried. "See what I mean, Augie? She'll slip on the turns in the wet when she's nearly empty. Gotta remember that. Here, you try it." With that he stopped and sort of climbed over me, making me slide under his fat butt and get behind the wheel.

I put her in gear and started out cautiously after what I had just seen, but right away there was Lenny cajoling me to go faster and not worry about anything. "Not worry about anything, are you crazy?" I asked him. "We nearly toppled back there!"

"Ah, but we didn't," he replied. "It was all just a lesson for you, old son." He looked away after he said this, so I dug in my heels and replied, "If you ask me, it looked like you were the one getting taught a lesson!"

I think I really got off a zinger with that one and was about to capitalize on it when he let go a sigh and said, "Just get us in one piece at Ollie's place in a hurry and we'll pick up the boys. Nicky said he'd meet us there. We better hope this rain slows down a bit or we'll have a rough time unloading all these cars today."

I then drove as fast as I could, all the while being careful on those turns that seemed to have taken the wind out of Lenny's sails for a spell. I turned from Grand Street onto Communipaw Ave at the Five Corners and began the long, gradual ascent west. I enjoyed the feel of the T going through the deep streams of water at curb side at first but after a while all things become common, and you can grow tired of them. Plus, it was slowing us down, what with all that water hitting the undersides of the running boards with a loud "Whoosh" sound. I began riding the center of the streets where they seemed clearer of water and gave better purchase to the tires. Lincoln Park loomed ahead, with Ollie's place just to the north. I turned right onto West-Side Street to skip the park when I suddenly braked and slid to a stop. Lenny looked up and was about to have something to say when he saw the large pond of water in front of us. The lake in the park, swollen from all the rain, had moved its reach about a hundred yards eastward.

"Holy crap, Augie, but let's find another way," was all he could say.

I put the Flivver into reverse gear, backed out of West-Side Street unto Communipaw, went east a block and found a better route. In no time at all we were in front of Ollie Olson's place. I squeezed the horn-bulb a few times, and out came the boys. We were on the way quickly and were not surprised to see smokes and coffee coming out from under their wet slickers. I wondered if Lenny would like me to take the next turn without slowing down but kept my prior caution in effect. The rain was relentless, and visibility was difficult, so I concentrated on keeping the car afloat while they traded pleasantries.

We got to the Yards without further incident, other than witnessing the spectacle of the Hackensack River at full flood tide, torrents of water cascading out of storm drains on both banks. High tide was already in and the Hacky would not start to drain back into Newark Bay for about an hour. Meanwhile all sorts of debris, picked up off the banks from the rising water, was pushed midstream in the muddy river. The force of the deluge emanating from the hills created an ugly glop of flotsam that swirled and eddied, jumbled together, and separated again. Gulls seemed to be attracted to something in the mix. There were lots of bottles, several large kegs, branches still full of green leaves, wooden crates, a few nearly black waterlogged tree limbs, a wash tub, and whatever else I knew not what. Just as I was about to remark on how filthy man had made this once pristine river Lenny went and tossed his cigar out into the flow.

The Yards themselves were sodden and the ruts were full of brown water. It appeared that the rain lightened up a bit but maybe it was just because we had come to a halt. We deployed much as we had yesterday and got right into the fray once again. One difference we noticed right away was that someone had off-loaded all the boxes from between the ambulances. That must have been Pete's boys and Nick looked relieved at that knowledge. While Ollie went to check planks on the second train, Nick got to cranking for me and Lenny. We got into that same rhythm as yesterday and finished the final eight or nine flatcars of the first train in about an hour.

Ollie returned soon after that and gave Nick a break with the hand crank task, enabling him to drive the first T off the second train. Nick looked as nervous as I was on that first effort and while I went through it only yesterday, it seemed a long time ago. He came back from the parking field beaming. I "could nae blame him," as he would say.

It turned out the rain did not hamper us in the least as we all "walked the tightrope" in our ambulance cars. We were all cautious and took our time. With the three of us driving it wasn't long before the second train was half emptied. I volunteered to trade spots with Ollie for a bit, thinking he was having too big a workout with all that cranking. But he just laughed at me and told me not to worry, that he was a born crank.

We took a break at half past one and were headed toward Ollie's tool shed where we could shelter within the open doors with our lunch pails when the rain began to let up, pause, come down lightly again for a minute, and then suddenly stop.

"Well, would you look at that," chimed Lenny. I thought he was talking about the rain having stopped, and about time that it did. But then he pointed toward Manhattan and, looking past the doors of the shed — with a backdrop of white, grey, and black clouds, above the rain-sodden cattails and marsh grasses — arched a magnificent double rainbow, stretching all the way from Newark Bay northwards toward Hoboken and beyond. It was a thing of beauty and I feel we all took a moment to reflect on God's greatness. I looked at the men around me as they viewed the heavens. I took in the mud-encrusted boots, the scarred hands, the worn-out work clothes, but above all, the smiles and wide-opened eyes of their faces. We were men, but we were still boys at heart. We worked hard as hell, but we still played when we could. We cussed up a storm at times, yet we could offer a prayer of thanks for a thing of such beauty.

We got back to work shortly after that and by 5:00 had both trains entirely off-loaded. There were now 160 new Ford Model T cars of various configurations lined up in eight rows on the parking field, twenty in a row, much like a company of soldiers awaiting inspection. Most of them were ambulances; all of them were facing east, the direction they would soon be heading, to who knows what sort of adventures? Other formations of Ts stared at us from various parts of the Yards, with their twin headlamps imploring us not to forget them; that they, too, were prepared to go "to the sound of the guns."

By the end of the day, we were tired, sore, dirty, and yes, cranky. But we were done with the unloading task, and tomorrow would indeed be another day.

10

The Black Tom Warehouse: 7/4/16

INCLUDING WHAT WE OFF-LOADED, there were now over 240 Model T Ford cars of various styles parked around the Yards to bring out to the docks. Once you account for several flat beds, tankers, staff cars, and two with large winches for towing, a total of 209 needed to be packed with medical supplies and equipment before driving them through town to the Hudson. There were another two dozen Buick C4 cars, all decked out as ambulances, to be included in our charge. These had a different gearshift system that Ollie was familiar with, so he claimed responsibility for those.

It turned out we would not be putting any overtime in at the docks, what with our ferrying duties, and that suited us fine. Driving was a lot easier than all that heavy lifting. Originally, I thought once Peter got back from South Jersey, he would be joining us in our task, but instead he was needed in the Newark Yards, as he is high up in the chain of command there. That left me, Ollie, Lenny, and Nick as drivers. That worked out to about eighty cars apiece (one car would have to make the return trip). If we could squeeze in seven or eight trips each per day it would take us between two and three weeks to get them all packed, moved, and shipped to France.

We had our work cut out for us and would be driving from dawn to dusk, keeping a steady flow of vehicles going from Kearny Point over to the National Docks. The plan was to always have one auto bring back all the drivers for the next round. That car would ferry additional medical supplies in boxes and crates on the way over. Conveniently, that would also be the hooch car and it would make several stops along the way. To cover the extra time it would take for Lenny to drop off the White Lighting, he instructed the three of us to maintain a slow speed on the way to the river. We could open the throttle up wide heading back, to make up some time. "Nobody's gonna know the difference," he said.

Peter's crew began loading the boxy Fords that Tuesday morning and we commenced our plan with the non-ambulance types first. One tanker was missing, having gone to South Jersey for a big gulp of moonshine, but four remained. We took three on the first go-round, with Len riding in a black staff car in the rear of our little convoy. When I looked back after crossing the Hackey, he was no longer there, having already turned off for his first delivery. We got to the Hudson dock complex in about 45 minutes, passed through the National gates, and were directed to a wharf on the Central Railroad of New Jersey Docks, where a black and white cargo vessel was tied up. The foreman signed for the Fords, and we collected our things and walked the hundred yards over to the National Dock offices. Lenny would be by shortly to pick us up and we settled down for a smoke and to compare notes on our accomplishment.

"My," Nicky began, "that took longer than I imagined it would. After speeding around the meadow paths, you'd think the city streets would have been a bit quicker."

"Well," I pointed out, "that slower speed had a lot to do with it but maintaining a column like we did was a totally different way of motoring for all of us. Each time Ollie braked in front, I had to come to a stop, and then you behind me. I couldn't see what was causing him to halt, and you had it even worse from back there."

Ollie chimed in and said, "Yar, but if a lovely lass is about to cross the street, a gentleman must yield to her; it's only right."

"And what if it is a little ol' lady?" asked Nick.

"Ah, they may be slower to cross, but quicker to back away if you keep on going."

"Ollie!" I cried. "You've been taking lessons from Lenny!" It was true; this wasn't Ollie talking.

"I'm just having a go at you, my good man," he replied. "You'll find that we Swedes are known for our sense of humor."

I still could not get used to the British accent coming out of this big, blond-headed Viking, but nodded in assent and took a drag. I was about to ask him if he spent time in the British Isles when Nick tapped my shoulder and pointed at the track crossing behind us: a black staff car was approaching, Lenny at the wheel, with the rear seats crammed full of chicken cages. The birds raised a fuss as he crossed the tracks with a double thud, pulled up and placed her in park.

"Be a good lad August and drive these here birds on over to Black Tom for me, would ya? I gotta have a quick word with the guys loading those tankers on the ship."

He started to hurry off when I replied, "Sure, Len, but who gets 'em?"

He turned back and said, "Ah, yea, right. Just go down the island until you pass the Lehigh warehouses. You'll see a grain elevator on the right and just past it, a long wooden structure with a big pile of crates in front of it. Ask for Karl. Tell him I got all the chickens he wanted but they didn't have any geese. I'll owe him. But I still want those five cases of Havanas we talked about. He's a stand-up guy; he'll fork 'em over."

With that he went over to the three tanker Fords we just dropped off and started talking to the boss over there, a very tall fellow I didn't recognize. We don't normally deal with the Jersey Central dockers, but Lenny seems to know everyone around here. Must be the *Marketing Business* he goes on about. He started pointing at one of the Fords, then to the hoist, then back to the Ford, and put his hands on his hips and started jabbering some more at the guy. I'd hear about it later no doubt and paid him no mind. Then I hopped in behind the wheel and trundled off down the wharf with the load of cackling cargo to find Karl. *Cigars*, I was thinking. *What's he got going now?*

I headed south on the riverfront toward the Lehigh Valley Railroad terminus just a bit downstream called Black Tom. It was a long wharf that jutted out into the Hudson River about a mile or so. It once was a separate island, just like Ellis or Bedloes — the one with Lady Liberty on it — and an old slave named Tom supposedly used to live there like a hermit. About fifteen or twenty years ago, they filled in the river there and connected the mainland to the island. Now there were a couple dozen huge warehouses and a bunch of shacks lining both the north and south side, with two or three sets of tracks running straight down the center. There was a constant flow of carts, trucks, dollies; most anything with a pair of wheels on it. Barges and tugs were tied up and other river traffic kept coming and going. Right now, there was a row of Lehigh Valley box cars being pushed in by a pair of locomotives and I was going to have to wait for them to clear the dockway before I could pull on to "Tom."

As I approached, I braked and sat back to watch. There were only about thirty-five box cars, but they were slow going because of the contents. The red flags on them indicated high explosives, either TNT or three-inch shells, no doubt. We did not work on this part of the docks but lots of the fellows would frequent Sullivan's or Packy's Tavern and share a few pints and stories with us. They claimed it was perfectly safe stuff to handle – if you were careful and took your time. They had their share of the normal accidents that we were all exposed to, but you wouldn't find me or my buddies hauling all this black powder and such. Hell, they won't even let you smoke on the job!

I contented myself in looking across the Hudson at Manhattan across the way. What a view! The sun was brightly reflecting off the windows of the Woolworth Building – tallest building in the world, they say. Can you imagine working in a building sixty stories tall? Holy smokes, that's a lot of stairs to climb down if the elevators ever broke. Pop and I had to go to the Singer Store on Broadway last year to get a new part for Mom's sewing machine. The shop was across the street from the Woolworth skyscraper, and we stood in awe with our necks craned back looking up at it. I felt dizzy after a minute or so but kept looking back up. Pop laughed at a big gathering of pigeons at the third-floor level, saying, "Gee, Augie, those birds have the whole building they can fly up and roost on, but they decided that height is all they need. Makes you wonder if they know something we humans don't, eh? And look at that brand-new shiny building with a big load of bird dung trailing down over those windowsills. Bet ya old man Woolworth isn't going to put up with that for long!"

That was a fun trip with Pop. We took the ferry back after dark and got caught in a sudden rain squall halfway across. The river was very choppy that night, and we shipped a lot of water as the craft was tossed up and down in the big waves. We were drenched and made it ashore all right, but I couldn't help but be amazed at a life where you could be marveling at a manmade Wonder of the World in the morning and nearly perish that same night in a simple wooden boat. Yup, makes ya think hard, it does, about our insignificance on this planet.

I heard the chugging of the locos getting louder as they began to cross in front of me and got ready to get the T moving again. I waved at the engineer, but I really had no idea who the heck he was. It's just the way we are down here on the river.

Once the train passed, I still had to wait for the flagman to signal the 'All clear' before I could cross. Boy, do they get ticked off if you don't wait. Accidents do happen, and it's almost always due to carelessness or lack of patience. The docks play for keeps.

I eased over the rails and made a careful left onto Black Tom Wharf; the slowly moving train just about ten feet to my left. You never know what you may find on the boardwalk here, I swear. So many obstructions crop up from one day to the next you really must move cautiously. A whole load of gun wadding stood right in the center of my pathway, and I had to squeeze through between it and a neatly stacked pile of kegs. What was in these small barrels I couldn't guess, but I doubt it was moonshine. A couple of docker dogs began to chase me once I cleared the wooden kegs, and I accelerated a bit, leaving them behind.

Funny thing is, the stacked kegs and gun wadding would probably be gone in twenty minutes or so. That's how quickly things get moved around here. It gets dropped off by train, wagon, truck, or small boat, and is then stored in the warehouses for a time. Then it almost always gets loaded on the south side of the pier onto sea-going freighters bound for Europe. While National Docks handles things like barbed wire, entrenching tools, medical supplies, food, and now ambulances, it's all explosives over here on Black Tom. The warehouses are full of it: large projectiles, TNT, mortar rounds, gun cotton, three-inch shells, wadding, 30.06 Enfield rifle ammunition, linked machine gun ammo belts, black powder, and who knows what else. It boggles the mind how much is stored here, what's already been shipped, and what's due to arrive next.

Gee, I could use a cigarette. Maybe later would be better, eh?

I came to a sudden stop when a mule darted in front of me. The skinner was having trouble controlling him, having let one of the reins slip. He pulled a carrot out of his back pocket and waved it in the air. The mule responded as the handler expected, and like that, they were out of my way. I wondered just who was handling who?

The Lehigh train took a switch track to a siding on the far left and I felt less hemmed in as I continued with my fowl freight heralding our passage.

I spied the grain silo up ahead and, just as Lenny said, the long, low warehouse across from it; a few hundred crates were piled up in front of the unpainted structure.

Pulling up next to a huge wagon overflowing with burlap bags, I noticed Spanish printing on them. I could make out the words "Havana" and "Tabaco" all right, but the rest was lost to me. A man came out of the warehouse carrying a tray with several glasses on it, smiled in my direction, and then frowned suddenly and said, "Now where in the hell is that scoundrel Leonard?"

Not being Lenny's protégé for nothing, I immediately deduced the situation, reached down, grabbed a jug of Lightning and said to the man "With Leonard's compliments, sir, I am to share a drink with you as we transact business. My name is August Landesmann. Would you be Karl, then?"

And that's how I met Karl Eisener, native of Stuttgart, and, as it turned out, one of Pop's customers. It seems the contents of his warehouses, consigned to Imperial Germany, were stranded here for the time being due to the British blockade efforts that increased the past year. Where neutral ships used to be escorted by the Brits through the minefields after inspection for contraband, now nothing was allowed through their blockade. Karl was literally sitting on a fortune of tobacco, and the ironic part of it all was — he didn't smoke!

As we carried the noisy crates of chickens into the warehouse I explained about the missing geese. He casually waved the news away with his hand and said, "Tell him next week will be good, but they'd better be fat." The warehouse was very long and divided up into compartments; most were overflowing with tobacco sacks, but occasionally I noticed things like furniture, books, a rusty sleigh that looked like it hadn't been pulled by a horse in over a century, and even a spinning wheel.

"When my wife left me, I moved our things into here and sold the house," he said. This did not seem the sort of thing to comment on as we only just met, so I merely nodded, and said, "Uh-huh." (Mom would know how to handle that situation; I'd try to ask her tonight. Pop would have probably just nodded without further comment. I'm a bit wordier than he.)

We put the cages in an empty stall and went back for the rest. On the way he handed me three crates of La Corona cigars. He said they were hand-wrapped just two months ago, and the finest in his supply. He carried two more and we went out to my waiting Model T to stow them aboard. Once we finished the Marketing Business, we sat down on a bench and poured out a few glasses of hooch. He told me a bit of his previous dealings with Lenny and said, "When he lifts his left hand to show you some-ting, just keep an eye on his right." I told him a few tales, too, as we sipped on our drinks. I was getting used to the burning sensation after all, just like the guys said I would, but I nursed mine while Karl had several. I left him the rest of the jug and another unopened one as "Free samples," and was on my way. All in all, a profitable transaction, I should wonder.

My drive back to the boys was uneventful. If there were any chugging locomotives, kicking mules, or dogs chasing me, I didn't notice. Maybe it was the effects of the 'shine but I was more worried about losing my way than I was about hitting anything with the T. Weird, that, because it was a straight run north along the river and not like I could take a wrong turn or anything. It's just that there was so much activity on the docks.

I didn't see the Model T tankers any longer but noticed a group of people alongside the black and white freighter. I pulled up, shifted into park, and hopped on over to where my buddies were laughing it up over something with the tall boss and some longshoremen lads of his. Lenny noticed me and said, "Ah, here he is now — you can forget about sending the telegraph message to the light house – he won't be floating out to sea after all." The dock boss got a chuckle out of that, waved 'So long' and turned on up the gangplank. I'll bet he was glad to get back to work after that long interruption.

We all hopped back into the staff car with Nick at the wheel this time, and left the waterfront via Johnston Ave, then back onto Grand toward the Hackensack and Kearny beyond. I told Lenny about Karl's fat geese comment, the Coronas and leaving the jugs and he merely nodded and said, "Good, good." He then added, "Nicely done, Augie. It would make sense to include Karl's warehouse as one of your own personal stops when I assign your routes."

"Oh, will I be dropping off chickens all the time?" I asked.

"Heck no, Augie," he replied. "Those birds were just an icebreaker to get him to try the moonshine. You did well to have a few with him, as I figured you would. I'll do the same when I bring those fat geese in a few days and work out a deal giving weekly swaps of Lightning for Cubans. He's old school, that one, and up to now has just sat on the tobacco of his, saying it was supposed to go to the Vaterland. Well, I think I may have convinced him otherwise last week, what with the war news, and the chicken trade was the deal maker. He likes his eggs and meat, he does, but those birds will last him a long time and the hooch will be key to continuing our Marketing Business with him.

He just doesn't know it yet. He may not let us deal in large volume, but at the least we'll be all set for our own personal tobacco use. There's a case here for each of us and one for Pete, when he gets back."

Wow, I'm thinking, *what a haul — wait 'til Pop sees these! He adores a good cigar, and we can sit out on the porch after one of Mom's nice dinners, smokin' and shootin' the breeze.* Things were shaping up nicely in the delivery business.

11

The Mix-up: 7/5/16

T HAT WHOLE DAY WAS A whirl of spinning wheels — steering wheels, train wheels, wagon wheels, Ford wheels, and the big wheel behind it all, Lenny. Once we got back from dropping off those Model T tankers, he was all over the Yards, inspecting the packing job Pete's boys were doing, updating Boss Charlie on events, doing something in the reefer car, looking at the Buicks with Ollie, and filling the staff car with jugs of Lightning. He even got us settled with our ambulances (he assigned us certain cars by serial number and maintained a logbook, more to impress management than for any other reason – typical Lenny).

A group of fifteen Fords was fully packed as called for and marked with a white chalk "X" on the front left fender. Ollie would be joining me and Nick in driving Model Ts today, as none of the Buicks were yet loaded. That omission would soon be rectified and wasn't the only error Lenny discovered. All the boxes, bottles, tools, cans, and things appeared to be in perfect order. Yet, none of the ambulances had stretchers inserted in the racks built into the rear of the cars! The eldest of Pete's boys, an Italian lad called Giovanni, was put in charge and swore he would put things to right.

Len shook his head, hopped in the staff car, and took off ahead of us saying he'd meet us at the Hudson in about an hour.

Giovanni ("Call me Geo") soon gave us the go-ahead and we left the Yards on our second delivery at 1:00 p.m. exactly. With Ollie in the lead this time, we got to the river at just before two, and made a very brief drop off at the Jersey Central Docks, getting the tall fellow to sign our chit immediately. I had the feeling he didn't want to get caught up chatting with Lenny for any length of time and he didn't seem to mind that he hadn't shown up with us. In fact, his crew members were nowhere in sight, and we figured they must be having their lunch break. As before we settled on some boxes and had a smoke.

It was getting warm, and I was feeling a bit lazy looking out over the wide river and watching a couple black cormorants doing their dives. They swim mostly submerged, with their long neck and head above the water. Then they'll disappear under the waves, and you'll look and look for them to surface. They'll pop up about thirty feet away, often with a fish in their bill sticking out sideways. With a jerk and a shake, somehow, they navigate that fish down their gullet, and *gulp*, it's gone. Lenny once had Nick convinced there was a U-boat periscope in the river looking our way, moving slowly to our right, bobbing in the waves. He had him going, too, until the cormorant began to run on its webbed feet across the water and took off downstream! Right now, there were a few of them sitting on top of bulkhead poles drying their wings off. They hold them out wide to let the air and sun dry them, looking like some sort of prehistoric monster. Spooky looking things, they are.

My reverie was once again broken by the tootle of a Ford horn. We looked up and were surprised to see Lenny waving us aboard, in a hurry-like. He pulled right out almost before we got settled and got the Flivver moving at a fast clip, saying, "Pardon the hurry, boys, but time's a wastin'. We've only moved six of these babies so far today and here it is nearly two-thirty. We'll make four more trips before dark and cap it off at eighteen, but I'm gonna have to ease off on the hooch delivering for now."

"Eighteen Fords," I said, "including the tankers, right?"

"Oh yea," he replied. "And if we can give them a dozen and a half on the first day it won't look like we've been slacking the way we've been. Starting tomorrow we'll up it to a full two dozen and make some haste. When Pete comes back, we'll slow down again, and I'll make the drop-offs. It'll work out."

We bounced on the cobbled roads once we crossed the Hacky and turned back into the Yards like the devil was after us. Lenny pulled up at the parking field, we jumped out, got cranking, and took off again within ten minutes with him in the lead.

His saying, "Make it fast boys and see if you can keep up with me!" was all it took to motivate us. We were off like the Dickens in our group of green-clad Ford Model T ambulances, resplendent in our brass radiators, sparking headlamps, gleaming windscreens, and tastefully painted red crosses on large white circles. We buzzed by carts, wagons, a few running kids, a drunk or two, and a group of nuns from Our Lady of Czestochowa, paying no mind to anything but reaching the docks. We made it in about a half hour this time!

We spotted the black and white freighter, the foreman, the longshoremen, and some lady in a nurse's outfit grouped together. Lenny pulled up first in a kind of sideways slide. It looked impressive and would be something to learn from him when we had some time. Nick, Ollie, and I pulled up behind him, switched off the machines, and the four of us wandered over to the group. This nurse lady appeared to be giving the business to the tall boss man, who got sight of us approaching and pointed at Lenny. She was shaking a paper at the foreman in her clenched fist when she turned to look at us. She had a terrible scowl on her face, looked angry, and was beet red. I fell in love with her at once; it was the girl from the docks!

"Who is responsible for this mess with the ambulances?" she demanded.

"That would be this man," Lenny said, and pointed at me!

"Oh, and can you tell me where you found the baboons who packed the medicines?" she asked, focusing her vitriol right at my face!

"Ah, oh, er..." was all I could say.

Lenny then jumped in (the bastard!) and came to my rescue (what a fellow!) just as fast as he had abandoned me to this hellcat and said, "Oh, that mess. No, that wouldn't be this lad's fault at all. When you said 'mess with the ambulances,' I thought you meant the machines themselves. Young August Landesmann here is the convoy commander and is responsible for their maintenance, fueling, and transit to the docks. The medicinal supplies are packed in the Kearny Rail Yards by an entirely different group! What exactly is the problem?"

With that her face changed back more closely to the angel I recalled from the dockside, she uttered a sincere, "Oh, I'm so sorry, Mr. Landesmann," then turned to Lenny and said (still a bit sternly), "And just who the hell has totally messed up the supply system here and what are you going to do about it?" (You gotta hand it to Lenny and his way with women.)

"Ma'am," he replied, "I'm certain we can straighten things out lickety-split. If you'll allow me to make a list of the problems, August and I will do our best to accommodate you."

She hesitated just for a second there, took a deep breath, and continued with, "Well, for one thing, each machine is supposed to have three gallons of ethyl alcohol packed inside. There is not a gallon to be found on any of these ambulances you delivered earlier today. Then, one machine had all the bottles of peroxide, another had all the salve, and in the third was all the distilled water. None have antiseptic! The bandages and stretchers were fine, but there are no splints or thermometers! Just how in the world are we going to treat wounded men at the front when monkeys oversee the packing?"

"No splints or antiseptic?" he asked. "You've got to be kidding!" He stuck both arms out wide and went on "And, no alcohol? No thermometers? This is a disgrace!" he stamped his foot."August, write this all down, would you?"

"I don't have a pencil," I replied. "But I think I can remember it all."

"Oh, I have a list right here for you men," said the nurse shaking it in Lenny's face. "How about we take a quick peek at what's inside these cars and see if I need to add to it!"

With that I opened the rear doors of the first car in line and she stepped inside. "Yup," she yelled back at us. "Just as I thought — no alcohol here either. And look in that box right there, Mr. Landesmann. You'll find no splints, I'd wager."

"Call me August, Ma'am, if you would," I said. I opened the box, looked inside, and added, "By God, you're right; I don't see any splints in here."

"And what do you see inside the medicine locker over there?" she asked.

"Well, it looks like it's full of distilled water, Ma'am."

"No peroxide? No salve? No antiseptic?"

"No, Ma'am."

"Molly."

"What?"

"My name is Molly. Call me Molly. Ma'am won't work with me. If you want to get along with me, you better call me Molly."

"Yes, Ma'am."

"Molly."

"Yes, Molly."

And that is how we met.

12

The Fix-up: 7/5/16

THE OTHER TWO CARS WERE similarly stocked: well, mis-
stocked. Molly crossed her arms and impatiently began tapping
her foot. It did not look like a happy rhythm either.

Lenny took charge at that moment, ordering us into the staff car
and telling Molly we'd return in two hours' time with the missing
items, and three more ambulances, "All properly outfitted." He asked
if she, "…would be so kind in the meanwhile to correctly distribute
the salve, distilled water, and peroxide among the six ambulances already delivered?" He promised there would be no further packing mis-
takes and that he was going to "…give it to those monkeys but good!"

This seemed to satisfy the lady, who thanked us but also asked if
we could please hurry. She then formally introduced herself as Miss
Molly Johnson, student nurse, and told us her father had given her the
task of ensuring the ambulances were loaded properly. She said he
was an official with the American Field Service in Paris, and that she
would be joining him there once all the Fords from Kearny Point were
successfully delivered to the docks — properly outfitted, inspected,
and approved with her signature. She put her hand on my arm and
squeezed, looking from me to Lenny, to Nick and then Ollie and said,

"I hate to come across as mean or angry, but while we're chatting
away here, there are boys on the Western Front who lack proper medical care. They lay dying from horrible wounds and diseases. I need
to get to Paris and the Field Service as soon as I can, but first I must

get more than two hundred ambulances properly equipped and sent to Le Havre. From there they will be distributed to newly formed volunteer ambulance sections in France and their good work can begin. I really need your help in this, and you must not allow this sort of mischief with the supplies to happen again!"

"Aye, Ma'am," said Lenny in reply. "Not to worry a bit, Ma'am, as me and the boys will see to it."

"I'm counting on you. Lenny, is it?"

"Yes, Ma'am, Lenny. Lenny Krulikowski."

"Well, I'm counting on you Lenny; you and August and the other fellows. Pray do not let me down."

"Oh, no, we won't, Ma'am!" we chimed in unison. With that she backed away and we were off as fast as the Ford staff car could take us — back to the Yards and some hard work. I noted that she didn't ask him to call her "Molly" and smiled to myself.

We rode in silence for the first half mile or so, each of us lost in our own thoughts. Ollie was the first to speak, "She has a good point, you know."

Nick answered for the rest of us by saying, "Just how do you mean? It's not like we've been loafing. We've been working hard enough. It's not our fault Pete's boys goofed up with the supplies."

Ollie replied, "Well, on that level I am inclined to agree with you, Nicolas. We have been working hard indeed. However, do you recall that bit she said about 'chatting away?' I don't think she meant just at that moment in time, while we were having that discussion.

"More likely, her feeling is of the big picture — here we are in America, safe and sound from the Great War that is devouring the flower of European youth. We're free to come and go as we please, have a couple beers Friday night, eat what we want, work how we choose. Why, we even sit at the docks having a smoke while waiting for Leonard to come pick us up. All the time while we are vigorously living our lives, many chaps over in the trenches are cold, wet, and hungry. They're likely to be torn apart by shellfire, mutilated by machine gun or rifle bullets, ripped by shrapnel.

"See what I mean? We're safe and well-fed in New Jersey while fellows our own age are bent over with dysentery, fevered with malaria, or suffering from shell shock. That is where she is coming from. Her motivation, what she is gearing up her life's work to be, lies across the sea in the carnage in France and Belgium. She wants to save lives and help stem the flow of blood, and here she is dealing with the work of, what did she say? Baboons!"

"By Christ, lad, I wish I had checked those supplies better!" blurted Lenny. Although he did not take his eyes off the road when he spoke, we all could hear by his tone that he was sincere.

"That's all right, Len," I said. "We trusted those young lads to use their noggins and they were careless, as boys will be. A few raps on their thick skulls is all it will take and we'll be supplying the machines just fine. What we'll have to do from now on, is a double check of the items before we put the chalk marks on the fenders. If it's that important, heck, we can check 'em again at the docks while waiting for you to pick us up!"

He brightened up at that, and added, "Aha! That would do it Augie. And, if anything turned up missing at the docks, I'll carry extra supplies in the staff car to put things to right! Yes, that will do it!"

With that he smiled again, as only Lenny could, with that big Pollock grin of his, and we rode once again in silence. Before you knew it, we arrived at the Yards.

He skidded to a halt in front of the remaining Ts in the formation and had us jump out, "Check them all, lads, and make a note of any missing items. We'll start with this bunch, and I'll have Giovanni here inside a minute with his boys. We can do this; we have but nine of them left for today. We'll need to make three trips and the last one may be after dark."

While Len trotted off toward Boss Charlie's office, we went through the Fords in the parking field. Each one had items missing, just as we feared. At least all the stretchers were aboard, I'll give them that.

We heard a commotion coming toward us and looked up to see

Lenny leading a group of five disheveled boys carrying boxes and crates. Giovanni was in the rear pushing a dolly stacked with boxed gallon bottles of alcohol. Len had them pile up the crates in front of the ambulances, put the lads at a rough form of attention, turned to Ollie and said, "They're all yours, sir."

Ollie beamed, and in his dirty coveralls started pacing before the group and began to address them: "Men, your hard work and attention so far have been much appreciated. Boys like you are fighting and dying over there in France and what you are doing is a great service to them in their hour of need! Sadly, certain items are not getting to the front in sufficient quantities. We must ensure that each ambulance is outfitted with all the medicines and equipment on the checklist. Giovanni, step forward!"

"Yes, sir?" said Geo.

"I need you to be personally responsible that each Ford machine has every item on this check list. I want you to take charge of this pencil given to me by Boss Charlie himself — don't lose it — and make a check mark next to each item on the list. You can read, can't you?"

"No, sir!"

"Drat, and double drat!" said Ollie. "I never thought of that." He turned and resumed pacing and said in his powerful voice, "Is there anyone among you who can read?"

A few seconds went by when suddenly a hand shot up. It was Lil' William. Lil' William was from Poland, like Lenny, but outweighed him by a good one hundred pounds. He was tall with dark hair and dressed in a motley collection of dirty rags. Nobody knew much of Lil' William, only that he slept somewhere in the Yards.

"I can read, sir," said Lil' William. "I used to be in Seminary."

"Good Lord," chimed Lenny.

"Precisely, sir," added Lil' William.

"All righty then," said Ollie, and resumed his stance. "Lil' William, I need you to be personally responsible that each Ford machine has every item on this check list. I want you to take charge of this pencil given to me by Boss Charlie himself — don't lose it — and make a check mark next to each item on the list. You can do that, can't you?"

"It would be my privilege, sir."

"Very good," said Ollie, "come with me." They went off to one of the ambulances and looked inside. Ollie handed Lil' William the clipboard with the check lists on it, made a show of giving him the pencil from Boss Charlie, and patted him on the back. Meanwhile Lenny had the boys pile the rear seat of the staff car with various boxes and two large crates of rubbing alcohol in gallon bottles. He was off in a flash in the staff car, but suddenly stopped, put it in reverse and shouted over the engine to us, "Augie, get moving as soon as you and Ollie personally double check the contents in these cars. Nicky, you may as well do a triple check this time around, just so you know all the things to look for. I'll see you all at the freighter!"

With that he was off.

In no time at all we had the missing items replaced and did our double check. There was only so much you could stuff in the back of the ambulances anyway. It was just a matter of knowing what went where. Nick thought he caught us for a moment, but the items were all there, just placed inside the lockers in a different order.

Ollie gave the boys a final harangue and ended with an admonition that tomorrow all the Fords had better be fully equipped or, "Heads will roll." Coming from a big guy like Ollie that sort of thing might keep them up at night.

We felt the boys would perform satisfactorily, but we would still verify the contents before driving off the next group in the morning.

We left in a big hurry, as before, but with Nicky in the lead. He was a natural dancer, as I've said before, but a convoy leader he was not. He seemed to hesitate at intersections, almost as if he was confused. I pulled up to him after the second instance and asked him what was going on. He said, "I'm not quite sure of the way, August, and don't want to take a chance on getting us lost."

"Just follow me then, Nick," I told him. "We're all nervous right now, and all of this is new to us." I took the lead position and hit the gas. In no time at all we got to the docks and spied Lenny and Miss Johnson standing together by the ship. We pulled up in line and shut down the motors as they approached. We got down from the cars and stretched.

"Hello, lads, there's the good boys. You just made it in the two hours, as promised!" Lenny looked relieved as he said this. Can't say I blame him.

"We'd have made it sooner," says I, "but we got stuck behind a horse."

My joke fell on deaf ears, so I carried on with, "You'll find everything stocked in the cars as ordered, folks. Come have a look for yourselves."

Things got quiet as Nurse Johnson opened the first set of doors. She climbed inside and began opening the boxes and lockers. She kept nodding her head affirmatively, very business-like, as she peeked inside. Lenny kept pumping his fist in the air at each successful audit and when she stepped down and went to the next car.

Thank God for our double checking back in the Yards, as we passed the test with flying colors, save for one incident: as Nurse Johnson emerged from the third car, she had a quizzical look on her face. She was holding a bottle of White Lightning. "This one bottle seems to be unlabelled," she said. "Any idea what it is for? It has a strong smell of alcohol, yet another strange smell in it I do not recognize."

Lenny was on top of it at once and said, "Oh, that's for the radiator, Ma'am. It helps keep the engine from freezing in the frigid winter. Ollie, one of the mechanics must have left it in there, be a good chap and put it in the fender box, would-ja?"

Ollie gave us his best "Yar," reached for the bottle and went around to the driver's side fender box to stow it. I noticed he stuffed it down his overalls instead. We were all rogues, the lot of us.

Lenny wrapped it up then, and said, "If we may, Ma'am, we must be getting back to Kearny Point to make the last two runs of the day. Be assured that our packing will pass muster from here on out. We sincerely apologize for all the mix-ups. Will you be here when we return?"

"No, Mr. Krulikowski, in fact I'm boarding the next H&M train to Newark and from there a fast walk to Saint Michael's, so I must hurry down to Exchange Place. Leave the ambulances right here and I'll have them loaded aboard in the morning after I check the contents. I've already told the foreman that plan."

"Yes, Ma'am," replied Lenny, "and have a great evening then."

Things were looking up now that we had the details worked out, and it began to look like we had the lady's confidence after all. As I passed by her on my way to the staff car, she said, "Nice to meet you, August." My heart fluttered but I managed, "You too, Molly. Good night."

I caught Nick smiling at me out of the corner of my eye and gave him a wink as I hopped in next to Lenny. Molly was already walking upriver toward the Hudson & Manhattan Station as we pulled away from the dock.

Just a few weeks ago, I was loading bales of wire onto freighters. In just a short time, I'd learned to drive a motorcar, tried my first moonshine, been given a case of Havana cigars, and was now smitten with a woman. What more could a man want?

13

The Decision: 7/5/16

AS WE DROVE WEST THROUGH Jersey City I was once again lost in thought. I wondered if Molly would say Yes if I asked her to go on a picnic or something. Nick's group was always having things like that on summer weekends; they'd still play their fiddles and such, but it would be out in the open air in the park. There'd be beer, hot dogs, potato salad, baked beans — the works. Why, they have a big pond there and I could take Molly out on a rowboat. And a lovely little island in the middle where…

"Wake up, Augie, yer dreamin' again." This, a voice from over my shoulder, made me start. I looked back and asked, "What's that, Nicky?"

"You don't have me fooled, August, I'm in on yer little secret."

"Well, yes, I guess that's true, but keep it from Lenny, would-ja? I don't need him busting my horns."

"What's that, August?" asked Lenny. "Something wrong with the horn?"

"No, go ahead and tootle it; it should be working fine."

Ah-ooo-gah, ah-ooo-gah!

"Yup," he said, "Sounds ok to me, too."

"Oh, good. I must have imagined it."

• • •

We got back to the Yards just as darkness was falling. We still had three more Flivvers to deliver to the river. That sounded funny —

Flivvers to deliver. I could always ask Pop if he wanted me to deliver any liver in my Flivver to the river. He'd get a kick out of that.

"Boys," said Lenny, as he smacked himself on the cheek to ward off a mosquito, "we'll be heading out in about twenty minutes. Take a break, have a smoke, whatever. I'll be in with Boss Charlie for a spell and see if he heard from Pete on the office telephone."

With that he strolled off while lighting a Cuban. I got down, too, but decided to walk around a bit and stretch my legs. If we had one more round-trip to make, I needed to get my blood flowing again. I was getting stiff from sitting as a passenger. When you're driving, there's a lot of motion involved. As a passenger, you tend to sit still and just look around.

I headed over toward Ollie's equipment shed. Earlier I had seen a small flock of goldfinches chomping away on the sunflowers he planted in his small garden. You see these yellow and black birds all over the meadows in summer where they nest. This group left husks of seeds all over the ground, and you could see the carnage they wrought on the flower heads themselves. I'd pull off some seeds for my own use but was not sure they were ripe yet. There were some red cherry tomatoes, so I put ten or twelve in my pocket to munch on later. All the big beefsteaks were still green.

As I turned the corner of the shed a small possum bared his teeth and hissed at me. This was a cute little feller, but in no time at all he'd be as ugly as the rest of them. They grow fast down here at the Point and are quite numerous, but I've yet to see one actually "playing possum." They've got to be the world's ugliest creatures and look as though they were created from a spare-parts box by some maniacal demon. Their large, rat-like head, the shaved tail, big pink nose, matted fur, uggggh. I picked up a shovel from the side of the shed, scooped him up, and sort of swung him into the marsh grass in a swooping motion, where he scooted off. The canes spoke of his passage.

"Friend of yours, August?" This was Ollie Olson. He must have seen the little critter and my confrontation with it.

"We only just met," I replied. "And I don't look forward to any further acquaintance with him."

"I'm quite surprised at your gentle toss of the little creature into the brush. Some chaps around here are prone to smashing in their skulls. I cannot say I have the taste for that method and prefer the approach you just employed. When I come upon one of the local fauna, I will stamp my foot once or twice to scare them off, or else I take a slight detour not to interrupt their endeavors. For all we know, Mother Nature herself may have sent them on that errand. Why, that one, miserable creature may be the last chance of survival for that species in the local environment — or even on the entire planet. Perhaps it was just on its way to mate and any attempt at disruption, nae-ye-mind destruction, could spell doom for its lineage. And what about its place in the food chain? Predators that catch them for their meals would lose a source of nourishment. Scavengers who dine on their carcasses would have to find something else or go hungry."

"Ah," I interjected, catching on, "and don't forget the useful function they themselves perform, eating insects and mice, scattering seeds in their dung from plants they eat that will in turn sprout new growth. Each one is part of the whole natural plan; an important part, and if wantonly killed by such as we, it becomes a crime against nature."

"Aha!" exclaimed Ollie, "a man after my own heart. That explains your cautious toss of the little animal — you are a naturalist."

"Only to some extent, Ollie. I confess I have shot the odd rat around here and will continue to do so. They spread disease, get into the storage bins, and are filthy animals. Even though I feel bad about it afterwards, I still do it now and again."

He nodded, put his hands in his overall pockets and surprised me with something out of Genesis: "And God said, let us make man in our image, after our likeness: and let them have dominion over the fish of the sea, and over the fowl of the air, and over the cattle, and over all the earth…"

"…and over every creeping thing that creepeth upon the earth," I finished.

"Precisely," he said. "Such is the lot of man that he must act as judge and executioner at times, over the animal kingdom, in his role as steward of the earth. You are not to be faulted at all, August, over your occasional sniping of vermin. Look what rats did to Europe in the Black Death! And today they're getting fat on rotting corpses on the Somme battlefield, wreaking havoc in the trenches with the wounded, and spreading who knows what kinds of disease among the troops and refugees. I imagine both sides are fighting the rats when they're not trying to kill each other!"

I popped a cherry tomato into my mouth and nodded as he continued. "Much like that possum we just philosophized about, have you ever thought of the effects this war is having on humanity? Why, just the death of one man can alter the path of history, don't you think? Torn bodies and destroyed lives yes, but what about the loss of intellect, deeds left unfinished or never begun? What budding inventor will be buried by a shell, leaving humankind without the benefit of his machine? What young physician may be killed by a bomb dropped indiscriminately from an aeroplane in the heavens above, killing his future contributions to medicine along with his corporal self? What literary works will never be published, art produced, music written? Even the lowest private of little or no schooling being machine-gunned down in No-mans-land, what of his contributions to the world?"

I did not know what to say. I merely stared at him, expecting him to go on.

He took a breath, and continued, "Kaiser against King, Tsar versus Crown Prinz, Field Marshall pitted against general, diplomat and, well you know, all the politicians, all the elites making statements to the press, or in Parliament, against the foe, all the while ordering the movement of troops around the globe. Sending a regiment to their deaths here, ordering fleets to sure destruction there, forcing entire battalions, nay, entire divisions, to remain in positions while enduring intense bombardments.

"Two weeks ago, on the opening day of the Somme the British generals had wave after wave of men attack in straight lines, at a walk, behind officers holding riding crops or kicking foot balls. When they got in range the Germans opened-up with criss-crossing machine gun fire, then pre-registered artillery, all in broad day light! Frontal assault like that is madness, and the General Staff knew that already! Why are they throwing away lives like this? A whole generation of our youth is being tragically wasted by leaders who are too slow to learn how to adapt to the 20th century weapons that are being used to great effect. They talk of patriotism, but where is their patriotism grounded, on the blood of the innocents being spilled? On their vaunted honor and medal –bedecked chests?

"No, true patriotism beats in the hearts of the common man who endures these dangers and hardships, either for love of country or the belief that by doing so they are protecting their homes and loved ones. These brave souls are joined by those blinded by hatred of the enemy due to state propaganda, and those forced to do so by threat of imprisonment! So, a mixture of patriots, the hateful, and the unwilling, all being led by the incompetent, in a human tragedy of epic proportions, one that will set back humanity for eons, no doubt, and happening right at this very moment, affecting every living thing on this planet. And you, young August, although Prussian by birth, are American by the grace of God. Have you ever thought where you will fit into this tapestry? How will your fibers be woven into the history of this global conflict, you who cannot hurt a small possum but will occasionally shoot the odd rat because you feel it necessary? If America joins the allies in this war, how would you feel about battling your old homeland? Do you think you could fire a shot in anger at a possible relative or old neighbor? They will not be rats; they will be people. What will you decide to do when the time comes? Will you be a patriot? Ah, but to which country? Or will you instead be a hater, or perhaps, the unwilling?"

Again, I did not know what to say. I merely stared at him, hoping he'd go on. But he didn't speak. He just stared back at me, with his hands in his overall pockets. I remembered Pop in the kitchen the other day and his similar questions. I thought about Lenny and his schemes, I recalled the *Lusitania* and other ships that had gone down,

I smiled at the thought of Molly and her compassionate need to get to France. I thought about my cousin Max in Stuttgart and my Uncle Ernst in Elberfeld. I saw images of rats scurrying from my rifle shots. Suddenly, it all dawned on me. I knew the answer. It was there all along. I looked Ollie in the eye, took a breath and said, "I'm going to be an ambulance driver."

"Good God," he remarked. "I never thought of that. What a wonderful idea! The shovel and the possum should have given me a clue. Well, you're certainly young and strong enough. Of course, it will be very dangerous for you, up at the front and armed with a Model T Ford instead of a rifle."

"Yes, but it's something I can do; something I can contribute without having to shoot anything or anyone."

"Well, let's hope it stays that way. Wars have a habit of changing the way people think about things. Meanwhile, it would please me greatly to spend some time giving you instruction in engine mechanics. As you said, it is something I can contribute, and you may find yourself in need of such knowledge one day, having to make a field repair in great haste. Beyond that possibility, there are certain modifications you can make to your personal vehicle that would get you out of trouble faster than the factory-made Model T."

I must have looked at him strangely, for he patted my right shoulder and said, "Just because Mr. Ford built these cars a certain way does not mean the talented mechanic cannot alter them to increase horsepower and performance."

"Oh?"

"Oh yes, indeed. Starting tomorrow I'll give you the basics on the internal combustion engine and drive train. From there we can get into some experimental ideas I've employed while working on Prince Gustav's racing car."

I was about to ask him about the prince when Lenny came back from the office and smacked me on the back saying, "OK, gents, we're good to go. Let's get this last bunch to the river and call it a night." He went off calling for Nick who had disappeared somewhere.

Ollie and I followed in his tracks, the occasional mosquito buzzing in my ears. I noticed the smudge pots were not lit yet although complete darkness had fallen. These help keep the bugs off if you're not moving around. There were, however, several metal barrels blazing, as is the norm in the Yards at night. If we don't burn up all the empty crates you find around here, they tend to pile up and give safe harbor to rats and other critters, so we're always feeding the fires.

As we walked toward the waiting ambulances Ollie said, "Young Molly is going to be right in the thick of things when she gets to France. I hope she stays far back behind the lines."

That startled me. I had not thought of Molly being in danger and it shook me. I found my tongue and said, "I imagine she'll be safely staying at one of the main hospitals in Paris." That — my humble opinion when I said it — turned out to be the case. Well, while in France, anyway. It was only later I learned that, during a U-boat encounter on one of her passages to England, the two ships on either side of hers were sunk.

No one, nowhere, nohow, was safe anymore.

14

The Dark: 7/5/16

WE CAUGHT UP TO LENNY who had us board our machines "lickety-split." Nick cranked for everyone while Len went about with a box of stick matches lighting the kerosene in the lone red taillight on each rear bumper. The staff car would lead us through the dark streets with its headlamps fully lit, but all the other Fords had yet to have the acetylene generator tanks on the running boards filled with calcium carbide, so their headlamps would not be working. As Ollie explained earlier, by turning a simple valve, water mixes with the calcium carbide in the tank below to create acetylene gas, which flows up through rubber tubes to headlamps that need to be lit by match to help see at night. He also said that they cannot use them at the Front anyway, because the lights attract artillery barrages. Better to careen about in the dark than be blown to bits by a shell, I suppose. Funny thing is, the 1916 Model T has electric powered lighting, but our ambulances were all built in 1915 and have the old style.

Without further ado, we were off with Lenny's staff car headlamps lighting our way through the Yards, out the massive gate, and onto the cobblestone road. The moon had gone above the clouds, leaving the meadowlands black with night. The lone set of headlamps threw illumination forward and a bit to the sides, brightly lighting the marsh grass that hemmed us in on both sides as we bumped along the cobbles toward the Hackensack. I was bringing up the rear, closely following Nick, who was tailing Ollie, who was about thirty feet behind Len.

All but the lead Ford were focused on the little red taillight ahead. This was going to be an odd game of "Follow the Leader."

We kept a tight formation until we climbed the Hackensack Bridge. Then Lenny picked up speed before Ollie realized it and really flew down the ramp to the Jersey City side when we were about halfway across the span. Ollie opened his throttle and took off after him, but I was hemmed in by Nick, who was probably skittish crossing the span at any pace, as he seems to be shy behind the wheel. "What the hell," I thought, and cut loose myself, passing him on the left side and picking up speed as I hurtled down the bridge after Ollie. "He'll catch up eventually," I figured, "But I'll keep looking back at him." Well, in my effort to catch up to Ollie, I misplaced Nick after the first block. Len's headlamps were clearly visible far ahead as I turned onto Communipaw Avenue, and I could also now see Ollie's red tail lamp. Lenny had stopped in front of a saloon but, since there are several in a row in this part of the Avenue, I wasn't quite sure yet if it was Hannity's, The Black Garter or that one with the weird name I can never remember. Ollie pulled up behind him and I thought I'd brake where I was to give Nick a chance to catch sight of me before moving forward. I heard a series of *ah-ooo-gahs* behind me, getting closer and closer, turned my head and saw the glint off his brass radiator from a nearby gas light. I put the Flivver in gear again and headed up toward the parked Fords, Nick right behind me. Lenny and Ollie were out of their cars and walking to meet us as we both pulled up. Lenny was waving both arms in a cross pattern to get our attention and called out, "Leave 'em running, chaps. One beer is all. I'll be back in ten, fifteen minutes tops. I'm off to Adler's to give some samples to the Madam and I'll give you the skinny on Pete when I get back." With that he turned on his heels, remounted the staff car, and took off into the night.

"Leave 'em running, he says, and takes off like Cupid's arrow to the whore house." This from Nick, who seemed out of sorts for some reason, which is understandable if you get my drift. He hopped off the Ford and stuck his hands in his pockets.

"Don't be sore, lad," said Ollie. "He's got more on his mind right now than carousing with the ladies at Adler's. It takes a lot of energy to stoke as many fires at one time as our friend Lenny is, and he means well by us."

"Oh, I'd believe that only if he was buying, but there he goes off and leaves us," smirked Nicky. His expression changed when he saw Ollie waving a handful of greenbacks, who laughed and said, "He told me to get us some sandwiches while we were at it!"

I got down from behind the wheel, straightened up my overalls and joined the boys as they climbed the wooden steps and passed through the doors to the noisy confines of The Black Garter. Now, with a name like that you may conjure up visions of black-stocking-clad dancing girls kicking their legs up high over their heads, bloomers showing. Nope. It's just a big joke that would bring a strong man down if it weren't for the excellent beer on tap at this place, and the marvelous sandwiches. The only black garters visible were on the shirt sleeves of the owner, Patrick Ryan, who was always impeccably attired in a starched white shirt, red vest with gold watch and chain, with black, pin-striped trousers, white spats, and patent leather shoes. The man parts his bushy red hair down the center and has a handlebar mustache to boot. He is an Irishman's Irishman, if you know what I mean. He is very generous (but not if you ever cross him), quite religious (curses religiously), patient as a saint (but not toward drunks) and has been known to help immigrants from the Isles (unless they're English). He was in quite the happy mood this evening, and immediately asked for Lenny.

Nicky said, "Oh, he'll be along shortly, Patrick. He's stopped at Adler's for a spell."

"Ah," replied Patrick, arching an eyebrow inquisitively. "Then maybe it will be some time before he makes an appearance, if he is looking over the new ladies there?"

"Not at all, my good man," chimed in Ollie Olson. "Lenny is merely distributing our new product for Madame Sylvia to sample, much as he will shortly do for your fine establishment."

"English are ye?" asked the owner with a scowl.

"Not at all, sir. I'm a Swede."

My ears perked up at that. Maybe now I'd hear the truth about his oddball accent.

"A Swede, you say? Then, pray tell, what is the national food of Sweden?"

"We call it *Lutefisk*."

"Aye, then; a Swede ye be. Only a Swede or Norseman would know of the strong-smelling cod called the *lutefisk*. Are you also aware of the effect it has on the wee animals in these parts?"

Ollie looked stumped, and Patrick continued. "Well, we had raccoons in the trash barrels making a mess every night, until I hit up on the idea of tossing the leftover *lutefisk* in the bins at closing time."

"And?" Ollie asked.

I jumped in and finished this old joke for him: "Well, the raccoons went away, but now they've got a family of Norwegians living under the saloon!"

This earned me guffaws from Nick and Patrick, but Ollie stood open-mouthed until it dawned on him, at which point he smacked his forehead with his palm, shook his head, and laughed aloud.

"Sorry, lad, but when one discusses *lutefisk* it's open season," said Patrick.

"I'm fine with that, my good man, and beg your forgiveness at my slow response to catch the humor of the thing. Truth is, I cannot abide the smell of *lutefisk* at all, so I felt badly for the poor raccoons and was lost in reflection at their fate. The Norwegians, now that's funny!"

This, too, resulted in laughter, and a round of beers soon appeared, one after the other, from the hand of Mr. Ryan himself, who smiled broadly and said, "These are on the house, gentlemen."

Ollie then plopped down ten dollars and stated, "Lenny recommended your corn beef and cabbage, and asks you keep it coming. He will join us shortly but ordered us not to wait."

Patrick called back to the kitchen to let his wife Maureen know how many plates to prepare, then changed his mind and asked her to just bring the entire platter so we could help ourselves. He then had to go down the other end of the bar to attend to several other patrons and begged our pardon.

They didn't have any dancing girls in this place, but they've got one heck of a piano player who has a fine tenor voice. Nick's eyes lit up as soon as Sean O'Meara got started up on "Londonderry Air," and if I didn't stick a beer in his hand he may well have joined in singing. That was when we first heard the new words to the song, penned just a couple years back to the older tune. These days they were all the rage:

> *Oh, Danny Boy, the pipes, the pipes are calling*
> *From glen to glen, and down the mountain side,*
> *The summer's gone, and all the roses falling,*
> *It's you, it's you must go, and I must bide.*
> *But come ye back when summer's in the meadow,*
> *Or when the valley's hushed and white with snow,*
> *It's I'll be here in sunshine or in shadow,*
> *Oh, Danny Boy, oh Danny Boy, I love you so!*
> *But when ye come, and all the flowers are dying,*
> *If I am dead, as dead I well may be,*
> *Ye'll come and find the place where I am lying,*
> *And kneel and say an Ave there for me;*
> *And I shall hear, though soft you tread above me,*
> *And all my grave will warmer, sweeter be,*
> *For you will bend and tell me that you love me,*
> *And I shall sleep in peace until you come to me!*

Sean finished with a flourish, to the applause of all present. Nick had listened with rapt attention and went right over to Sean to get a look at the words for himself. Maureen came out from the kitchen, carrying a large platter of corn beef and cabbage, with her teenaged daughter Kathleen carrying a pile of plates and silver. The words to another song — "I'll Take You Home Again, Kathleen" — went through my mind as I admired her long red hair. Her mother caught my eye and smiled, and I think my complexion suddenly mirrored Kathleen's locks, and I quickly took a swig of my beer.

Although there were plenty of tables in the large room, we ate right at the bar — something frowned upon in other places. Kathleen set us each up with cloth napkins, forks, and sharp knives, while Maureen dolloped out large portions of meat and vegetables, including carrots, potato, and cabbage. Nicky came back to join us, and we dug right in. It was so hot I burned the roof of my mouth on the second bite, a potato. My Mom likes to say, "There's nothing hotter than a hot potato." Well, she's right.

A loud voice from the doorway attracted our attention as it declared, "God bless all here." It was none other than Lenny, arriving with a large box in his arms. This Emerald Isle greeting is seldom heard outside of the Irish pubs in town, but here it fit right in, resulting in a chorus of replies, nods, and other greetings in return, such as, "God bless you kindly."

Nick whistled his dockside signal and Lenny gave the thumbs-up and smiled, then turned and followed Patrick behind the bar into a small room in the back. Knowing the contents of the box he was carrying, we all went back to our hearty dinner. Moments later the two chaps emerged, and Lenny joined us while Patrick drew a few more glasses from the tap and carried over a tray of foaming mugs. Maureen reappeared and served Lenny a large portion of corned beef and fixings, followed by her daughter carrying a platter of sliced rye bread and butter.

"Well, then, I expect you lads are all set for a spell," declared the handsome bartender. "Should you require a refill just give a holler. And my sincere thanks for the delivery, Leonard. My, ah, back's been aching something awful and I expect a cure is within reach." With that the Ryans went this way and that, clearing the empty glasses and leaving us to our own devices.

"Gents," Len began between bites, "I spoke to Peter on the office phone earlier. He's leaving the Barrens at first light and ought to be back in town the day after tomorrow."

A chorus of "That's great!" greeted the news. We then resumed eating with abandon.

"Were there any problems with the tanker car?" asked Ollie, who after all, is the mechanic of the group and would be the one to have to make any modifications to the Fords.

"None at all, and Pete took care to follow the advice given by the Piney moonshiners. Seems you can't fill the tanks all the way up and they must be vented. Sounded like good advice, too. We ought to be aware of how we store the booze, though. He also stacked several crates of bottles on the jump seat. I just hope he can keep his mitts off it on the way back north. We wouldn't want him winding up in a ditch somewhere, eh?"

"He's hopping back onto the Penn Railroad, right, not driving all the way back?" asked Nick, who already emptied his second mug of beer and was looking for one of the Ryans for replenishment.

"Oh yes, he's picking up the northbound PRR at a siding in the Pines, actually; an unscheduled stop where the ticket is a trio of bottles for the engineer, fireman, and conductor. He's also bringing a bushel of cranberries, of all things."

I excused myself as the piano player launched into a familiar Joplin Rag, as I had to hit the men's room at the rear of the place. "Cranberries," I said out loud as I walked down the length of the bar. "What the heck is that all about?" I smiled at an elderly gentleman and his wife at a small table whom I've seen before, and avoided tripping over Ol' Roy, an Irish Setter who could always be found snoozing back here. Just then I was jostled roughly by a fellow in a plaid jacket and bowler hat who said, "Watch out, pal," and quickly made his way past me to the men's room, slamming the door shut. Not wanting to start anything in Pat Ryan's place, I bent down to pet Ol' Roy, who thumped his tail at my approach. "What's with that guy anyway, Roy? Must have to pee bad, if you ask me." Roy just looked at me and I could read in his expression that he agreed. I rubbed behind his ears, and he closed his eyes. I always heard dogs liked getting scratched behind the ears. Not sure I'd like it myself, though.

Mr. Pisser came out from the john, leaving the door wide open. He rushed right past me and Roy without even looking at us. *What a shmuck*, I thought, and got up to go do my own business.

By the time I got back to the boys they had polished off most of the platters. I tossed some more veggies on my plate and grabbed a piece of rye bread to sop up the juice. Nick had finished and was talking music with Sean at the Wurlitzer. He was going on about syncopation and *Basso continuo*, whatever that is. Ollie and Len were discussing the Civil War, of all things. I'm thinking, *Cheez, Augie, you go take a leak and when you get back yer out of the loop.*

I decided to grab just one more piece of corned beef and put it on two slices of bread to put in my pocket for later when a loud quarrel began at the front end of the bar. I got up to look and was not surprised to see Mr. Pisser in the forefront of it all. He was slamming his fist on the bar and going on about something I couldn't quite hear. Patrick joined the young barman who was bearing the brunt of the onslaught. The kid looked quite upset. I wrapped my sandwich in a piece of newspaper and put it in my side pocket when suddenly, Mr. Patrick Ryan grabbed the lout by the jacket collar and man-handled him past several patrons and straight out the door! "And don't ye ever come back!" he exclaimed. He wiped his hands-on a bar-towel, poured a shot of whiskey, and whipped it on down. He next poured one for the red-faced barman, patted him on the back and handed him the shot.

Lenny looked up for a moment but went right back to talking about "Little Round Top" and a guy named Chamberlain. Nick ambled on down toward Patrick and I guess was trying to be a calming influence in his own way. I'd already heard Len carry on enough about Gettysburg back on its fiftieth anniversary, so I figured I'd take a stroll on over to hear the news on Mister Pisser, or Shmuck as I now might call him.

As I approached Nick and Patrick, I could hear some of the fellas nearby discussing the recent events. One of the longshoremen recognized the cad and said he'd been known to cheat at cards, sucker-punch fellows, things like that. Nobody seemed to know where he lived or worked, but several guys said they'd seen him around the waterfront the past few months.

I went over to tap Nick on the arm and asked, "What's going on?" Patrick looked at me and said, "Here, old son. Look at what that sonofabitch tried to get away with." He flipped a coin at me with his thumb, giving it a nice tumbling spin in a high arc. I caught hold of it and said, "Hmm, a five-dollar gold piece?"

"Not quite. Take a closer look."

Well, I've seen the odd gold piece myself from time to time, at Pop's store, but greenbacks are all the rage these days. I peered at the date – 1883; nothing wrong with that. It had a large Roman numeral "V" on the rear, just like the nickels you see all around, but those say "Five Cents" on the back. I handed it back and said, "So?"

"Lad," he said, "you're too young to remember, but when the V-nickel was first minted, it did not say 'Five Cents' on the backside. Some fellows got the idea to gold plate them and pass them off in shops or taverns as five dollars. They'd then take the change and head off to roll another victim. It took some time before folks caught on and raised enough fuss that the government added the 'Five Cents' to the back of the thing. I haven't seen one in over thirty years, but Johnny here dropped it on the bar and thought it sounded wrong. He took a close look at it and called the guy out on it."

"Yeah," added Johnny, "and he told me to go to hell, which is fine, but he said it right off the bat, confirming my suspicions. Had he claimed innocence and paid with a half dollar instead I would have believed him, but don't be telling me to go to hell like that."

"That-a boy, Johnny O'," chimed Patrick. "Yer a sharp lad there and I appreciate it. Why don't you have something to eat and go on home early tonight? You earned it."

Johnny got a big smile at that, took off his apron, thanked Mr. Ryan, and went on off toward the kitchen. Patrick scurried down the bar to fill some glasses and Nick rejoined the piano player, who had started up a familiar waltz that sounded Viennese.

What the heck? I thought. *Maybe I'll get some air.*

I exited the front door and immediately found the cool air refreshing after all that tobacco smoke. The moon had reappeared through a break in the clouds, which were moving fast. I could hear crickets and a night bird on a roof somewhere. I gazed down at our Fords. Lenny's staff car had been switched off; lights extinguished. Ollie's red tail-light still glimmered, as did mine. Nicky's was, what? Nicky's was gone! Holy crap!

I ran inside and called, "Lenny, Nick! One of the Fords is gone!"

15

The Search: 7/5/16

I WAS BACK OUTSIDE IN A flash, looking up and down Communipaw Ave. for that tell-tale red light on the back bumper, to no avail. Nick was next, saying, "Where? What?" — followed closely by Len and Ollie, who both wore faces of concern. I hopped in my still idling Flivver, revved the engine and said, "I'm headed toward the Hudson." Lenny gave me the Thumbs-up, told Nick to get up to the front of the staff car to crank, and ordered Ollie to get behind the wheel. He then went over to two old men who were sitting on rockers out front and asked if they had seen anything. I saw one of the old gents pointing eastward so I tore out of there and down the road so fast I didn't even see what happened next.

I don't know why I had guessed the thief would head toward the big river but since the car was pointed that way to begin with, it just made sense. That, plus we had just come from a relatively quiet section of the city and the closer you got to the docks the more action was to be found — bars, brothels, gambling — the works. I figured it was that shmuck Mr. Pisser and I'd bet he was out for a night on the town pawning off more fake gold pieces or some such scheme. I was also betting he was not that experienced at driving Model Ts and that my pushing mine to the limit would catch me up before long.

Jersey City is quiet at night — unless it's summer and you're on one of the main drags, and Communipaw was as main as you could get after sundown. There were lots of folks out on their porches, walking arm in arm on the blue slate sidewalks, sitting on benches, or, to my dismay, crossing back and forth across the street. I tootled the horn repeatedly, but people just seemed to look up without moving, so I had to slow down to avoid hitting them. When they cleared out, I gave it the gas only to have to weave around a wagon with a team of draft horses, or a guy on a bicycle cutting in front of me. It was frustrating. I was beginning to doubt the shmuck went this way after all when suddenly I came upon an upended vegetable cart with cabbages and beets strewn all around the street. The driver was holding the reins of his frightened horse, patting the animal's neck, and doing his best to calm the poor thing down.

"What the hell happened?" I asked him.

"Why, it was an ambulance, just like yours, the bastard! Who was that sonofabitch that banged into me? I'm gonna kill him with my bare knuckles!"

"I'm after him myself, buddy," I told him. "Did you see which way he went?"

"Hell, yeah, I did. Straight on down toward the river he went, after he took the north path at the Five-Corners."

There's a bunch of "Five Corners" spots in Jersey City, but this man must mean the nearest one — a few blocks away — which turned northeast on Grand Street.

"When did this happen?" I asked.

"Shit, it just happened. About five minutes ago."

Well, wasn't that something? I put the Ford in gear and got moving. For some reason, I had a big grin on my face. I got to the Five Corners and hung a left without slowing down, raising the Flivver up on two wheels. She held in there, coming back down on all four tires without missing a stroke. That was invigorating! I peered forward through the windshield for any other calamities that might befall me at this pace, but this part of Grand Street is residential, and the way ahead seemed clear at last. Large sycamore trees line both sides of the thoroughfare here and the only illumination is from the occasional gaslight post or house windows. It began to drizzle.

I thought I saw something a few blocks ahead that reminded me of a glowing coal in the midst of a dying fire; an ember that wouldn't quite go out this summer's eve. I went even faster. As I watched, it appeared to get bigger and was swaying slightly from side to side.

It was a red taillight.

It had to be Mr. Pisser.

Thinking back to that day in the meadows where Lenny and then Peter slimed me with the giant mud puddles, I accelerated and planned to surprise the schmuck on the left side, giving him a blast of horn and then cutting him off.

And catch up to him I did.

I roared up on his left and hit the bulb on the horn — *ah-ooo-gah, ah-ooo-gah!* I noted the surprised look on his face, took in his stupid looking bowler hat and that flashy plaid suit. His hand went inside his jacket and came out with something black. He pointed it at me.

I wasn't born yesterday. I hit the brake pedal and pulled back on the handle, screeching to a halt. He shot past me and picked up speed. I was aghast and angry both at the same time!

At that moment, I heard a very pleasant sound indeed — the sound of two more Ford Model Ts pulling up behind me!

"August!" yelled Lenny from behind the wheel of an ambulance. "Are you all right?"

"He's got a gun, Lenny!" I yelled.

"Well, old son," he said, "so have I. Nicky, drive this thing, wouldja? I'm going with young August here." With that he got down, reached into the back, and pulled out the biggest buffalo gun I'd ever seen. He climbed aboard next to me with the rifle and said, "I'm riding shotgun, eh? Now you get me in range, and we'll fix his wagon, the bastard!"

Ollie had taken off ahead of us to keep the mangy cur in sight, and we at least could see him in the staff car, still up ahead on Grand. I peeled out and Nick followed; I noticed that they hadn't re-lit the headlights of course, being in such a hurry. This was a weird situation we had here.

Ollie turned to the left up ahead and I followed just a minute later. He was still on the guy's tail, and we were playing at "Follow the leader" all over again. I didn't know the name of the street, but it was paved with red brick and the tires were humming a tune. We were headed north, anyway.

"Was it the lout with the fake gold coin?" asked Lenny as he checked the loads on his rifle. It was a big gun all right.

"Oh yeah," I replied. "I'd know that rat-face anywhere. I can't believe he pulled a gun on me!"

"You did well to slam on the brakes," he offered. "I knew something bad had happened the moment I saw you do that. How'd you ever think that one up?" He had a tone of amazement when he asked that, but I didn't think anything of it. These Fords we were driving were becoming like a second skin, or like riding a horse, you know? You think left, you go left, you think *STOP*, and you stop. Right about now I was thinking, *Go, go, go!*, and damned if it wasn't going like a bat out of hell.

Ollie was matching the rat's pace and was not attempting to overtake him, being unarmed as he was. I noticed that we were catching up and was about to say so when the guy pulled a sudden right turn at the last second in an attempt at evasion. Ollie reacted quick-as-a-whip and made the fast turn onto Wayne Street, a cobbled thoroughfare that began a gradual descent to the river.

"He's headed toward the Hudson," remarked Len, as he fingered the elephant gun. "He'll have to decide right or left in about a minute. Hmm, if he goes south closer to the river he'll run out of room when he gets to the canal and be forced to turn right or go swimming." This was a reference to the Morris Canal, a left-over from the last century in use before the railroads took the shipping away from the canal boats coming from West Jersey. Now it was just a good place to go fishing and you could catch some nice soft-shell crabs at low tide. It emptied out into the Hudson just a few more blocks from here.

As chance would have it, Mister Pisser did turn south a minute later, prompting Lenny to say, "Augie, don't follow them — take this first right instead. We'll go parallel to them so we can cut him off when he turns right at the canal. Let's get there first and nail him!"

This sounded like a plan, so I hard-turned the wheel and accelerated at the same time. She felt like she was spinning gears for a second but took off, nonetheless. At the next intersection I slowed, and we looked to the left and — sure enough — Pisser passed by a block away, followed by Ollie two seconds behind him. I scooted down the street yet again in time to see them repeat the process. It was about 200 feet now to the Morris Canal. Nick was still a bit behind us and was not going to be much help back there.

Lenny said, "I figure we'll block the road and let him come on at us. I'll knock out a tire or something."

"What if he rams us?" I was thinking I'd be sitting on the side that would take the force of a collision.

"Oh, don't worry about that, pal. One shot of this cannon and that Tin Lizzie is history!"

That remained to be seen. Meanwhile, we caught a glimpse of both Fords as they crossed the final intersection before the canal, where they'd be forced to take the expected right turn along it. There the land juts out just a bit and they'd have to slow to navigate the bend. We hurried down to the water and took a blocking position on the road next to a streetlamp and a pile of cord wood. Lenny got down from the T and rested the big gun over the hood. I thought it prudent to join him there, although I left the motor running.

It all happened so fast. No sooner had I gotten down from the passenger's side, the lead Ford appeared, driven by that scoundrel in the plaid coat. Ollie was right behind him, and he tootled his horn to acknowledge our presence. Lenny was lining up a shot and said, "Wait for it…steady, steady…" when Mister Pisser must have figured things out, for he suddenly jumped the curb and was driving the T on the grassy embankment along the canal to avoid us. The ground slopes down toward the canal on an angle here and, although littered with boards and boxes, it was giving him sufficient purchase to drive around us!

"Freakin' sonofabitch won't get far, laddie," Lenny muttered. He squinted down the sights of the massive gun and fired. Nothing happened. I looked at Lenny; he looked at the gun. Pisser bounced over a crate and held on with both hands as he passed us with a big shit-eatin' grin. That's when Nicky flew by us on the right with a screech of his brakes and hit Mister Pisser broadside. The stolen Ford flipped down the slope, tumbled over, and landed on its side in the dark water with a huge splash!

Nick's battered T came to a halt at the verge of the bulkhead, and he got down shakily. He was bleeding from the forehead and stumbled to the water's edge. We went over to assist, and Lenny grabbed him by the arm to steady him. Ollie pulled up and went to the canal with a hand-held battery torch light.

"Nicky, are you all right?" Lenny said, still holding the big gun in his left hand.

"Arrrrrrgh," he replied.

"Must have been a misfire," I said, pointing at the rifle.

Ollie said, "I don't see a thing down there."

"Sheeesh," croaked Nick. "I saw your taillight and tried to stop, but I must have hit the gas pedal instead of the brake. I did pull the handle way back, though."

"We're lucky you didn't go over the bank too, lad," added Ollie, "or we'd all be in the drink trying to pull you out."

We all looked at the black water. The tide was in, and only faint shimmers cast by the street lamps reflected off its surface. Ollie's light played back and forth until he hit upon the boxy rear of the ambulance floating halfway across, mostly submerged. It appeared to have come unbolted from the chassis, which must have sunk.

"Let's get that cut cleaned up, old son," said Lenny, who handed me the useless rifle and took Nick back to our ambulance to get the bandage box out, along with a bottle of moonshine, no doubt.

Ollie then handed me the torch-light and began picking up bits and pieces of the two cars. I first shined the light at the front of Nick's T and was surprised to see that, other than both front tires being flat, the fenders being twisted and bent, the headlamps missing, the radiator off-kilter, the windscreen cracked, and the hood crumpled, the Ford looked OK. On second thought, it didn't look OK at all, but you could still hear the engine. Somehow Nick had thought to take her out of gear after the smash-up, and the motor was still purring!

I then shined the light back at the water and right away caught sight of something round floating on top. It was a derby hat.

A fitting end to Mister Pisser, I'd say.

16

The Cleanup: 7/5/16

I WALKED BACK TO SEE how Nicky was doing. The fellows had cleaned and dressed the gash in his forehead, and he was sitting in the passenger seat of the damaged car holding a jug of hooch. Ollie asked to see the faulty rifle and deftly broke it down to inspect it. At that moment, Lenny decided to give instructions to get us moving. I leaned on a bent front fender and yawned.

"Boys," he began, "we've had quite a rough night and it could have ended worse, what with Nick getting injured and all. However, we are still short on delivering three vehicles promised to Miss Molly Johnson."

"Aw, damn," was the chorus in reply, among other such expletives.

"Therefore, I've come up with a plan that will remove this deficit before the lady ever discovers it and has cause for complaint. It should not take us too long to rectify the situation if we 'divide and conquer,' as the saying goes."

"And what would that be then?" chimed in Nick, who then took a huge belt of White Lightning and grimaced.

"I was just coming to that, old son," replied Lenny. "If you gents will hold comments to the end, please, I'll give you all your assignments. Augie, you'll take this banged-up machine back to the Yards and swap it for the next one in line. If the supplies are not yet loaded in that one, you're gonna have to move them from this car yourself. It would be a great help if you could drop Nicky off at his home on your way back. See he gets inside all right, eh?"

"Sure, Len," I replied. "You betcha."

"Nick," he continued, "you go home and get to bed. Don't overdo it with that booze or you won't be any good to us tomorrow."

"Arrgh," Nick replied, and said naught else.

"Ollie," Len went on, "we just have this one brand new T ready to deliver to the docks. If you wouldn't mind putting that gun back together and drive her over there, I'll be along shortly with the staff car and pick you up. Then we'll head over to the Yards and get a hold of one of those special Fords with the winch attached to the back. While you get one all oiled- up and ready to run, I'll join Augie and check the supplies in another new ambulance and then we'll follow him over to the drop-off point. We'll ride with you from there in that tow vehicle, come back here and try our hand at fishing."

I groaned. It looked like it would be a long night.

Ollie looked thoughtful, nodded, and then replied with a quick, "Yar, Leonard, that will be a cinch, but first we need to change both of these flat tires." He then handed me the buffalo gun and asked if I wouldn't mind putting it in his shop so he can look at it later. There was something odd, he said, about the firing pin.

I smiled and said, "Yar, Ollie," which Len thought was funny. I then hopped off the fender, stashed the rifle behind the front seat, and went to fetch the tire jack. Ollie undid the spare from the left side of Nick's T and Len grabbed a second one off the staff car. We changed both within fifteen minutes but had to be careful to chock the wheels as Ollie did not want to shut the motor off. "She's running now but may not restart after the shock of the collision," he said. "For all we know, there may be problems with the starting mechanism, being right there at the point of impact." With that chore complete, we got moving to carry out the other plans Lenny had laid out for us.

Through it all, Nicky remained slumped in the front seat with the hooch. I imagine he had a few swigs while waiting. Finally, I mounted the crinkled-up Flivver, looked at Nick and asked if he was ready. He merely nodded.

I backed away from the canal, put her in forward, said, "Tally Ho!" and off we went.

●　●　●

Nick was nearly asleep when I dropped him off at his row house. His brother Clarence was there visiting and was sitting on the front stoop having a cigar with their Pop when we pulled up. Clarence gave me a hand getting Nicky down, but I think the unsteadiness in his gait had more to do with the hooch than the gash (I made sure he left the bottle in the car, too, for Lenny did not want him to overdo it). They offered me a cheroot and Clarence struck a match off his heel to light me up. I told a short version of the mishap, and his Pop told me not to worry, and that, "Mother would look at it." I asked to give my regards to Mrs. O'Halleran and got going after a few more pleasantries.

It wasn't long before I arrived back at Kearny Point Yards and pulled up at Ollie Olson's shop. He wanted the mangled Ford pulled into the small barn to keep it out of sight from the boss, so I shut her down and "Closed the barn door behind me," as they say.

Before leaving, I noticed Nick's cap lying on his seat and picked it up, cramming it in my pocket. There was a small notebook down on the floorboards, too, amid a smattering of blood droplets. I stuck it in my waistband to look through later.

I next put the so-called Buffalo Gun on Ollie's workbench, after checking it was no longer loaded. He keeps a nice, neat shop, he does. Lots of things hung up or laid-out neatly in rows — wrenches by size, for example, and many jars of nuts, bolts, and other hardware. I could probably learn a lot about mechanical things from him and, since he offered, decided I'd take him up on it.

Pulling up a stool by the light of the lamp, I flipped through Nicky's pad to see what he'd been up to. I was surprised by the volume of pencil drawings he had made in it. I'd seen him sketching birds and horses before but didn't know he was interested in drawing our Model Ts as well. They were all there: ambulances, flatbeds, tankers, staked sides. Everything but our staff car version of the Ford. Ol' Nick was full of surprises. I'd get this thing back to him as soon as I could, poor sod.

It was a warm, humid night and the rain had let off, although it was still cloudy. I made my way to the carpark and checked the rear of the next Model T in line. Yup, it was totally packed with medical supplies. Pete's boys were doing a much better job now. I poked my head in the next few, too, and again was satisfied at their efforts.

The sound of an engine approached, and I looked toward the gate and waved as the staff car entered, Ollie at the wheel this time. They pulled up near me and Len motioned for me to climb aboard. We headed off to the west end of the Yards where the non-ambulance vehicles were gathered. Ollie gave a once-over to the towing car, had me crank her while he fired up the engine, and the three of us squeezed into the front seat for the hop over to the ambulance park. He then waited at the gates while Len and I cranked each other's Flivvers to life. Then the big Swede led the way and we caravanned to the docks with the two fully loaded ambulances, dropped them at the ship, and headed back to the Morris Canal to pull out the sunken vehicle. I was hoping we'd find the remains of Mister Pisser behind the wheel, but as it turned out, that was not to be. At any rate, we backed the machine up to the bulkhead and began tossing a few lines down toward the wreck.

We've done this sort of thing before, of course; a load will sometimes break through a loose cargo net while winching crates aboard ship, for instance. Depending on whether being dunked would ruin it or not, we may drag the bottom for it if the water is not too deep. Sometimes you hit it right away, other times we simply give up. If the drag poles are too short, we'll toss in long lines with grappling hooks on the ends and pull them to shore from different angles until we feel a decent snag. We once salvaged a couple dozen crates of corned beef that way, figuring, hey, it's canned, so a little water won't hurt it.

For a target as large as a Model T, it sure took long enough to get a hook on her. We all had differing ideas on where she went in. Once snagged, it was a snap to snare the car at two other points as well. These three lines were then joined to the winch chain, and we began hauling at her. When we got her dragged to the edge of the bulkhead Ollie stripped down to his skivvies and jumped in. He got the hook and chains from the winch attached down below and scrambled back up the bank. About a half hour later we were on our way back to the Yards with our catch.

17

The Lessons:
Early-to-Mid-July 1916

THE NEXT TWO WEEKS SHAPED themselves into an endless repetition of trips back and forth from the Yards to the docks, ferrying our Fords and delivering Jersey Lightning to local establishments. We'd always come back in the staff car as a group and sometimes stop off for a quick beer or a sandwich. Being mid-July, it was very hot and, after all the rain we had, the humidity increased substantially. The mosquitoes were abundant as well, and my arms were starting to look puffy from bites.

We'd grab mugs of coffee each morning and gather to begin the day with a lesson in mechanics while Ollie used the Ford we rescued from the drink as a guinea pig. He had taken the entire motor and carburetor apart to clean and oil and, as a result, we benefited from watching him reassemble the parts while delivering a step-by-step explanation of the various gears, levers, wires, and other moving parts. We all got a chance to turn a wrench or drive a screw this way, too, and there was no possibility of our fouling things up under his tutelage. His plan was to make a generator out of the motor to run lights in the Yards, which would be helpful for night work. He assigned me the special duty of salvaging parts from this car to repair the damage to the one Nick had crashed. It was a piece of cake changing the fenders and headlamps, but boy did I have trouble with that brass radiator. Several of the bolts holding it were bent and had to be sawn off with a hacksaw. Then, I needed to weld in new bolts to hold the replacement. It took some time but eventually that Model T rejoined the ranks for transfer to the docks, which made me feel proud. I made a mental note of the car number painted on its side — "508." *Maybe one day I'd see her again in France!*

Nicky joined us the day after the accident, looking like what the cat dragged in. Len thought it best to leave him back in the Yards but after a few cups of Ollie's Swedish coffee he seemed to come around. He shouldered his load as always and seemed to even drive a bit faster than he had before. "Maybe clonking his head like that got him over his driving demons," said Lenny.

A few days later while Ollie was giving us a lesson in taking off a driveshaft, we spotted a Model T tanker car coming through the main gate. As expected, it was Peter, but we were surprised to see the odd-looking passenger sitting beside him. The man was holding a weird club, had an old stovepipe hat on his head, and two long black braids of hair hanging down to his shoulders. He was wearing buckskins, of all things. A large Bowie knife hung on his hip. They pulled up to us and shut down the Ford, which chugged to a noisy stop.

"Hey, Pete, what took ya?" asked Lenny as he walked on over and clapped him on the shoulder. It had been at least a week, I guess, but it seemed like two.

"Boys, it's good to be back home, I'll tell you," Pete replied. "I've been sitting at that wheel for so long I think I'll have to sleep sitting up the next few days. Me and the Chief here rode up on the flatcar to Newark, of course, but the train had no caboose and no place else to sit but in the T. Oh, we stretched our legs a few times, and walked the flatcars and gondolas, but that was a long hundred miles with a few stops for water and coal, too."

"And who, may I ask, is the Chief?" said Ollie.

"Oh, forgive me, fellows, this here is the Chief. His name is 'Falling Leaves in Autumn Rain' but it's easier to just call him Chief. It's not a rank or nothin', just shorter to say than all that 'Falling Leaves' stuff. He seems to like it, anyways."

"Ugh," said the Chief; at least, it *sounded* like that. Or maybe he said, "Yar?"

Pete went on with, "He's an original Piney, is the Chief, and he runs the distillery operation at that end, having a group of locals brewing up the Lightning for us. I wanted him to get a feel for the scope of our endeavors, so he'd have a better idea of how much to produce with his crew."

We all mumbled our understanding at this, nodding intelligently as we are wont to do.

Ollie stepped forward at this point and addressed the Chief with, "*Yut ta hey*," to which the man replied, "*Wanishi, hey*," and extended his hand for a shake. We all stepped up and shook his hand while Pete continued his introductory remarks: "He has a large family down in the Barrens and is second-in-command of what I guess we'd call a tribe. His father is actually called a Sakima and heads the group, and wanted to come see our operation for himself, but his wife wouldn't let him."

"Yea, Mom won't let the old guy out of her sight for a minute," said the Chief.

We all looked at him dumbstruck.

"Oh, come on, fellows," he laughed, "I'm a Jersey-er like yourselves; I just happen to be a Lennie Lenape of the Unami Clan. Hey, is there anything to eat around here?"

Lenny answered, "We've got coffee and burnt toast if you'd like, but in about a half hour we'll be on our way to Jersey City to begin our day's work. We'll stop in at Max's Diner on Raymond Boulevard and get you boys some bacon and eggs. You must be famished."

"You read my mind, bro," said Pete. "We haven't eaten since some time last night; we started out with some corn cakes and cider, but they were so good they didn't last."

Pete and the Chief went off to Ollie's shed for some coffee and we soon wrapped up the driveshaft lesson. Ollie told us he'd go over it again in the morning as there was an important point he'd yet to make about the ring gears.

About fifteen minutes later we were once again in convoy headed over the Hackensack River Bridge — Lenny and Peter in the staff car up front — followed by the rest of us in three newly outfitted Ford ambulances. I was honored to have the Chief ride with me and asked him loads of questions about the Pine Barrens and the moonshine business. I was surprised to hear that he didn't touch the stuff himself, and that quite a few of his extended family also stayed away from it. "Too much money at stake," he said, "to take a chance at falling victim to the 'clear liquid that burns.'" Well, I know too well a lot of guys who get falling-down drunk so often their marriages suffer, and sometimes whole families fall apart, so this bit of wisdom from the Pinelands made a lot of sense to this city boy.

A few times he referred to the Pinelands as simply "The Barrens" or even "The Pines," but now and then he used an odd term that I couldn't quite mouth myself, so I asked him to teach it to me.

"We Lenape call it 'Popuessing' — it's common among all the Delaware Tribes," he told me.

I repeated it a few times until he nodded affirmatively, and then asked him what it meant in English.

"Popuessing," he said, "means 'Place of the dragon,' to put an American flavor to it."

"Place of the Dragon!" I exclaimed. "You mean like, the Jersey Devil?"

"What is it with you white men anyway? That's all you talk about when you come down to the Barrens. It's never about the cranberries, the peat bogs, the sand, the pine trees, the deer or wild boar. It's always about this Jersey Devil legend. Cheesh."

I felt bad and said, "Sorry, Chief, I guess it's just a silly superstition. Forget I asked."

"Superstition?" he replied. "No, not at all. Why do you think we call it, "Popuessing'? I've never seen him myself, but I've seen deer torn apart, and have spoken to a few of the elders over the years. What they told me has kept me up at night when I heard strange sounds outside my cabin. I always sleep with a shotgun at my side, and I always carry this club." With that he brandished this strange, curved club of his. I looked at it occasionally out of the corner of my eye as I navigated the streets of the city, and noticed some strange characters carved into it. He saw me looking at it and explained, "The runes on the club date back several hundred years. They are a part of our mythology, what we call the *Walum Olam*. It tells of the Earth's creation, the beginnings of man and the animals, the origin of the Lenape. My grandfather's father carved some of them on this war club because they have special meaning to our clan, the Unami. See this one? This is our totem – the Turtle."

I thought this was interesting, and figured it was akin to the Egyptian hieroglyphics I've seen at the museum in the city. I merely nodded my understanding without making further comment. I would have asked if there was a dragon on it but didn't want to set him off again.

We pulled up in echelon outside of Max's Diner, shut down, and went inside for breakfast — a real treat for a change.

• • •

The Chief stayed with us for several days, sitting in with the mechanic lessons and going with Lenny on some of the moonshine drop-offs. Ollie gave him some serious driving lessons, too, but the Piney could not grasp the concept of going in reverse. Every time he tried it, he'd give it too much gas and smack into something, or he'd go backwards in fits and starts. Peter finally got him squared away by lining up barrels in an empty area to bang around in, but it was not easy. In the end the Chief became an excellent driver and left the Yards in an empty tanker outfitted as before with extra gasoline, water, and food. Pete rode with him to the Newark Rail Yards to put him on a flat car to Philly. Lenny made some sort of agreement with the Chief, and we would be getting a new tanker car each month, "… unless things heat up," he said.

That evening we dropped off the last Fords of the day, climbed into the staff car and were about to drive off when I saw Molly Johnson and a well-dressed gentleman coming down the gangplank. I grabbed

Lenny by the elbow and had him hold off, telling him she might want to address some concern or other about our work so far, but I really wanted to just say hello to her. I hopped out and said, "Hello, Miss Johnson, did you need a word with us? We were just finishing up for the day."

"Why, Mister Landesmann, how nice it is to see you again. In fact, I'm delighted to see all of you fellows this evening. If I may have a moment of your time, I would like to present to you my father, Doctor Edward T. Johnson. He is the liaison with the American Field Service in France." With that this great big hand seized mine in its grip and squeezed my knuckles tightly together.

"Hello, son," said Doctor Johnson. "How the hell are you?" He shook my hand and I managed to stay on my feet. I replied that it was indeed a pleasure to meet Miss Johnson's father, and that he had a hard-working daughter.

Lenny, Peter, Nick, and Ollie got down in turn and introduced themselves. Molly waited for the introductions to settle down with an amused look on her face, and then interjected, "Dad, these are the gentlemen I told you about who are ferrying our ambulances to the docks from the Kearny Yards."

"Ah, splendid!" he said to all of us, beaming as he did. "I've heard good things about you boys from the inspectors on board the *Edward Luckenbach*. She sailed out of here last Saturday and I received a signal just this morning. You've done quite well, I must say. They reported that everything was fit and proper, from the supplies inside the cars, to the air in the tires, oil in the engines, and the minimal amount of gasoline in the tanks. Keep up the good work, gentlemen."

Well, we were all beaming at that but then Molly said, "Mister Landesmann is the convoy commander, but to hear him tell it, it is really a group effort."

I think my face was showing a bright red by now and felt obliged to speak. I said, "Ah, er, well, yes sir, it really is a group effort."

He took my hand again and said, "Well done, lad," with yet another pumping of my mitt. Lenny jabbed me in my ribs and Nicky kicked me in the leg, but still I maintained eye contact with Doctor Johnson and felt confident enough to say, "So, ah, well, if you need anything else, please don't hesitate to ask."

And then my life changed.

He said, "Why, now that you mention it, there is something you can do for me, well, for both of us, in fact. Molly says that we've stayed too late on the ship and have now missed the very last Hudson and Manhattan train back to Newark. This was my entire fault, of course, but with so much to attend to I lose track of time." He pointed up at the ship, and after a sweep of his arm, continued, "The problem is, we need to get to Harrison, as my wife is expecting special dinner guests and we're sure to be in the doghouse if we're late once again! Would you boys be able to drive us there?"

Lenny stepped forward, and, God bless him, offered my services and the staff car, saying he would drop off the gang in an ambulance and get it to the docks afterwards, noting that I'd have to pick him up in the morning on my way to work.

The good doctor was delighted and thanked us profusely. He helped his daughter get into the middle seat, handed her up his medical bag and an umbrella, and climbed aboard next to her. We were off to Harrison quick as a wink.

18

Harrison: The Soiree

“HOLY JESUS, HOLY JESUS, GOOD God Almighty, I can't believe it I just can't believe it! Jesus Criminy!”

I was talking to myself this way the whole ride back from Doc Johnson's house. I would also shoot my fist up into the air and yell, “Hoorah!” every few minutes. I was excited. The evening had been amazing. I was ecstatic. Holy smokes, a lot went on at that party. To top it off, Molly kissed me!

Dang, I thought I'd just run over something; oh well. Maybe it was a rat. I told myself to calm down and concentrate on driving the staff car down this dark stretch of the Newark–Jersey City Turnpike. I'd better be careful not to hit a deer. At least I took the time to light the carbide lamps on the front of the car. I could see pretty good in front of me with them lit, but everything to the sides was behind a curtain of darkness.

Doc, I thought, *he wants me to call him Doc, but I must call Molly "Miss Johnson" in public.* In a way, that made sense to me, and I would adapt easily to that sort of thing. On the other hand, she insisted I always call her Molly. This was what my Pop would call a conundrum. Maybe I'll ask him what he'd do in my shoes.

I was driving at a good clip on nicely laid Belgian Block cobbles. This was a straight stretch of road through the meadows and was once a cedar plank road. It floods now and then but seemed quite dry tonight. Up ahead I could see the lamps on the bridge over the Hackey. I would probably be home in about twenty minutes, but first I had to stop and take a leak. I pulled over next to a salt marsh and noticed it was ornamented with the flashes of hundreds of lighting bugs. They were in the trees at the edge of the marsh, in the cattails and reeds, and at varying heights in the still air. They appeared to be celebrating something. It was the prettiest piss I ever took!

I hopped in and continued, thinking back on events at the Johnson's house over on Sussex Street in Harrison. Did I just meet Thomas Edison? Did I really dance with Molly twice? Was that red-haired fellow in fact a British general? Was I still wearing Molly's brother's seersucker suit?

The answer to all of those was a resounding, "Yes!"

I had taken the Johnsons across the Hackensack and down this turnpike road through South Kearny and into the small town of Harrison just about four hours ago. We made good time, and the Doc was so thrilled to be pulling up at the house at exactly 7:30 like his wife expected, that he pulled me out of the staff car and invited me to dinner! Naturally, I deferred and pointed out my clothes were dirty from a day's work and if it'd be all right, I'd just be on my way. Molly wouldn't hear it, though. She grabbed my arm and said, "Now you listen to Dad, please, and come on in and meet Mother. You can wash up and we'll fix you up with some of my brother James's duds, not to worry. Why, wait until you taste her fried chicken — it's superb!"

Well, fried chicken, what could I say? I love fried chicken. "That would be great, Miss Johnson," I said, "I'll just…"

"Molly," she demanded.

"Miss Johnson," corrected the Doc.

Molly stood her ground, put her hands on her hips and said, "Dad, I would really like him to call me by my name when no one else is around, ok?"

"Fine, fine, don't get excited," he answered as he faced the house and fumbled with his key ring. "Gee, you're just like Mother." He turned then, and asked her, "And when do you plan on telling me his given name?"

She smiled and said, "August."

"What? When? Why, that's two weeks away!"

"No, Dad, that's his name. His name is August!"

"Oh, yes, of course. Augustus Rex!" With that we climbed the front porch of the huge house, where I noticed a variety of rocking chairs, planters full of red and white flowers, wind chimes, and even a large bird cage with a big green parrot inside. When I passed the cage, the big bird acknowledged me with a squawk.

Molly said to me, "Zinga likes you."

I looked at her sidewise and said, "Wait until he finds out I ate fried chicken." I thought that would have gotten a laugh from her, but she rolled her eyes. The Doc chuckled and gave a thumbs-up.

We entered a central hallway that was adorned with flowery wallpaper, a large pedestal mirror, a chair, and a potted palm tree. A white-haired man in livery approached the Doctor and took his bag and umbrella, placing the medical bag on a special little table beside a closet, the umbrella in a brass stand.

"*Buono sera, Doctore, Signorina Johnson*," said the man.

"Hullo, Angelo," replied the Doc. "Please see that this young man is attended to straight away. Molly, would you handle this for me? I've really got to get into the parlor to meet any early arrivals."

Molly said, "Why, certainly, Father, we'll be only a few minutes." She took me by the hand and said, "This way, August," then looked over her shoulder and beckoned Angelo to follow us up to James's room.

We climbed a carpeted stairway that turned twice at spacious landings, then went down a long hallway decorated with paintings of ocean-going clippers and mountain hunting scenes. We came to a closed door at the extreme end of the hall and Molly turned the knob and tossed the door open saying, "James's room, just as he left it three months ago."

This was curious, but I held any questions until I knew more about James and any fate which may have befallen him. Molly went across the room and swung open a closet. She reached in, pushing some hangers back and forth, until she pulled out a few items.

"I think a blue jacket would suit you fine, August," she said, handing me several hangers full of blue cloth and a white shirt. A narrow black tie slithered and fell off one of the wire hangers. I picked it up and looked at it. She continued her instructions saying, "Angelo, would you run some hot water in the sink and get a towel and washcloth for August? I'm afraid there won't be any time for him to shave, as things will be starting downstairs shortly." She turned to me and said, "Just wash up and put on this suit and Angelo will show you down to the parlor." With that she left me with the white-haired gentleman, who took the clothes from me and lay them on the bed. He said, "*Andiamo, Senore*," and motioned me with his finger toward the open doorway.

I followed him out to the hallway bathroom and got started up washing my face and hands. When he went back to the bedroom to prepare the suit for me, I stripped off my dirty shirt and knickers for a quick, "whore's bath," as they say on the docks. Once sponged down, I wrapped the large towel around me and went to see how Angelo had fared. Boy, was I impressed! He helped me on with the pants and shirt, then tied the tie for me, and got me into the jacket in no time at all. Luckily, there were several pairs of black shoes lying on the closet floor and I was just barely able to squeeze into a matching set of them. *James must have small feet*, I thought to myself, just as Angelo suggested, "You must have bigga feet, Master August!"

It was my turn to laugh.

He said I looked, "*Molto bene*," and gave me the old "*Andiamo*," again, so I followed obediently, and we left the room for the hallway. His pace on the stairway was slow and measured, which gave me the needed time to satisfy my curiosity about brother James. Lenny always said, "If you want to know something, Augie, just ask folks questions. It doesn't pay none to be shy in this world." With that in mind I asked Angelo about Molly's brother James and where he went three months ago.

"Oh, it is a sad-a thing, but could have been much, much sadder," he said.

Now, that did not sound good at all.

Angelo went on to say that James left home in March for France, volunteering for Le Escadrille Americaine, a group of American boys who formed a fighter squadron to fight the Hun in the skies over the Western Front. Poor James was shot down over the Argonne Forest in May and was currently in a hospital in Paris, all wrapped up in bandages with some severe burns and a broken leg. "He was on the way back from his second mission when he got-a shot down," was how he put it. That was all I could get from Angelo on the matter. I wisely decided that it was the sort of thing that not even Lenny would bring up, despite his boldness. Under the circumstances, I would have to wait for the Doc or Molly to mention James again before asking any questions.

We got to the bottom of the stairs, and I followed the old man from the landing to a pair of richly paneled mahogany doors which, although shut, were emitting the sound of voices and gramophone music. "This-a way, Master August," he said, sliding the rightmost door open. As he entered the large room, he stepped aside and assumed an attitude of attention, nodding his head toward where Molly and her father stood. I smiled and took a step in their direction, wondering what she would make of me in this blue suit she had me put on. However, as I made my way over toward them, they were approached by a man in uniform with lots of ribbons and braid. He had a red stripe down his trouser legs and a type of stick tucked between his left arm and his ribs. He kissed Molly's hand, which I didn't like, but when her father seized his hand in the Doc Johnson chokehold, I was pleased to see the man's unexpected grimace. Amused, I decided to look around at my surroundings until such time as the soldier retreated.

The place was a veritable carpenter's dream. Lustrous panelling adorned the walls such as I had never seen. Much like the stairwell I had just descended, there were beautifully carved shapes in the woodwork: scrolls, squares, circles, and finials. The wide plank floors were highly polished oak. The wallpaper looked velvety and was enhanced by gold etching. Oriental rugs were strategically placed by the sofa, divan, and near a group of large armchairs. It was all very impressive. There were palm trees big enough to hide behind!

A young maid carrying a tray of drinks offered me something called a cordial that I quickly grabbed and tossed down. I reached for a second one, putting the empty glass back on the tray with the other hand. The stuff tasted a bit like almonds and, although a bit sweet, went down smoothly. The maid warned me to go easy on the stuff, but I just chuckled. No doubt she'd never been within a hundred miles of moonshine, nor ever would be. Hah, if she ever tried a swig of Lightning it would probably knock her over, and to think she was warning me about this juice? Not wanting to look foolish, I kept the liquid in the glass and ambled over to Molly and the Doc the moment the soldier moved away. From the beeline he took toward a group of people huddled around the overstuffed armchairs (where a few well-dressed ladies were seated), he either saw someone who owed him money, or they had begun serving food.

Molly glanced up at me with a look of surprise, and exclaimed, "Why August, you look wonderful!" My head grew large, and I began to float around the room. Well, that was how I felt. Instead, I had the composure to reply, saying, "Thank you, Miss Johnson," which had the effect of simultaneously placing both a frown on her face and a smile on the Doc's. He saved me, clapping me on the back saying, "Yes, my boy, you do look rather nice in blue. Now, would you two excuse me for a moment? I need to freshen up my drink." With that he went off in search of the maid and I found myself alone with Miss Johnson, uh, Molly, at last.

She opened with, "What's with this Miss Johnson business again?"

I countered with, "The Doc said to call you that in public."

"This isn't public," she said, "this is my home."

"This isn't public?" I was perplexed, and added, "I thought it was public if you were in front of a lot of people you didn't know."

"Well, maybe you have a point there, but I'd be pleased if you would call me Molly from now on if my father is not present, public or otherwise."

Finally, I had a set of rules I could live by, and affirmed my understanding with a nod and a, "You betcha, Molly." This had the desired effect and she smiled sweetly. I thought I was home free, and could now enjoy some pleasant moments with her, when suddenly she grabbed me by the arm and said, "Come, let's go meet some of the guests. You simply must meet my uncle." She looked around the room and said, "Aha! There he is!"

With that we were off toward the Victrola cabinet, and the group of people gathered around its large horn, swaying a bit to an instrumental I recognized as "The Maple Leaf Rag," by Scott Joplin. This was one of my favorites and I began to whistle it as I drew near.

She tapped a gentleman on his shoulder and said, "Uncle, I'd like to introduce you to my friend, August Landesmann." He turned toward us, smiled at Molly, looked me in the eye as he grabbed my hand and said, "Any friend of Molly's is a friend of mine!" I was expecting to have my mitt torn off again by one her relatives, but this fellow was a bit gentler and quick with a shake. Before I could say, "How do you do?" the record playing machine gave a loud thunk, and then stopped altogether. "Drat, there it goes again," exclaimed the uncle, and proceeded to remove the arm from the record, pulling a screwdriver out of his jacket pocket. The other folks must have just gone through this procedure, for they seemed disinterested and melted away. Having tinkered with my mom's music boxes before, I commented that it might be the main spring. "Think so?" he asked. "Well, you're right — that's precisely what it is; the grease is caked up and it's going to have to be taken apart and redone — a very big job. I've had it with this infernal Victor contraption." With that he put the screwdriver back into his pocket, closed the shiny wooden lid, and said, "Molly, your friend here looks like a strong chap, do you mind if I borrow him for a few minutes? I need to go across the street."

"Oh, please do, if it would mean we will have more music. If I cannot dance with August this evening, I will be sorely disappointed." I managed to get a look at her just as her uncle grabbed me by the wrist and said, "Come along, son, time's a wasting." With that we were out of the parlor, down the hall, and out the front door in nothing flat.

The crickets in the front yard stopped their chirping as we descended the front steps out onto the flagstones. The sky had cleared but you could see there had been a passing shower. He stopped to search for his keys, and I had a moment to ask, "Where are we going, sir?"

"I work across the street here, in the Lamp Works. We've got one of those 'Victrola Talking Machines' in the office and nobody will miss it. You're going to have to carry it yourself unless we can find a hand truck. If I could just find my keys…well, no matter, there's another way in." With that he led the way across Sussex Street toward the Edison Lamp Works building. This is a monstrous red brick building that takes up an entire block. In fact, this was one of several such buildings, but right across from the Johnson's house. We headed down to the corner, rounded the block, and ended up at a steel door boasting a huge white sign with red letters that stated, "No Admittance!" He tried it and it was locked. *Well*, thinks I, *that's that.* To my surprise, he pulled out a black case, unzipped it, and removed a small silver tool, saying, "Just a minute, me bucko."

A moment later he pulled the tool out of the keyhole, turned the doorknob and said, "Voila!" He went inside and said, "Come on, son, time's a wasting."

He mounted the steel staircase two at a time and I could not help thinking how spry this old fellow was. He made the landing and slowed down on the next flight, but not once did he stop. Finally, we got to the third floor, and he led the way down a shadowy hallway. "Over here, August," he said, turning to a dark doorway, which was open. He hit a wall switch and the room was suddenly ablaze with electric lighting. There were different sized bulbs on the ceiling, on the walls, on lamps, on tables, on poles. It was fantastic.

"What is all this?" I exclaimed.

"Welcome to the Edison Lamp Works," he said, and began laughing. "We've been working on improving exterior lighting in the streets of old New York — as the song says, 'East Side, West Side, all around the Town.' Here's where we test out various lighting devices and configurations. Careful now, or you'll 'Trip the light fantastic!'"

I looked all around the room; I had never seen so many different sized bulbs, so many bright lights, so many wires! He interrupted my reverie after a few seconds and said, "Come on, the Victor machine's over here. They sent it to us from Camden as a gift, but they were just rubbing our faces in it, with their flat disc records. I've got to admit, it plays a lot better than our gramophone cylinders and even our new discs, and it's become all the rage, so what the hell? Still, nobody in this office would dare play this machine, so we may as well remove it."

I had to know, so I asked, "Why wouldn't they play it, would Mister Edison get upset?"

"You bet he would!"

"Gee," I said. "Never thought he'd be a cranky old cuss." *I mean, who wouldn't appreciate Victrola music?*

"Oh," he continued, "you don't know the half of it. Here, let's get this thing up on that hand truck over there. Come on — time's a wasting."

I grabbed the hand truck and wheeled it over to the dark brown cabinet. He closed the lid down and folded the horn over by loosening a nut on the side. While he tilted the cabinet forward, I moved the hand truck into position and tied a rope around the mid-section. I tested the weight and found it not too heavy after all.

He picked up a box of records and said, "Let's go, August, I've got what I wanted." I began to push the hand truck through the doorway and got stuck on the edge, crunching my finger. A nice old German word escaped my lips, namely, "*Scheisse!*"

"Ah, the old words are best," he said, adding, "Be careful son, we've a long way to go." He opened the door wider so I could get the machine through, and I heard a distinct click, plunging the room into darkness.

As I pushed the machine out into the hallway, I suddenly felt a large hand grab my arm, and heard a loud voice in my ear demanding, "What the hell are you doing?"

Looking to the left, I saw a huge brute of a man in a blue uniform, with a policeman's cap and a stern expression. He was wearing a silver star on his chest that was inscribed "Night Watchman." I froze.

Molly's uncle intervened then, saying, "It's all right, O'Malley. He's with me."

"Oh, Boss, it's you! Sorry about that. I saw the lights on from down the hall and was not expecting anyone after hours."

"Well, you're just doing your job, Joseph, just like always. Now, if you wouldn't mind going ahead down the hall for us and ringing up the Otis, I'd appreciate it."

"Sure thing, Boss, it's as good as done." With that, the hulk practically sprinted the length of the hallway toward the far corner, where he tapped a button on the wall and waited for us to catch up.

I pushed the hand truck as Molly's uncle walked beside me. He put his hand in front of his mouth so O'Malley couldn't hear him and said, "I don't know why I'm whispering this, because he's deaf as a tree, but he's a good man and scares off a lot of would-be burglars."

I can attest to that; my first impression of Mr. Joseph O'Malley was that he was about to pound me into the ground.

The "Otis" turned out to be a freight elevator, made right here in the Town of Harrison, according to a plaque on the doorsill. O'Malley opened the metal gates, and then the doors. I pushed the Victrola on board, followed by the uncle, who I'd prefer to think of as "the Boss" from now on. Everyone seemed to be my boss these days.

"Down to the street, please, Joseph," said the Boss.

"Yes, Boss, right away." Night Watchman O'Malley closed the outer gates first, then the inner doors, and punched a button labelled "G". There was a sudden jolt, then a whir, and then a whine. After another jolt, she began descending. A minute later we were at the ground floor level and O'Malley opened both the doors and gates once again. I backed out of the elevator carefully, followed by the Boss and the Watchman. I spun around slowly and followed the two of them toward a door that led to the street we came in on, but not the same entrance we used earlier. The guard opened the door for us, and we felt the fresh night air at once.

"That will be all, Joseph," said Molly's uncle, the Boss.

"Yes, sir, Mister Edison," replied Joseph. "Have a good night."

My mouth dropped open as I tried to think back to what I just called Thomas Edison upstairs. Why do I always do things like this?

I quietly pushed the hand truck as he led the way to the corner. I had to figure out an apology and fast! As he turned the corner he began to chuckle. At least, it started as a chuckle. By the time we got to the street it had turned into a full-fledged laugh. I started to blurt out an apology, but the words were failing me. Not only had I insulted Molly's uncle, but it was Thomas Edison! I had called the Wizard of Menlo Park a "grumpy old cuss!

"Mr. Edison," I began.

He interrupted with, "Don't you mean cranky, old Mr Edison?"

That was it — I had said "cranky," not "grumpy." I get that way when I'm upset.

"Sir, I really must apologize," I offered. "I would not dream of…"

"Stop right there, son," he said while still laughing. "It's not every day I meet a man who will say what's on his mind, and it's refreshing. But that's not what I was laughing about."

"Well," I said, "I am truly sorry nonetheless, but just what is so funny then?"

He said, "You should have seen the look on your face when O'Malley grabbed you! I thought you were going to piss your pants!"

I'm glad he thought it was funny, but when I mulled it over a bit I began to laugh, too. I mean, dang, they're not even my pants. A sense of relief overcame me as we approached the Johnson home, and we began the walk up the flagstones to the porch.

Mr. Edison opened the front door for us, and I angled the hand truck into the foyer, being extremely careful not to scrape the woodwork. Angelo met us and led the way into the parlor, where folks were still milling about with their drinks, chatting socially.

It wasn't long before the Victrola was hooked up and the strains of Stephen Foster's, "Old Folks at Home" were filling the air. Molly and I danced twice that night, but I don't remember the music, only the light in her eyes and the feel of her in my arms. Dinner was eventually served, and I remember eating most of it, but again, I recall more the touch of her hand and the occasional rub of her foot against mine under the table.

When it was time to go and guests began to leave, she called me aside and said, "Uncle Thomas was very impressed with you, but he wouldn't say why. Do you know?"

What could I say but, "Well, he likes a man who will speak his mind." That's when she kissed me.

19

Morning Pickup:
Mid-July 1916

"**I**'M TELLING YOU IT WAS Thomas Edison!"

"Yea, laddie. I believe you. Tell me then, was he dancing with Queen Victoria when you met him? Did you remember to bow when you were introduced to Her Majesty?"

Lenny thought I was full of it, which I often am, but not today. Today I was righteous and proud.

"No," I ventured, "the Queen couldn't make it; there's a war on... actually, she died twenty years ago, didn't she? Mister Edison, though, couldn't get the Victrola to work properly, so we broke into his factory across the street."

This got me the "Lenny Look," so I continued to clear things up. "He's got electric lights strung up all over the place."

That got me yet another look from Lenny, the one with the "Big Eyes."

Nothing to lose, I went on and said, "No, really, we got up into his shop and carried a new Victrola back to the party so we could all dance again."

"And?" he asked imperiously, as we pulled up into the Yards.

"And he was outside when Molly walked me out and even cranked the Tin Lizzie for me."

"Really, August. You've outdone yourself this time. Have you been hitting the hooch this morning?"

"No, not at all, Len. You'll believe me when the batteries and head-lamps get here." I shut down the staff car and hopped out. Lenny followed and as I looked over at him, I saw I had gotten his attention with the bit about the batteries. Mister Edison did crank the Ford for me last night, but not until after he caught sight of me striking a match to light the lamps for the dark road home. He asked me what I was doing with carbide lights on my machine in "this day and age," so I filled him in about the 1915 Fords being the last ones built without electric lighting, that at the Front they wouldn't be using lamps anyway, and that we're stuck with having to light the ones we use for ourselves.

"Why not modify them then?" asked Mister Edison.

"Oh, we're just going to have to put up with it until they start sending us the 1916s. It's not a big deal lighting the lights, but we've run out of water or calcium carbide a few times already. That's bad news if you're out at night with a long way to go."

Then he asked me something I've thought of many times since and have taken to heart. He spread both arms out, fingers splayed open and said,

"Why constrain yourself within the current boundaries of technology?"

I had no answer for that, and fell back on my standard, "Well, ah, um," which works both in English and German with my parents. To my credit, I did put together an intelligent response, and asked him, "What?"

He looked perplexed for a moment at my reply but was quick to re-cover. I guess he realized I wasn't one of the inventors he knows, so he restated his question with, "Why don't we rip out the carbide crap and install some battery-operated lamps and switches for you?" He then went on a bit about the wiring, battery placement, magnetos, and things like that, and I found myself wishing Ollie were there. He even offered to provide four or five complete sets of apparatus for us, and send them to the Yards, but we'd have to install them ourselves. He would include a diagram showing the connections so there would be no confusion and added, "Even a child could do it."

Well, not to be outdone by a child, I told him I would get the first one done myself.

Finally, Lenny asked me what I meant about the batteries, so I began to fill him in as we went through the door into Ollie's shed. Ollie was up already and had the coffee going but was nowhere to be seen. I poured while Lenny looked for the sugar bowl and he spooned some in as I finished the tale of Mister Edison's offer.

"This is too good to be true," he opined.

"Well, it's true all right, and we won't owe him a cent either, but I may have to give him a ride now and again."

"Hah, I knew there'd be something attached," he added. This is typical Lenny — he always has an angle himself, so he thinks everyone else does, too. So, I up and told him, "It's no big deal, buddy. He's Molly's uncle — I'd be happy to help him even if he wasn't the Wizard of Menlo Park."

"Uncle? Molly's uncle is Edison?"

"Yup, and he's going to send us a box in a few days."

"Hah!" he laughed. "I'll believe that when I see it."

20

Bottles and Batteries: A Few Days Later, July 1916

NOW THAT OUR FIRST HOOCH wagon had arrived, Pete's boys proved very useful to us. They were not only stocking the ambulances perfectly (after all our efforts and continued coaching) but were also put to work filling the jugs and smaller bottles of White Lightning, boxing them up, and loading them into the reefer car for storage, or into the staff car for distribution. Happily, their young taste buds did not react well with the stuff, but Pete kept a watchful eye on them anyway.

Two of the more muscled boys went to the docks with Nick for a couple of days training, to sort of fill in on some of the tasks we used to perform. Lenny explained the move, saying, "It wouldn't do to make things look like they're backing up too much at the river." Nick came back with the assurance that the current crew were doing just fine but would welcome using the boys in those lesser roles that crop up over the next couple of weeks. It looked like we'd be doing Yardwork and ferrying Fords for quite the time after all, so this was good news indeed.

Lenny was in his element delivering the juice to the local customers, and the cash began flowing. Of course, cash flows in two directions and payoffs needed to be made, yet each of us began collecting folding money for our future. My boat idea was beginning to look better and better!

The procession of Fords kept going to the docks, and we'd hop back in the staff car after the drop-offs for the haul back to the Yards. Each night we stopped and ate at a different tavern. The meals were all paid for by Lightning Enterprises, so it did not come out of our earnings.

True to his word, Mister Edison's box of batteries and headlamps arrived one morning — Friday, July 21st in fact. Ollie called us together for mechanic class and went over the diagrams. We then brought five Ts into a circle so we could all work on the installations within earshot of Ollie's instructions. These included two of the staff car types, one tanker (the other being in South Jersey), our work-ambulance (painted black, used to transport items privately), and one of the winch cars for towing. The batteries were the same as used in home telephones — dry cell number sixes. These were the familiar "Eveready" ones. Each car had three batteries installed in a metal holder especially designed to store them under the seat. We wired them up to the coil box and there was a switch up on the dashboard, allowing you to turn them off and on immediately. What an improvement! Ollie told us one day batteries would replace the hand-crank in starting the cars, but these number sixes would not accomplish that task. Still, what a luxury it would be now to merely flick the switch and have instant light!

Later that day it began clouding up, and lightning flashed toward the west. We were about to leave the Hudson for the Yards when I pointed to the dark blue and purple clouds headed our way from Newark. A huge bolt of lightning stabbed the earth in the direction we were looking, causing a few exclamations. The wind picked up, too, and whirls of dust danced by on either side of us. We decided to put the canvas roof up on the staff car and button up the side flaps as best we could. We got it all up in no time, too, with the four of us somehow coordinating the effort without tripping over each other. We hopped in as Nick cranked the engine to life. Just as the first large splats of rain pelted the hood and windscreen, a young boy in overalls and a tweed cap handed me an envelope and said, "Miss Molly asked me to give-ya dis." With that he took off for the shelter of the dock shack just as the curtain of rain hit us full force. Lenny had the wheel and headed north to put us in the lee of the wind behind a massive warehouse. He laughed and switched on the headlamps, singing, "Ta da!" We kept northward on the river for a bit until he decided to cut a left turn onto Johnston Ave, which leads to Grand Street. The moment he turned into the torrent we lost most visibility and Ollie began operating the hand lever to wipe the windscreen. This helps a lot but is tiresome to the cranker. We trundled through the streams of water that were headed down the hills to the Hudson, occasionally honking at some poor unfortunates who were soaked to the skin. Soon someone passed a small bottle of moonshine around. Nick began telling a tale of a storm he recalled from his Belfast days when I looked down and saw the envelope sticking out of my vest pocket. Molly's note!

I pretended to listen, nodding my head and smiling as Nick dove into his tale, but instead gave a furtive look at the writing on the envelope. It read, "Mister August Landesmann," and was written in a feminine hand. Since it was addressed to me personally, I opened it right up and unfolded the papers within.

> *Dear August,*
>
> *Each year our family goes on vacation to the Pocono Mountains in Pennsylvania. We stay in a cabin on the Delaware River and enjoy many outdoor activities without all the hustle and bustle of the city. My father told me yesterday that we would be going next Friday night, the 28th instant, taking the train up to Calicoon, N.Y., where we will be met by his brother for the car ride to the cabin. We will be gone for ten days.*
>
> *I know it is short notice, but if you are not working Saturday, do you suppose you would like to attend the moving pictures with me and my cousin Lillian? The Warner Theatre in Harrison is showing* The Tramp, The

Bank, *and* By the Sea *with Charlie Chaplin and Edna Purviance. I am a real big fan of Charlie Chaplin! You have not met Lillian, but you would like her (but not as much as you like me, I hope).*

I do not ever ask gentlemen out on dates, but after all, it is 1916, not the Victorian Era. I know how busy you boys get down at the docks and in the Kearny Yards, and next week will fly by just as the last few have, so I am not sure I will be seeing you before we take our family vacation.

If you choose to attend the moving pictures with us tomorrow, please come to the house at 2:00 and you may have dinner with us. Mother is making a pot roast, with string beans and mashed potatoes. My father would be delighted to have a chat with you and Mother did not get much chance to speak with you at all the other night. Lillian and her mom will also be joining us. Her father is already in the Poconos.

If you cannot make it, I will understand. You may feel befuddled being asked by a woman to a date, but as I said, we will be gone for such a long time, and I really did enjoy your company when we danced the other night.

Sincerely,

Molly Johnson.

p.s. Bring one of your Ford cars; I would like a short driving lesson!

•   •   •

"A driving lesson!" I exclaimed.

"No," said Nick. "But it was a driving rain, I'll tell you that. Why, by the time we got to the pub we were wet as codfish, and a good thing it was that Flaherty had a room upstairs and several extra kilts for the three of us!"

That got a laugh from the group, so I feigned agreement and

laughed along. It's not too hard with these fellows to keep your feel-
ings to yourself. I put the letter back into the envelope and into my
vest pocket. I would ask Len about using one of the cars later, when
we got a beer or two into us. We were headed to a place over on
Bergen Avenue called "The Buffalo Tavern." It's right across from
the Liberty Fire House and the firefighting lads spend more than a bit
of time there, so the owner went and named it after the Buffalo Boys
— what they call the volunteers around here. They aren't paid much,
like the full-time fellows, but that doesn't keep them from fighting
blazes or helping their brothers in other ways. They're a tight-knit
group, this lot, like us Dockers.

We shut the T down completely and mounted the steps to the porch
of the place. Nick led the way this time, as he's a Buffalo Boy himself.
We were met by a strong smell of frankfurters and sauerkraut, laced
with a bouquet of beer and whisky. The men were gathered around
several tables playing poker, with a pair at the bar as well. We took
seats at the bar on either side of these fellows, who greeted Nick
warmly and seemed to know Lenny, too. Ollie and I were introduced
and quietly nodded. Beers appeared without having to be ordered —
one of the nice things about this town. It turned out that the two were
both chiefs of Liberty Fire House and were going over things at the
change of shift. The boys playing poker were through for the week
and looked like they were going to be spending some time here.

It wasn't long before we went through a platter of franks and kraut,
plus several mugs of beer when I had to hit the men's room. On the
way back it was Lenny's turn, so I used the moment to ask him for the
use of a Ford tomorrow afternoon, once we had put our four hours in.
He started to nod his assent when suddenly he had a bright idea and
said, "The whole rail yard is full of Flivvers! What was I thinking?"

"Huh?" I offered.

He said, "Pick one."

"What?"

"You know, your own Ford. Which one would you want to drive
home and back each day? I'll give you first choice and take the next,

then we'll tell Nick and Ollie. Why are we bothering to pick ourselves up each morning and then do a drop off at night? We have loads of cars — let's use 'em!"

This was great! This would work out well, what with all the back-and-forth we were doing. I was going to be all humble as usual but thought to myself, *To heck with that,* and came right out and said, "I'll take one of the staff cars with the new lamps!"

"And I'll have the black ambulance," he replied.

When he put the idea to Nick and Ollie, they both didn't care one way or the other, so Len assigned the other staff car to Nicky and told Ollie to think it over, that he, "could have pick of the rest o' the litter."

And so it happened that I was all set for giving Molly a driving lesson. Heck, as many lessons as she could want!

21

The Preparations: 7/22/16

SATURDAY MORNING DAWNED BRIGHT AND sunny, and I rolled out of bed with a purpose. Today I would see Molly again, have dinner with her family, give her a driving lesson, and see the moving picture show. But first a bit of coffee and I'd be listening for my pick-up arriving out front.

These half-day shifts on Saturdays gave us a chance to catch up with our drop-offs at the dock in case we got behind, but more than likely we'd spend them in the Yards going over mechanic lessons or helping Ollie get new arrivals road ready. In fact, a new trainload would be arriving Monday followed by yet another next week. Lenny would be gone all day delivering jugs of Jersey Lightning to our favored customers so it would be just Nick, me, and Ollie tinkering on the cars.

Pop was at the store already, but Mom was up, and as I heard her coming down the stairs, I poured two cups of coffee.

"Why, thank you, *Liebchen*," she said. She liked to call me that when no one else was about. "Did you see the note your father left?"

"Note?" I responded. "What note?"

"Over on the cupboard there, son, he wants your help today after work."

Oops. That could be a problem. Pop seldom asks for help from anyone, so if he needed a hand, it could be something big, and I had plans for the first time in my life. I put down the mug and made my way over to the cupboard where I saw a scrap of yellow paper held down by an African violet plant in a clay pot.

"Aha!" I smiled as I began reading the note. "He wants to know if I can drive him over to Harrison to pick up a new meat slicer. I was planning on going there anyway!" Then it dawned on me – if I had to bring him there to get the slicer, he'd need a ride home as well. This could be problematic for my plans with Molly. Well, maybe there was a way I could handle it and still get it all done today.

I thought it over and said, "Why sure, Mom. I'll drive over there after my shift and see if he needs to come along or if I can get the slicer myself. Did he say if he picked one out already?"

"Picked it out already? Oh, I see where you're coming from; he wouldn't have to leave the shop early if you could pick it up for him. You are such a good son, Augie!"

This was the sort of thing a son loves to hear, and I could have gone with it and told her, "You know how hard he works, Mom. I just need to feel like I'm a good help to him," but I didn't. I simply said, "It's no big deal, Mom, I'm on my way there already and I can handle it for him if he's already picked it out."

She hugged me and said, "You're a good man, August. We are so proud of you." Before she could get any mushier, I heard a Ford engine approach and the loud *ah-ooo-gah* saved me.

"Don't worry, Mom," I told her as I pecked her on the cheek, "I'll stop by and see him about 12:30." With that I was out the door and down the steps, wearing the big grin of anticipation that comes from having both something pleasurable to look forward to, and the ability to handle a sudden responsibility.

Nick was driving, which I thought strange, but then I realized Len would be stocking up the car to make his deliveries and we probably wouldn't see him until Monday. Ollie would be in his shed, and Pete was off in the Newark Rail Yards these days. It was just us two boys this morning. I climbed in and we drove off.

Other than exchanging pleasantries, we rode in silence most of the way. Nick likes to concentrate on his driving, I noticed. Lenny looks right and left, as if he's afraid of missing something. I guess that's my style, too. But Nick? His eyes are glued to the front of the car, and I swear his ears are tuned to the sound of the engine. He gets nervous if someone crosses in front of him and I'll bet he still hasn't lived down getting those two flat tires the first time he drove.

It was a bit cool for July, I thought, and noted the sky was clear except for one cloud that wasn't moving a bit, so there weren't any storms brewing. If the rains came again, it would put the kibosh on a driving lesson, and I wanted to impress Molly with my new-found abilities.

Pulling into the Yards we noticed Ollie Olson up on a flat car with a two gallon can of oil in one hand and a funnel in the other. Lenny was nowhere in sight, so it looked like we'd be getting right to work and skipping our usual coffee-chat. We ambled on over to get our orders and within minutes were imitating Ollie's movements at different parts of the same trainload. These Fords came in during the week and were all flatbeds with stake sides instead of ambulances. Yet, they were Model Ts and still had those carbide headlamps.

We spent the entire morning topping off oil in the engines and pumping up the tires. Then we started to drive them to a new parking area, over the planks just as before. To think we were so afraid of falling off between the railcars just a few weeks ago and now it was a cinch. Lenny never even showed up to see what we were doing, so he must have had his own hands full. At noon, the whistle blew, and we went our separate ways. Me to check on Pop's plans, Nick to one of his band practices, and Ollie over to Manhattan for a Broadway play with a lady friend. I imagined that he'd change out of his coveralls and wondered what he'd look like spruced up.

I was delighted to drive out of the Yards alone in my own car. I waved, wished the guys a nice weekend, and was out of there like a shot. In two minutes, I was over the Hackensack River and headed into the city. Well, Jersey City. Around here when you say "The City" it always means New York City.

The sun was glinting off the river once again and I offered up a prayer to God that all would be well with my loved ones, my friends, and Molly of course. In today's world, you just can't take things for granted. Just look in the newspaper! Shootings, stabbings, theft — not like it used to be. And things must be heating up over in Europe because rail shipments keep increasing substantially. Besides the influx of our Fords, we were seeing many more trainloads of shells passing through to the docks. Nope, that can't be good.

A few minutes later I pulled up in front of Pop's store and went inside to see about the slicer. If I played my cards right, I could get it on the way to Molly's before the driving lesson.

I waited patiently in line (no mean feat) behind Mrs. Kirkpatrick and Mr. Wolhzinsky as they filled their orders for pork chops or chicken parts. Mr. Wolhzinsky was a neighbor and always had a kind word for us, so it was fun to hear his exchange with Pop. "Mrs. K" used to be so cranky that we kids called her "Old Lady Kirkpatrick" when we were younger. She hasn't changed. Pop filled her order quickly and, as usual, gave her his big smile. When she left the shop, he just shook his head and I know just what he was thinking. He turned and rang open the cash register, placing the bills and coins inside. With that he turned to me and said, "Well, August, did you read the note I left you?"

"Sure did, Pop. If you want, I can pick it up myself since they've given me my own car to use for back-and-forth trips to the Yards. In fact, I was headed over to Harrison right now, having a few things to do there this afternoon and into the evening. What do you need then, just a meat slicer?"

"Oh yes, indeed, a slicer, but not just any slicer. It's a Berkel — and almost brand new, too!"

I'd heard him discussing slicers and stoves over the years and knew how much he wanted one of these machines to replace the old one that came with the shop. I let out my usual *Hoorah!* of approval.

With that he pulled some greenbacks from his wallet and said, "Gee, son, I'd really appreciate it if you could get on over to Wilken's Hardware and pick up the slicer for me. That way I can spend the rest of the afternoon moving shelves around. I'd like to put it on the left side of the meat counter instead of taking all that room up in the center. I've already spoken to Jim Wilkens about it and he's even throwing in a new set of carving knives for free. Remember the last time we went there together? It had to be in '09 or '10, and we stopped at Polsky's for chocolate sodas."

"Yea, Pop. That was fun. He gave us a big basket of peanuts to go with them, remember?

"Sure do. What a nice combination that was, too."

"I'll take care of it this afternoon, Pop. How about I bring it home with me tonight and then give you a ride here Monday morning?"

"Now that's an idea. That way I get chauffeured through the neighborhood and folks will think I've hit the Big Time!"

"Oh, Papa. What are we gonna do with you?"

"Yah, Augie!"

Excusing myself, I went to the back room to change into some decent clothes I had the foresight to put in a cloth bag. When I emerged, he gave me a smile and nod of approval and said, "My compliments, son. When I wrote that note about the meat slicer, I secretly hoped you would dress for the occasion. Just wait until Mr. Wilkens gets a load of you!"

"Well, I'm going to a picture show with a few friends tonight. We're going to see Charlie Chaplin in *The Tramp.*"

"Would one of these friends be a young lady?" He smiled.

"Hence the tie," is all I needed to say. He laughed and wished me a good time. He also handed me a bunch of licorice and said, "For the young lady."

I left the store, and the engine was purring nicely at the curb. After the Mister Pisser incident, we began shutting down the first few days, but we're back to our old habits again. Whenever we can, we keep an eye on our machines, and will even post a guard at night if we leave 'em running, although we've gotten where we can start the cars alone if we choose. I pulled out from the curb and started whistling one of the Strauss waltzes Pop likes.

I went straight to Communipaw Avenue because I recalled seeing some nice flower arrangements and thought it would be nice to get a bouquet for Molly and her mother to share; something to put on the table. Mom always said we should bring something for the Lady of the House if we were invited to dinner. Since there were two ladies, I might have to get a larger bunch.

Spotting the flower shop on the corner, I pulled up and tootled the horn to get the attention of the young girl who was busy filling vases out of a watering can. She looked up and I signaled toward the large bouquets of red and white carnations, holding up one finger. She brought one right over and I gave her two bits, telling her to "Keep the change."

She said, "That will be another dime."

"Well," I thought, "I already got free licorice for later, so I can afford to splurge."

I handed her a ten-cent piece, plus a buffalo nickel and told her, "When I was a kid, things were a lot cheaper, but you can still buy yourself a soda with five cents, right?"

"I'm saving for a bike," she said.

"A bike? Well, I guess I'll be seeing you on the road then!" I tossed her another nickel.

She got a big smile at that, said, "Thanks, Mister," and I was off on my way.

Crossing the Hackey again I noticed the tide was in and I hoped there wouldn't be any flooding on the turnpike through the meadowlands. I wouldn't want to splash my good clothes. The cobblestones were clear, and everything seemed to be going my way. I had candy, flowers, money, clean clothes, a Ford conveyance. Yup, I had it all going my way. The sun was shining brightly and there was not a cloud in the sky.

Then I ran over a skunk.

I had not planned on that occurrence.

My luck held, as when I looked back, he was still sauntering across the road.

Whew! I drove a bit more carefully then but didn't slow down. To think a run-in with a skunk could have scuppered my plans at this stage! I shook my head in wonder, grateful that God has a sense of humor.

22

The Girls and the Park: 7/22/16

I GOT TO WILKEN'S HARDWARE and handled that business lickety-split. Mr. Wilkens commented on how big I had gotten, and how good it was to see me, but I noticed he still counted the money twice. I took no offense, as that's just business.

Taking my leave, I stowed the slicer and knives in a built-in wooden box behind the rear seat. I next went up Washington Street toward the Edison Lamp Works at the T-intersection. The sycamore trees on either side of this road were shedding their bark in strips of six inches to a foot, and I wondered if this was due to the heat or akin to snakes shedding their skin as they grew. Who knows? I sure enjoyed the smell of the bark, and it was always fun to step on these when I was a kid.

I made the right and parked in front of Molly's house, shutting off the machine. Hopping down, I adjusted my pants, checked my shirt buttons, picked up the flowers and made my way toward the front gate. The licorice was still in my pocket — that will come in handy at the picture show. Mounting the steps to the front porch I noted some of the potted plants could use a watering and made a mental note to point that out to my hosts. As I was about to grab the bell rope and give it a clang, the door opened abruptly. It was Angelo, who recognized me immediately and said, "Ah, *Signore* Augusto, how are you?"

"I'm good *Signore* Angelo. *Molto bene.*"

"*Veni, veni.* Come in, *Signore.* I go getta Miss Johnson for you. Come in and setta-down in the parlor."

I took a seat in a powder blue wingback chair, holding the red and white bouquet in my lap. Suddenly, from over my shoulder came that voice again. "Awwwwwk, give us a treat!"

Turning to look, I noted the parrot had been moved inside, his cage standing between two large palm trees. He seemed to be eyeing the flowers, walking left and right on his perch, eyes wide, and continued his squawking for treats. Knowing a bit of parrot-talk myself, I lifted the flowers higher and said, "Awwwwwk, Polly want a flower?"

I felt a tap on my shoulder, turned and there were three women laughing at me; Molly with her small hand over her mouth, her mother with two hands over hers, and the third woman — just a girl really — was holding a tray of lemonade and had a confused expression on her face. This had to be Cousin Lillian.

Molly said, "Hello, August. How nice of you to bring Zinga flowers!"

"Very sweet," added her mother.

Before the young girl could join in, I stood, presented the bouquet, and said, "Zinga doesn't seem interested in the flowers — would you ladies accept them instead?"

"Why, August, how very nice of you!" This from Molly's mother.

"Yes," Molly agreed. "'tis very sweet of you. Here, let me take them and find a vase in the kitchen. Lillian, just set that tray down there and meet August."

Lillian placed the tray on the small table, turned and curtsied. What else could I do – I bowed, and said I was delighted to meet her! I caught Molly's eye and saw her delight. Looking at her mother I saw the same sparkle. I was doing well.

Her mother took over and said, "Why don't we all sit and have some of the fresh lemonade that Lillian prepared for us?"

Molly went off with the carnations as I regained my chair. Lillian poured out four glasses of lemonade, using a wooden spoon to keep the pulp from splashing down into the glassware. I thanked her and tried to come up with a debonair toast for when Molly re-joined us. Ah, I had it.

As Molly returned, she smiled at me and took her glass. Before she could sip it, I stood and said, "To the most beautiful ladies in the world, and their parrot!"

Smiles all around, and a tinkling of glasses as we touched. To tell the truth, as a toast, it seemed to fall flat. Before I could dig myself deeper, Lillian asked how I liked the lemonade, as she felt she may not have added enough sugar.

"Oh, it's swell (I lied — it could use a bit of sugar), just like my mom makes at home." (In fact, my mom over-sweetens it and I find myself adding water to thin it down. You can't get decent lemonade in this state. I wonder if you mixed it with hooch?)

Mrs. Johnson got right to the point, saying, "My daughter tells me you'd like to take her and Lillian for a spin before dinner. So long as you don't drive too fast, that will be fine. Make sure, that you're all back before 3:30, as Lillian will be helping with the pot roast today. Dinner will be at 5:00 p.m. sharp."

"And," Molly added, "The picture show begins at 7:30, which will give us plenty of time, as the Warner Theatre is just a few blocks away."

"I can't wait to see *The Tramp* at last," chimed Lillian.

We all agreed that seeing Charlie Chaplin again would be a blast.

The doorbell rang, and Mrs. Johnson got up to look past the drawn curtain to see who had arrived. We heard Angelo's voice at the door, "Ah, *Signore* Thompson, a great pleasure to see you again. Come in, come in. I bring you right away to see Mr. Johnson. He is inna the office. *Veni, veni.*"

"Please excuse me, August," said Mrs. Johnson, letting the curtain close itself. "But I must greet Mr. Thompson. He works with my husband with the ambulance project over in Paris. He's only just arrived back in the States yesterday! I'll see you kids before 3:30 then."

With that she was gone, leaving me alone with the parrot, and, ah, the two girls.

"Come, Lillian," Molly began. "August is going to take us to the park in his Ford!"

"Oh, yippee!" was all she could say. This was going to be fun, I guess, but would not count much for "alone time" with my new girl. Oh well, it was a beautiful day, and I'd be with her, nonetheless.

"Sure thing," I smiled broadly. "We'll have some fun. Let's go!"

It never hurts to have a good attitude, no matter what you're doing.

I got the girls situated in the staff car, Molly in front next to me of course, and Lillian in the back seat. I cranked the Lizzie, "quickly and efficiently" as Ollie would say, and pulled away from the curb.

"Take a right here, "Molly told me, "and head a mile north — we'll cross the railroad on the 5th Street Bridge into the park."

We played ball in that park once, so I knew just where we were headed.

We coasted down the slight hill from Sussex Street toward the main street in Harrison, which is the same road as the Newark–Jersey City Turnpike. The locals call it Harrison Avenue, of course. Once across that we continued another five blocks until we reached the narrow span over the tracks below. The railroaders had cut right through the main ridge that goes north/south through the area. The bridge had to be fifty feet above the rail bed. I slowed down for safety. It was an impressive job, as rail cuts go.

I headed through the gates into West Hudson Park, onto a path with a slight decline and through a small tunnel. We emerged into a little vale with hills rising on both sides. At the top of one was a long, roofed gazebo. It was round on each end, like two normal gazebos, but these were connected by a roofed pathway that had to be 200 feet long. Amazing. I wondered if they used it for weddings or something.

I came to a halt on the pathway next to this little valley and asked Molly if she was ready for her driving lesson.

"I'm ready if you are."

"Well, then, allow me to demonstrate." I hopped out and went to her side to help her down. Instead, she just skootched over, so I climbed back up and sat on the passenger seat. As I was about to point out the throttle to her with admonitions as to braking, her hands and feet moved in such ways as I did not expect, suddenly putting the Ford in gear and into one hell of an acceleration!

"Hold on, Lily!" Molly cried.

"Holy smokes!" I grabbed onto the dashboard in awe as she took the Flivver right up the side of one of these hills, crested it, and on down the other side.

"Whoa, Molly, what are you doing?" I was astounded.

"Just want to see what ol' Henry Ford's got that Karl Benz hasn't. Hang on, we're about to find out."

With that we exited the small pathway and got onto the main road that runs through the park. We headed over a small bridge at a good clip and were picking up speed as we began descending a long hill that led to another arched bridge crossing a main street below.

"Molly," I pleaded, "slow down!"

"Don't worry, I've got it."

Lillian then spoke up, "She's done this before, you know!"

Well, no, I didn't. But as Molly said, we were about to find out. She'd slow down for the bridge, though. I mean, she'd have to — it was arched.

She didn't slow for the bridge. If anything, she sped up!

We hit the surface of the bridge briefly before rising into the air without the benefit of wings. My stomach dropped as my butt rose. It's a good thing I had grabbed the bottom of my seat, or I'd be in the trees with the squirrels. We soared for a few seconds but happily landed on all four tires, bouncing just twice. Molly held that wheel, and turned to me with the biggest, sweetest smile I had ever seen. What could I say? I was defenseless. Lillian was gleeful and made all sorts of happy, excited noises. I managed to get my breath back and was equally happy to see Molly slow down and bring the car off the main road into a short turnoff that led to a duck pond. She braked to a stop and shut off the motor.

"Nice controls," she said. "Thank you for the lesson."

"Lesson?" I managed. "What was that all about?"

"Oh, August, it was a great lesson! I had never driven a Model T before. My father taught us on a Benz while we were in England last year," she smiled demurely. "I didn't tell you?"

Like I said, I was defenseless. I just looked at her.

To break the silence, she said, "Come on, let's walk a bit. You can drive back."

"Are you sure you don't want to fly her yourself?" I had to ask.

"Oh, don't be sore. If I told you I could drive already, well, where's the fun in that? Why, just to see the look on your face made it all worth it."

This was a Molly I did not suspect. There was a bit of Lenny in everyone, I guess. What was there to do but give in, so I said, "I must admit, you're quite a driver. Who would have guessed? My compliments to your skill at the wheel."

There, that felt better.

"Thank you, Augie. That means a lot." *She called me Augie!*

"Can we do it again?" Lillian had to ask.

"No," I felt I had the right to say, "We've got to start back — it's 3:05 — we've got to get back so you can cook. Come on, girls."

And that's how I took charge, and to this day, I've never let my guard down around Miss Molly Johnson.

I got the ladies settled, cranked the engine to life, and wheeled the staff car out of the park and back toward Harrison, arriving at the Johnson home in plenty of time for Lillian to help make dinner. Oh, and I'd see about a stiff drink, if I could help it.

23

The Dinner, *The Tramp*, and the Drive Home: 7/22/16

T HE PICTURE SHOW WAS A lot of fun (and I really enjoyed the piano player). Besides the licorice Pop had given me, we brought along a tin full of cookies that Mrs. Johnson baked, so we stuffed ourselves. I sat between Molly and Lillian, so not only did I get to hold the chocolate chips, but I also got to hold Molly's hand.

As usual, Chaplin was very funny with his antics. We were laughing so hard at one point I dropped the tin, but it was already empty by then, so no harm. Still, the clanging got me some looks from the folks seated around us, and some giggles from Lillian and Molly. It would have been worse had we not finished the cookies.

While walking back the few blocks to her house, Molly and I held hands again, with Lillian traipsing around us. We all agreed we'd have another movie night once the Johnsons returned from their mountain vacation. It was nice to have a night out in a place other than a tavern.

I walked the girls onto Molly's porch, of course, and she sent young Lillian on ahead with instructions to "Rinse out the cookie tin and leave it on the drain board." I took both Molly's hands in mine and tried to muster up the courage to kiss her on the cheek, when she suddenly leaned into me and planted one squarely on the lips! I recoiled, albeit briefly, and she giggled again, saying, "Why August, you shouldn't have!"

"Shouldn't have?" I replied. "You surprised me once already today with your driving, this makes twice!"

"What's wrong with my driving?" she pleaded, making a frown.

"Why nothing, nothing at all."

"Well then," she continued. "What's wrong with my kissing?"

"I don't know. Try it again!"

And she did, but it was longer this time, and maybe we'd still be at it, but the door opened, and Lillian intoned, "Hey, I've got more cookies, want some?"

Molly stepped back about a foot, took the plate from Lillian's hand, and asked innocently, "Yes, August, more sweets?"

"I don't know, they seem to be making my face red. I had better knock it off for a spell."

"More for me!" declared Lillian, taking the plate back inside.

Another long kiss (while we still could) and then we said our goodbyes and I had to be on my way. Although she would not be leaving on her trip until Friday, Molly said it was not likely she'd get a chance to see me during the week, as she had much work to do for her father before their vacation. We had a lovely day together, to be sure.

These events kept playing in my mind that evening as I drove the Ford east through the Kearny meadows again toward home. The driving lesson was a blast, what with her big surprise. And we had so much fun together seeing the Chaplin films and eating up all those sweets. Then there were those goodnight kisses, of course.

How often I thought of that Saturday we spent together over the next few years!

I sighed, lost in reverie for a moment, but again focused on the dips in the cobbles ahead of me as the new headlights shone their beams in a much wider path than the old carbide lights.

Before my thoughts could return to Molly and Lillian, it hit me that, with all the excitement of the moving pictures and joking around with the girls, I had not had the time to think much about what was said during the pot roast dinner. Well, not the dinner now that I think of it. While we ate, the conversation touched on things like local happenings — the construction of the Town Hall, the latest moving pictures, the visit of President Howard Taft a few years ago, and then Lillian entertained us with some silly Knock-Knock jokes. No, it was after dinner when Mr. Thompson, Doc Johnson and I went to the Drawing Room to enjoy some cigars and brandy that serious discussion began. I suppose the gents felt it was good taste not to discuss business like this at the table.

There was much to ponder. The world is a cruel place.

I kept the car at a steady twenty mph or so and reflected on the things they shared with me about the American Field Service Volunteer Ambulance Corps and the situation at the Western Front. Since the Verdun offensive began in February, something like 300,000 Frenchmen became casualties! The Germans suffered similarly, of course, and it appeared both armies were being bled white, with not much ground changing hands. Doc called it a "meat grinder." Mr. Thompson said the British over in Flanders were going through similar hell, but it was the French Department of Alsace he and the Doc were focusing on right now, having to raise several new Ambulance Sections to augment or replace those there already. There was simply not enough transport to handle the unending stream of bleeding, broken men. The ambulance drivers were being killed or wounded as well, and the machines themselves were badly worn out. A few were blasted to smithereens at forward posts; some went out on a run and never returned, vanishing without a trace.

Doc had me explain my experiences to-date with the cars so Mr. Thompson would have a feel for my knowledge. I thought he'd be impressed with the skills Ollie had taught with basic mechanics, but he really liked what we did to modify the machines to run with the electric batteries and headlamps, and how we salvaged parts from the one that sank into the Morris Canal and straightened out the front-end of another (I blamed the Canal incident on a new driver). "A skill with improvised field repairs is key at the front!" was how he put it.

Mr. Thompson particularly enjoyed the way I described how the T could climb up steep hills, jump over small ditches, drive right through streams, and stop on a dime when you needed her to. These were all things we did with the Flivvers in the Kearny swamplands, of course, and were second nature to me and the guys, but he said I spoke of these maneuvers with such affection, that he could tell I was a born driver. When I told him it was my intention to volunteer to drive an ambulance, that while I was against the war I could not stand by and simply do nothing, both he and Doc nodded in assent and said I'd be a welcome addition to the Corps. I felt a glow about me after that, and it wasn't the brandy. Doc said he'd get things rolling for me and in just a few days would have the papers for me to sign. I'd need a physical, of course, and he would vouch for my background and abilities himself!

Meanwhile, Mr. Thompson seemed intrigued with my work at the docks and the Kearny Rail Yards. Evidently, cargo was getting tied up at the wharves in France and there were many bottlenecks from the French ports to the rail yards in the interior. This was somewhat due to the loss of important facilities to the German advances but was also caused by the lack of enough locomotives and rolling stock to handle the massive amounts of supplies coming into the country. Military conscription also played a role, causing insufficient manpower at the docks, rail yards, and storage facilities. "I wonder," he said, "If instead of driving an ambulance, would you possibly be interested in helping us resolve some of the confusion over there? The AFS will control its own section of the Saint Nazaire docks, but we've been given the go-ahead to recruit a Chief Harbor Master to replace one that got himself killed at the Marne. The French are in disarray in this regard. You may be just the man we need."

That was the last thing I wanted to do! I had to think fast on this, or I'd end up behind a desk. I did not want to appear ungrateful for their trust in me, but nor did I fancy myself handling trains or shiploads of shells or barbed wire.

As often happens, it came to me in a flash. I put on a serious face, took a puff of my cigar, exhaled, and said, "I see where you're coming from; we've had backups ourselves at the Hudson or in the rail yards.

Once it happens, it can be a bear to untangle and set things right. You need a man with experience in these situations, a man of action, one who can think on his feet and boldly make decisions at a moment's notice."

They enthusiastically shook their heads in agreement.

"I'm not the man you seek. I am a driver, nothing more. No, the man you want is right here in Kearny, N.J. His name is Lenny. Lenny Krulikowski."

24

The Turn at the Docks: 7/24/16, Monday — 7/25/16, Tuesday

"WHY ME?"

"Well, Augie, we're gonna all have a turn. Nick went last week for a few days — we've got to mix it up."

It was Monday morning and Lenny had just sprung the news that each one of us had to rotate over to National Docks a few days at a time for the near future. Turns out the foreman, Tom Delaney, suffered a fall from a derrick and had a few ribs and an arm broken. He was home for a bit because he was having trouble breathing. This is the sort of thing that happens at the docks, and we were all used to it. Although I'd be filling in as foreman during that time, I'd still rather be driving.

I had gotten spoiled.

I gave in, saying, "At least Nick's there today." But I had to clarify, "So, I just go there tomorrow morning through Friday, or do I need to put in Saturday hours, too?"

"Looks like you'll have to, lad. If something changes, I'll let you know. I'll be there myself next Monday until Delaney comes back sometime next week. Ollie has no experience at the river, of course, so it's just the three of us for a couple weeks. No problem."

What can you do? It's the docks. On the bright side, I was able to drive Pop to the store first thing in the morning and carried the meat slicer in for him. I felt good about that, and never even bothered to mention it to the guys!

We ferried the cars with Ollie that day and I didn't see Nick until noon Tuesday, when he came with Len and Ollie to the Hudson with some sandwiches for lunch. I was happy to see them, and we went over to an old wooden table and benches in the shade of some freight cars and a huge catalpa tree for our meal.

"This heat is intense," Nick offered.

"It's as humid as shit," Lenny said.

"I'm sweating like a pig," I added.

We looked at Ollie for his opinion but all he said was,

"Anybody got any mustard?"

A hot breeze was blowing off the river as we commenced to eat in silence. A few nosey gulls hovered nearby but we ignored them. We learned long ago that if you feed them, they'll get too close and try to steal the bread out of your hand, the bastards.

As we ate, Lenny mentioned the fellow with the Cuban cigars over on Black Tom and said he finally got a hold of those fat geese for him.

"See if you can't get them over there tomorrow morning, wouldja Augie? I'll drop them off here when we make our first run but won't be able to get to Black Tom Island myself. They'll be some hooch, too, and he'll give you some more crates of cigars."

"You mean Karl Eisener?" This was the guy from Stuttgart with the chickens.

"One and the same," he replied, adding, "He asked about getting a case of *Das weissen blitzen schnapps*. I figured he meant the moonshine and told him I'd fix him up."

"*Blitzen schnapps*," I repeated and laughed. "White Lightning. Wait 'til Pop hears that one!"

"Yea, well, Karl mentioned a friend with a warehouse full of certain items we may be interested in and will share our product with him shortly. It sounds like a fair exchange, so as soon as I get the word, we'll need to fill one of the ambulances with a dozen cases of boxed hooch. With a deal this big, we'll have to play it a bit more on the sly, preferably after dark, so it will be after our shift is over, or even late Saturday night."

Nick asked, "What's he got in that warehouse?"

"You'll all find out soon enough. Let's just say that, like Karl's tobacco, this fellow has a building full of things the Germans ordered but the Brits are not letting through. Let's leave it at that."

It got quiet for a minute while Lenny's uncharacteristic discretion hovered in the air, so I broke the silence and asked, "Is that it with the geese then, or are you going to start sending him sheep, too?" I know how to start things moving along in these situations.

Lenny gave me that sideways look again, but just bit into his sandwich and shook his head.

A few minutes later they all climbed back into the Ford, lit up smokes, and took off. I went back to the boys at the docks to see if they had gotten into any trouble while I was away.

One thing was for certain, I'd get the lowdown on that mysterious warehouse from Karl himself tomorrow morning.

25

The Geese and the Indian: 7/26/16, Early Wednesday

T HAT NIGHT I DOZED OFF in Pop's favorite chair by the open window. It was hot and humid, and I was exhausted from my shift at the docks. I sat there thinking how bad the heat gets here each July, the sweat and hard work, and next thing I know I woke up with a start. Well, the cuckoo clock was announcing the stroke of midnight, so that explained what woke me. I stretched out my legs and began to gather my thoughts. Let's see, the clock is forty-five minutes slow at last count, so that would make it about quarter to one, Wednesday morning. Tomorrow's already here and I had better wake up and go to bed!

I stumbled out of the parlor and down the hall to my room. Collapsing into bed, I lay on my side and formed the pillow into a ball. I shut my eyes hoping to drift right off but began chuckling about Molly and the driving lesson. I can't believe she pulled out and took off the way she did! Then I thought of my talk with her father and Mr. Thompson for a bit. Next, I realized I hadn't mentioned anything to Lenny about recommending him for a job in France, of all things. I didn't want to bring it up in front of the guys yesterday as I had no idea how he'd take it. I had better get to that in the morning!

A few minutes later I heard the clock down the hall chime once, so a half hour had gone by since I left the parlor. It would be 1:15 a.m.

now, I think; funny how you automatically calculate things at times like this. I rolled over and tried to clear my mind. Charlie Chaplin was crossing the street with his cane and funny walk. He's so silly. I stopped the Ford to let him pass and he waved and smiled. A crow landed on the hood, and I scared him away. Lenny tapped me on the shoulder and offered me a cigar. I didn't want to take it. He tapped me again, saying, "Come on Augie, come on…Wake up Augie, wake up." I looked up and Pop was shaking my arm!

"Time to get up, son, " he said. "Here, I'll just put your coffee on the nightstand."

"Good golly," I yawned. "Is it 6:30 already?"

"Yes, and I'm off and running. Make sure you leave some coffee for Mom; I had an extra cup today and don't have time to make more."

"Sure thing, Pop. I'll just have the one. Enjoy your day!"

"You too, son. See you later."

I jumped up, found my trousers and belt, and pulled a fresh shirt from the basket Mom had left on my dresser. I grabbed a tan one because it would be sunny again today. Pop's coffee was always hot, so I took a tentative sip and carried it into the kitchen, where I splashed some water on my face from the faucet. I found some pumpernickel in the bread box and tore off a hunk, stuffed it in my shirt pocket, and was out of there in under three minutes, coffee mug in hand.

Starting a Flivver by yourself is not too hard after all, and we'd all mastered it by now. You simply must remember NOT to wrap your thumb around the crank, or it can hurt your arm. I put her in neutral, retarded the spark, put the key on, went to the front bumper and cranked, once, twice, and *Brrrrrr, Mmmmmmm, Rrrrrrrr*, she was running. I climbed in, advanced the spark and was off.

I got over to the docks in no time, since at this hour there are not too many folks about. I put the staff car under that catalpa tree to keep it in the shade for later and went over to join the boys. Today we'd be loading a couple thousand crates of canned goods unto a two-stacker. I got them settled and began poring over the manifest to see how far along we had gotten yesterday when I heard that familiar sound of

Lenny's heavy hand on a Ford throttle. Oddly, he was alone. That is, except for about a dozen honking geese.

"Laddie Buck," he began, "are ya ready to take flight with this gaggle?" Len is so poetic.

"Well," I said, "it's such a nice day I thought I'd swim. Think they're up to it?"

Hands on hips, he replied, "So long as you can float these crates of Lightning ahead of you, I don't see why not."

I laughed, saying, "Damn, there go my doggy paddle plans for the morning. I guess I have no choice but to load these into the staff car. How soon should I leave?"

"No time like the present, Augie. I told Herr Eisener you'd be along first thing. No need to move the geese or the booze, though. I'd prefer to swap vehicles for the day since Karl is giving me one of the Indians now and the second one after you deliver the full load of 'shine. We need to keep them hidden inside an ambulance during transport, so I'll just take the staff car."

"I'm supposed to pick up an Indian?" I was perplexed.

"Yes, indeedy doo. And wait 'til you see her!"

This was getting interesting. My face must have registered shock, as he went on.

"She's a real beauty, too, and purrs like a kitten."

"How can this be? Where is she from?"

"Massachusetts, I believe."

"Seneca? Mohawk?" I knew my Indian tribes.

"No," he answered, "Four Stroke."

"Four Stroke?" This was getting confusing.

"Yea and wait til you get her between your legs — she'll give you the ride of your life!"

"Lenny," I was aghast. "What that hell are you talking about?"

"Motorbikes, lad," he replied. "Built up in Boston, by the Indian Motorcycle Company. Karl's buddy has a few dozen that were supposed to go to the Kaiser's army, but they're gathering dust on Black Tom instead. He'll only part with two of the machines, but I'm hoping he'll change his mind in a few months. I'm not sure how we'll use them yet, but they ought to be fun to learn to ride."

"I've seen one or two of those over in Newark," I chimed in. "Nice machines. But you're not going to fit much stuff on them except with saddlebags."

"One is supposed to have a side-car — I'm keeping that one for myself, Augie, as I don't have good balance. I can fit a case or two in there easy. Anyways, I'm always open to new materials we might begin trading and these machines could be worth something along those lines."

I saw an opening here and jumped into an approach I had thought about while lying awake in bed last night. I asked, "Lenny, you know how we traded that ol' cow for a few cases of Johnny Walker, and then used that scotch to get the job ferrying Fords?"

"Yup," he smiled. "Business as usual."

"Right, and there were the cases of chickens for the cigars, and now hooch for a couple motorbikes."

"Yessir," he got a bigger grin. "I always try to build to the next level. Why do you ask?"

"Ever think of shipping overseas?"

He smiled and nodded, saying, "Well, now Boyo, that's a thought. Now that we've got a supply line and a local market a smart man would consider building on that, either across state lines via rail or by taking advantage of the ocean-going ships right here on the Hudson. Problem is, we don't have any connections anywhere overseas. I've thought about it plenty, believe me, but without a trusted accomplice on the other side of the ocean it's not a good risk."

I began my pitch, saying, "Well, I was offered a job at the Port of Saint Nazaire the other night, as the AFS Shipping Coordinator, Sea and Rail."

He asked, "Where the hell is that, Louisiana?"

"Nope. It's in France; about 250 miles from Paris, actually. Molly's dad and a fellow from the American Field Service offered it to me, because of my experience with you guys, but I turned them down."

"You turned down an opportunity like that? Why, you could make a fortune! You'd oversee scheduling, destinations and storage for ships, truck, and rail. We could ship you boatloads of hooch for the Frenchies! They'd give good money for that! Damn, what I'd give to have a job like that, even in France!" He seemed incredulous.

I shook my head, saying, "I know, but I told them I wasn't their man."

"Why on earth would you pass that up?"

"I want to drive an ambulance."

"Oh yea, the ambulance again. Yea, yea. Look, I know you've been going on about how you want to contribute, how you can't stand by and do nothing when so many are dying over there, and so on. But think of what you could do for the war effort if you oversaw all the shipping at that port. Think of what you could be doing for us! How you could…"

"No way, Lenny. I told them it's not for me."

"But think how you could help the war effort! Things are going badly; they need a guy like you!"

"No, not a guy like me. No way."

"Well, laddie, if not a guy like you, then who?"

"I gave them a name, so I'm out of the running, so forget about it."

"Wait, you gave them a name? Why didn't you ask me first? Didn't you even think about me?"

"Yes, I thought about you Lenny, I thought about you first. I didn't want to ask, seeing as you're so tied up over here and all."

"What? You gave them a name and didn't even bother asking me? Why, I could set Nick up in charge over here, take over Saint Nazaire, and have things running like clockwork for both the Frenchies *and* our bootleg, black market operations!"

"Really, Len?"

"Damn straight, Augie. You should have thought of me!"

"I did, Lenny, in fact, I meant to tell you — you've got an appointment tomorrow at 3:00 with the Doc and Mr. Thompson at Molly's house. Wear something decent. I told them some good things about you. Now, if you don't mind, I've got to get these fat birds over to Black Tom and see about that motorcycle."

"What? Appointment? Me?"

"Yup," I smiled, and added, "I told them all about you, except your private 'Marketing Business,' of course."

I hopped into the ambulance, setting off the honking geese again. Taking advantage of the clamor to cut short our conversation, I pointed at the geese, cupped my right ear with my hand, shrugged, and said, "See ya later."

As I drove away, I looked back over my shoulder. Just I suspected, Lenny had a big, wide grin on that mug of his. I wondered how long it would take for him to figure out I had played him.

26

The Indian: 7/26/16, Wednesday Noon

B Y THE TIME I GOT back from Black Tom and my visit with Karl, the boys had finished loading the freighter and were resting in the shade of that big ol' tree, it being high noon and hot as Hades. I parked the car over by the shed, switched off, and went around back to open the twin doors and take another peek inside at the "Indian."

This motorcycle was not at all what I remembered seeing tear down Broad Street one day last summer. That one was bright red with white-wall tires, gleaming silver-plated handlebars, spoke-wheels, shining engine and exhaust. I recalled when the driver went into a tight turn onto Market Street; I thought for certain he'd slide right under a trolley car, but he leaned over and kept going down Market with a thunderous roar as he opened the throttle — like a bat from hell, as Pop likes to say.

I was impressed with both the machine and the rider and often think of that afternoon's experience fondly.

This machine was just as big and powerful looking, but instead the paint was various shades of green and brown, with not a spot of silver on it. It had black saddle bags strapped across a metal deck over the rear fender, a metal toolbox attached to the side, and a headlight that was partially covered with a black hood. Karl and I had rolled it up a plank into the rear of the ambulance. Until then, I had not noticed that the stretcher shelves fold right up onto hooks, so we had lots of room for both the bike and the sidecar, which was not attached yet. We used that to help wedge the bike so it didn't tip over on a turn (it has a kickstand, but who knows how reliable that would be while transported in the back of a vehicle). As I looked her over again, I noticed a white spot right in the middle of the front fender. I thought *How odd is that to have an entire motorcycle painted green but still have a large white spot painted on the fender?* Then it blew off and joined the other goose feathers on the floor and I realized that I had been working too hard!

I opened one of the boxes of cigars Karl had given me and put a few in my pocket to hand out to the fellows at lunch time, normally about a half hour away, but by the look of things they took their break already. I shut the doors and put the padlock in place that Lenny had insisted upon. Well, he's the boss; I suppose he knows what he's doing. Karl had also urged discretion with these machines, so I have no problem with that. We had a nice chat together while moving the geese cages and moonshine into his warehouse, making several trips back out with crates of those nice Cuban cigars. At one point as we emerged with our arms full, he asked, "And so, how is your father doing?" I was about to answer him when who should I see clip-clopping by on a mare but Mr. Pisser! I stood agape until I realized I ought to follow him. Karl noticed my gaze and said, "*Ach*, that *scheisskopf!* He is a thief and a scoundrel we all must watch out for!"

Word evidently gets around. Shithead, eh? How fitting.

Well, we hadn't even loaded the motorcycle yet or I would have dropped those cigars, started the Ford up and given chase. Instead, I decided to abide for now and asked Karl if he knew that scheisskopf's actual name.

"Yah, his name is Kristoff. Don't know his first name. He is Slovak."

"How is it that he can ride freely on the docks here if you men know he is up to no good?"

"*Ach*," he replied. "He has good friends who look after him, men who are hard and tough. Otto Bremmer was almost beaten to death by these fellows after throwing Kristoff out of his warehouse for stealing. And there have been others, too, these past few years. We have learned it is best to lock things up and well-guarded keep them. We also have a gun nearby always, yah?"

I said, "Yes, a good idea that, Karl. One must be on guard with scum like him. But be careful with this man; he carries a pistol, too." I then gave him a brief description of that night where Mr. Pisser pulled a gun on me, and that we thought he had drowned in the canal.

Alas, Mr. Pisser was now reborn as Mr. Scheisskopf!

• • •

I had just handed out the smokes to the boys and struck a match when Lenny pulled up and waved me over. I lit my Cuban and ambled on over to him.

"I've been thinking about this Saint Nazaire thing, August."

"Yes, Leonard?" We were back to formal first names, it seemed.

"Well, I was thinking that maybe you were setting me up. I thought a bit about it later and felt like a bass on the end of your fishing line. Now, why is that?"

"I don't know what you're talking about, Lenny. I merely told them you were the best man for the job. Truth be told, they were trying to talk me out of driving an ambulance and almost had me set up in an office doing what I think you'd be that much better at anyway. Hey, you can always skip the meeting and not give it another thought. They'll probably pick some other fellow from here on the docks — it will be all the same to them. I just thought you'd like a hand in it yourself, being a patriotic American and all and knowing we'd soon be in it ourselves after that *Lusitania* incident. And what about your special abilities at delivering goods and services above and beyond the normal flow of materials on the docks? You know darned well about the shortages over there from the war, so there'd be lots of possibilities for the Marketing Business. They must have abundant things over there to trade that are not affected by the war; art, jewelry, tools, things like that."

"Ah, so it was in recognition of my patriotism, my abilities at organization, and my skills in addressing the needs of the masses."

"Correct, Lenny. And with Nicky back here on the other end…"

"…we'd have an endless supply of White Lightning, plus anything else we can conjure up!"

"Precisely."

He said, "Hmm," then thought for a moment, and said, "well, laddie, I think I'll go see those gents tomorrow and hear what they have to say. It seems like an opportunity in all the ways you mention, but you forgot one thing."

"What's that?

"I don't like the food."

"Nick can send kielbasa; you'll be fine."

"Oh, speaking of food, lad, why don't we grab something nearby and then you can get that Indian over to the Yards so Ollie can give her the once-over. Then maybe you can get some practice riding her on the dirt roads through the swamplands. I'll put the boys here to work the next few hours and you can take over in the morning."

With that we walked over to a small café up in the middle of the block just off the river. We had a bowl of stew each and some toast. He was quite surprised when I filled him in on spotting Mr. Pisser and asked me twice if I was certain. I assured him it was one and the same ape, with a new derby hat and another loud plaid jacket to boot.

Next, we agreed that calling him Mr. Scheisskopf was a step up from "Mr. Pisser" in this incarnation. I told him what Karl had to say about the beatings on Black Tom that this bunch was involved in and he shook his head, saying, "Ol' Karl had better watch his step — he's not one to put up with anything either. Maybe we ought to see if we can't pay a visit on this chump one of these nights ourselves. Perhaps we can find him in one of the local saloons where they don't know him yet."

"Oh yea," I recalled. "That's another thing — Karl says this clown's name is Kristoff, and he's a Slovak. Maybe we can start asking around about him?"

"Leave it to me, Augie. I have a guy in mind who will be a big help with that. He used to be a Pinkerton detective but opened a gunsmith shop now that he retired. Name's Malloy, Vince Malloy. I'll have him stop by and have a chat with Karl. It might be helpful for you and me to have a sit-down with Vince ourselves to describe this thug. I'll arrange it. Meanwhile, how's about you get that motorbike over to Ollie and spend the rest of the day tearing through the meadows?"

I nodded, and as I was about to get up, he added, "Pay the tab, wouldja Augie? I seem to be tapped out today."

I suspect my getting stuck with the tab was the price I had to pay for my afternoon fun in the meadows with that Indian.

27

The Morass: 7/26/16, Wednesday Afternoon

OLLIE LOVED THE MOTORCYCLE. HE checked the oil and brakes, put in a bit of gasoline, and was off like a rocket. I stood there listening to the roar of that engine as it disappeared behind the shed, then the water tower, and then rip right past me at high speed. Next, he took it around a long string of boxcars on a siding, and I steadily marked his progress by the sound of the fading engine as he sped down the length of the freight train. Then, detecting a slight pause, I saw him round the locomotive up ahead and come careening back to me lickety-split. The roar intensified until he pulled up to a sudden stop in front of me, declaring, "Blimey, what a machine!"

"You've ridden before, I take it?"

"Oh, indeed I have, August. It's one of the great memories I have of my time with Mr. Roosevelt; I had special use of a Harley-Davidson cycle of his on my time off. This one has as much power as that machine, but your newer Harleys would leave this in the dust. Still, a fantastic piece of equipment, this. Hop on and give it a shot!"

Ollie dismounted and held the cycle for me as I climbed aboard, saying, "I'm afraid I'm going to need to hear the basics first."

"Basics?" he replied. "Well, here's the throttle, that's the brake, you can't go backwards, you go like hell, then you stop. Those are the basics. Try it out!"

I did. At first, I felt wobbly, but once I got up enough steam, I felt steady after all. Before long I was trundling down the gravel paths alongside the tracks, getting my wings as it were. I had her up to a good clip in the Yards and then went out through the gates. She really handled well on the macadam, but I thought her a bit uneasy on the cobblestones (that will take some getting used to). After an hour or so I stopped by to see if Ollie wanted another turn but all he did was top-off the tank and wish me luck. I headed out into the meadows to see what she'd do in the muddy stuff.

OK, the muddy stuff was not so very wonderful. After the first few mud puddles I got up my nerve and let 'er fly through bigger and bigger messes until I hit a regular morass of about nine inches deep. Down I went, flipping over and getting covered with slime. I up-righted the machine and she fired right up again after the first two attempts. By the time I returned to Ollie I was unrecognizable, or so I thought. All he could say was, "Glad to see you took her through the paces, August."

I left the mud-spattered motorcycle with Ollie and hopped in Len's Ford for the ride home. All in all, I had a terrific workout with that machine and looked forward to doing it again. With any luck, I'd be back in the saddle tomorrow. I'd do my shift at the docks and stop by the Yards to see if I could spend another couple hours going over my lessons. Better yet, maybe I'd run over to Molly's house and get a chance to see her before her Pocono trip. She said she'd try to visit before they left but here it was Wednesday already.

I took a nice bath when I got home, even though I still had a couple days on the last one.

On a side note, when I did get to the Yards the next day, I found the Indian right where I left her. To my surprise, she was clean as a whistle, without a shred of mud on her. I don't know how he did it, or how long it took him, but I think Ollie set her to rights and it must have taken him hours.

From that day forward I vowed to treat any vehicle assigned to me with more respect than I had up till then, considering folks like Ollie would feel obliged to clean them up after my adventures. Little did I know what the Argonne had in store for me!

28

The Detective: 7/27/16, Thursday

I MET VINCE MALLOY THE very next day as I arrived at the Yards after work to get more practice on the motorcycle. I had just seen the cleaning job Ollie must have done and was about to say, "Holy smokes!" when Lenny called to me from Boss Charlie's office. I looked around and he waved me inside. There was still plenty of daylight left for a ride, so whatever he had in mind wouldn't be messing up my plans any.

As usual, the office was filled with smoke, and there was White Lightning being passed about. Boss Charlie wasn't there, having left for the day, but Nick and Ollie were seated on a couple stools near an open window. Lenny was showing the dock map to a rather tall fellow in an old beat-up cowboy hat. He was clad in blue jeans, boots, and what I always thought of as a western shirt, with Mother-of-Pearl snap buttons and designs of cattle skulls on either side of the front, above covered pockets. I checked for spurs, but I guess he drove into town today, rather than galloping in on "Traveler" or "Champion." The joke died in my throat as the man turned to me offering a firm handshake, after Lenny said, "Ah, Vince, here's young August now."

I've never seen a desert before, but when I looked at Vince Malloy's face and neck, that is the first thing I thought of. While the man was saying, "Glad to meet you, son," all I could see was the western desert etched on his face. His rough skin was several shades of tan and brown, as if he had spent all his life outdoors in the sun. Hundreds of lines — wrinkles of a lifetime's worries and smiles — appeared before me as the arid, cracked Death Valley terrain might look. The rolling Mojave foothills dotted with sage were represented by the flow of his cheeks, nose, lips, and chin, with various wisps of hair where a beard ought to be. Dark, piercing eyes drilled into me like those of a desert hawk watching its prey. A large, overgrown mustache dominated it all, like a defiant stand of cottonwoods at the edge of a barren expanse.

"How are you, sir?" was the best I could manage, as I simply stared at him.

Lenny jumped right in and got things moving along, telling me how he'd filled Vince in about the scene in the tavern, the theft of Nick's Ford, the chase, and the splash into the Morris Canal. He emphasized the pistol being aimed at me and my slamming on the brakes, calling it an act of genius, although I still felt stupid about the whole thing. What, did I think he'd simply pull over and give us back the ambulance, tip his hat, and wish us a nice evening?

Vince said he was, "…going over to the Black Tom Wharf next to see what this Karl gent has to say about the thief, just as soon as I get the lay of the land a bit more."

Lenny had me tell what I had seen when I was picking up the motorbike, how Mr. Pisser, er, Sheisskopf, was openly trotting down the wharf on a horse, like he owned the place.

"Seems to me that his boldness will be his undoing," said Vince.

"Yup," added Lenny. "If he's moving about that openly it shouldn't be too hard to follow his movements, day or night."

Nick chimed in with, "But who knows what he's doing behind closed doors?"

"Yar," Ollie spoke for all of us.

Vince nodded, took a swig of hooch, caught his breath, and said, "If you find out who a man's friends are, you find out a lot about the man. I figure Karl can point out more about this feller than he realizes.

He can then direct me to others on the wharf that can help complete the picture of this cur's comings and goings, who he deals with, where he eats, and of course, where he resides. In a few days, we'll know what makes him tick."

"And then we shut him down." This came from Ollie Olson, of all people.

At that we raised our glasses, drinking a silent toast.

• • •

We then went our separate ways; Lenny drove off with Vince Malloy to see Karl, Nick drove on home to relax, and I climbed back up on the motorcycle to get another thrill on a two-wheeler. Before I started her up, I hopped back off and went over to Ollie to thank him for his expert cleaning job.

"What are you talking about?" he said. "I didn't go near it."

"Huh? What? How can that be? Who else would have done it?"

"Aha!" he laughed. "Got you, didn't I? The fact of the matter is I did not touch the motorcycle. But when I noticed Pete's boys were done for the day and were just sitting around shooting the breeze — as you chaps say — I felt it would do them wonders to get familiar with the contraption in an up-close and personal fashion. I watched their endeavors for quite some time, too, and can vouch for their new-found respect of the fine machinery."

"Well, I'm sure their new-found respect would eventually dim should I return it tonight in the same condition. Therefore, I think I'll run her over into Harrison for a spell and perhaps show her to Molly."

Ollie gave me a thumbs-up and a big smile before he turned back into the office. I started up the bike and was on my way to see my girl.

29

The Race: 7/28/16, Friday Morning

AS IT TURNED OUT, MOLLY was not at home last night when I pulled up on the motorcycle. I thought it would be a sight, you know? I imagined her to be sitting on the front porch thinking of how much she would miss me while in the Poconos, my roaring up on the Indian, taking off my goggles, and her smiling at me, rising from her chair, and running down the sidewalk to throw her arms around me!

I went up the walkway and pulled on the bell rope. There was no answer. I pulled a second time. Again, no reply. I clanked down on the brass knocker a few times and waited. I knocked with my knuckles. Maybe I should have called? I turned to go down the porch stairs when I heard a familiar voice coming from alongside the house.

"I come, I come!"

It was the servant man, Angelo, but he was not wearing his good clothes this time. Nope, he was in a set of blue jean overalls, perhaps four sizes too large for him, with the pant legs rolled up and the suspenders tied in bows. His knees were dirty, and he was carrying a bunch of vegetables in a basket.

"*Buena sera, Signore Angelo,*" I offered.

"Ah, Signore Augusto! How you do, how you do? Oh, *espetto,* ah, wait, wait! Why you come here? Miss Johnson, she goes to see you at your yardie."

"What?"

"The Doctore, he takes Miss Johnson in the car to your yardie. Do you have tomatoes there, too?"

"No, Angelo, no tomatoes. But please, when did they leave this house?"

"Oh, they justa go. Maybe five minutes is all. They justa go now."

As I ran to the bike, I hollered back to him, "Thank you, Senore Angelo. *Arriva-derch!*"

I kick-started that bike and wheeled her around in a circle back toward the east and the Kearny Yards. I gave her the gun, thinking that by taking some short cuts I may even catch up to them before they made the main road. Tearing through several vacant lots on the diagonal, I made my way back to the Newark–Jersey City Turnpike just a few blocks north of me. I turned onto the 'pike and looked left and right, but did not see the Doc's black Buick, figuring they had such a head-start on me they may be well down the road toward the meadowlands already. Feeling comfortable now on the cobbles, I opened the throttle to get down the straight stretch ahead of me a bit faster. Since I did not recall any big puddles on my way to Molly's house from my ride in, I was encouraged to apply still more gas to the machine. Peering ahead I thought I could just make out a moving vehicle about a mile away. Leaning forward, I ticked up the throttle yet another notch. Eyes focused on the car far ahead, I had almost no time at all to react to the two deer that jumped out of the woods right in front of me!

I jerked the bike to the left, catching a bit of the second whitetail's rear quarter on the end of the handlebars. The bike didn't even wobble at that slight hit but kept going right off the cobblestones, up over the slate curb and into the weeds. It took flight for a few seconds, coming down with a *bruuuumph* on the soft earth alongside the turnpike. I almost lost control, but thankfully, a large oak loomed right in front of me. My knee-jerk reaction to miss this monster somehow restored my control of the Indian and I began to weave in and out of numerous white birch trees. Branches were reaching out for me, tearing at my shirt, and scratching my face and arms as I throttled down a bit to gain control. Happily, a path ran right by me and I raised the handlebars as I crested a slight rise alongside it. She rose easily and I continued slowing down to get my bearings.

I came to a stop at an old, overturned wagon to catch my breath and orient myself. "Wow," I thought, "That could have been a disaster!" My heart was beating a mile a minute and I felt sweaty all over.

From where I sat, I could hear the chug-chug of a loco over in the Kearny Yards and I remembered my mission. If that was the Doc's car ahead of me before, he and Molly may well be there by now. I pointed the bike in that direction and hit the throttle. Considering the dirt and scratches on me and my clothes, I had nothing to lose by sticking to the meadow paths and giving up on the cobbled road.

Within minutes I was at the edge of the Yards and could see the Buick near Ollie's shed. I slowed down to cross over the iron train rails and made my way slowly toward the folks gathered around the entrance. It occurred to me I could make a speedy arrival and try to impress everyone, but I was still a bit shaken by my encounter with the deer.

I may not have come roaring up after all, but I certainly was a memorable sight.

Molly was delighted to see me, so that's all that matters.

Ollie was curious about the tufts of white deer hide sticking out of the handlebar.

30

The Weekend: 7/28/16, Friday Afternoon

LUNCH CAME AND WENT, AND we had more boxes of hardtack to load on the freighter, but not until I handed out more of the stogies from Karl's warehouse and we all lit up. I had just finished regaling the lads with my mishap on the trip back from Harrison last night when Nick pulled up and called me aside. "We're having a get-together tomorrow night at The Black Garter. Lenny said we oughta bring dates, so you might wanna ask yer Molly."

"Well, Nicky, you wouldn't know as you had already left the Yards last night, but Molly's family is leaving on the train today to Pennsylvania, up to the mountains. Looks like I'll be coming alone."

"Ah yes, the Catskills. It should be nice this time of year."

"No, it's the Poconos — opposite side of the Delaware River — and from what she's told me, it's quite beautiful indeed. They'll be there a couple weeks or so."

"What, they got a cabin or something?" His eyes lit up at that thought.

"Yes, right on the river, too. Supposed to be nice."

He smiled, lost in thought for a moment, then asked, "So, you'll be there tomorrow, at the Garter?"

"Natch. And I'd expect it to turn into a poker game for those who hang on later."

"Natch." And with that, Nicky was off, probably to roust up some more players for tomorrow night's soiree.

I turned back to the dockhands and hoped for an uneventful Friday afternoon's work. I'd get out at quitting time but could go right home, since I was not involved at all with the day's ambulance ferrying.

Since the boys had their instructions and were anxious to get the job done, I took some time to myself and sat at the water's edge. The small waves were lapping at the bulkhead in a sort of quiet whisper. The sun's reflection off the water made it difficult to look directly at it, so I sort of gazed out across the river toward the New York side. There was lots of boat traffic today; ships heading out to the bay and the sea beyond. Small craft were ferrying folks back and forth between the two shores, bobbing peacefully in the water. Gulls were performing their acrobatics at the water's edge, as well as around the nearer boats. Some tired, rusty old hulk was making her way upriver, evidently loaded to the gills with who knew what cargo. Barges laden with coal were headed down to the tip of Manhattan, from whence they'd go right back up the East River to dock in Brooklyn.

I closed my eyes and thought back to my conversation with Molly last night, as we strolled away from Ollie and the Doc to get some time to ourselves. She had wanted to see me all week but there were so many things to get done for the Field Service before her family could get away on their vacation. Her father felt bad about it, so it was his idea to just drop everything last night and take a quick ride over to the Yards on the chance that I would be there. She took hold of my arm tightly and said, "When you weren't here, I was quite upset. Then, I looked up and you came roaring up like a White Knight on a steed, and I felt so happy!"

"White Knight on a steed? Roaring? More like a Dusty Duke dinged by a Dragon." She looked at me curiously, so I told her about riding the Indian up to her house hoping to impress her with my motoring skills, my conversation with Angelo, racing after her father's car, and my subsequent ordeal with the deer, trees, and brambles. That all seemed to go by the boards, as what she seized on was simply,

"You mean you dropped everything just to come and see me before I left?"

"Well, yea, sure! I'm gonna really miss you."

She put her arms around me and gave me a big kiss. I mean, a big, *big* kiss.

A horn honked somewhere behind us, and it was time for her to go. I walked her to the Doc's car and helped her in, shook the Doc's hand and wished them a wonderful time in the Poconos as they drove away. They both work very hard and deserve a nice vacation. I may take one myself one day. Meanwhile, those ten or twelve days would pass quickly and before you knew it, she'd be back in Harrison once more, and maybe we'd get over to that theater again, take a walk in the park, or simply sit on her porch swing and talk about the future. Yup, ten days was nothing.

31

The Heat:
7/29/16, Saturday

I GOT UP EARLY SATURDAY morning having to fill in for Tom Delaney and keep an eye on his crew as they finished loading that two-stacker. I'd rather be in the Yards listening to the lessons on motorcycle engines Ollie said he'd be giving today, but there'll be another time. When a docker gets hurt, the rest of us fill in where needed – that's a given. Tom would do the same for any one of us.

It would be another very hot July day and there was not a cloud in the sky. I grabbed my remaining tan button-down shirt as that would help reflect some of the sun's rays. With any luck a thunderstorm would blow in and cool things off, but that seemed an outside chance on this already sultry day. I had my coffee and got going.

We kept busy in the extreme heat and by the time our shift ended, most of us were shirtless and dripping with sweat. We finally saw the stern of that freighter as she headed downriver, fully loaded at last. I pulled out a bottle of hooch and gave the guys all a pull along with the usual Havanas, but we all kept going back to ladle some of the cool water from the water pail to better quench our thirsts.

Taking my leave, I buttoned up again and figured on a run to the Yards to see if the lecture was over yet. I hoped Ollie merely discussed the workings of the engine and didn't have the boys ride the Indian about much. I shuddered to think of Nicky riding that bike. Ah, she was sweet. Come to think of it, if I were riding her now, the sweat stains on my shirt would dry out. Seated in the front of a Flivver, the air does not pass through your body the same way, and I was wringing wet.

Arriving at the Yards, I climbed out and wandered over to the fellows assembled under the temporary shade of a canvas tent next to Ollie's shed. The Indian stood at the front of the classroom where Ollie was standing, a cylinder in one hand and a wrench in the other. Various parts of the engine were out on a table in front of him. Lenny and Nick were seated in front, with several of Pete's boys also in attendance. Everyone seemed rapt with attention as Ollie was discussing the "four stroke" principle. I hunkered down on a bench at the rear of the tent and relaxed to the cadence of his voice as he rambled on with his explanation. I closed my eyes and listened, feeling tired and sticky. There was a hot breeze blowing in, so I undid my shirt and pulled it out of my pants to dry it out a bit. I put my head down and folded my arms in front of me.

About a half hour later Ollie tapped me on the shoulder and said, "The lads are all gone, August. It's about time you get a move on as well. I guess you needed the rest, so if you want, I'll give you a private lesson on the engine another time."

"Ah, gee, Ollie, I'm sorry about dozing off there," I stated, frowning. "I really wanted to hear how she was put together."

"Not to worry, August. You've always been an apt pupil, and you've already had several hours on the machine. If anyone besides me knows how she's put together, it's you. Meanwhile, why don't you get on home and get some shuteye. It's going to be a long night once we get to card-playing later."

"Can I take the bike?"

"Ah, no, son. I've yet to put her all back together for one thing, and I wanted to change the oil for another. From what Lenny told me, you'll be bringing another one tonight. I would really enjoy us taking them on a day's ride together to break them in, you know? Perhaps sometime next week?"

"Break them in? You mean, they might go faster once we, what did you say, break 'em in?"

"Oh, yes indeed, they will. Once we put a thousand miles on them and change the oil a few times, the parts will coalesce a bit more and become more efficient, or so goes the theory. Meanwhile, you look as if you could use an oil change yourself. Why don't you go on home and take a nice, cool bath, eat a cheese sandwich, and then take a nap? You'll feel like a hundred bucks and be in good shape for this evening's festivities."

"Sure, Ollie, I may just take you up on that. I'm exhausted and feel like some slithering thing in these clothes. See ya tonight, then."

With that I was on my way once again in the staff car, creating my own breeze as I drove back over the Hack-bridge and on toward home.

• • •

Making my way through the familiar streets, I sensed a strange foreboding that I couldn't quite get a handle on. Trundling down the cobbles, I turned down a dry lane and raised a plume of dust behind me. Why did everything seem so odd? It was like driving through a ghost town. I looked left, I looked right, but saw no one about. There was nary a soul out today; that was it. Well, with this heat I'd be home, too, if I could help it. In fact, I was on my way!

I made the right onto Wayne Street and saw Pop out in front of the house with a watering can. I parked under the Sycamore tree at the curb and went on over to help with the garden, one of the chores I share with him.

"Hey, Pop, let me fill the other can for you and we'll both get out of this heat."

"Thanks, Augie. That'd be great. I'm feeling a bit slow from this humidity today. I, ah, left the big one over by the house, already filled up. I noticed the cukes were looking wilted and hit those already, but the beans and tomatoes could use some too. Doubt there'll be any rain for the next few days."

I lugged the bigger can over to the plot and watered the Blue Lake string beans we planted back in June, being careful not to get any on the leaves. The sun would burn right through any drops of water on the leaves, like a magnifier effect, from what Pop's told me time and again. He came back from filling the smaller can and went to work on the lettuce. We both went back and forth a few times to the spigot on the side of the house until we had good coverage of the whole garden, as evidenced by the darker color of the straw wherever we watered.

"Some iced tea, son?"

"Sure, Pop," I replied, as we dropped the cans under the porch and climbed the three steps into the shade offered by the small vestibule, and then into the parlor. Mom saw us on our way in and already went into the kitchen for the beverage, coming back with a pitcher of sweet tea and a bowl of frosty chips she had gotten from the ice box. She poured and then spooned in the ice chips.

"Ah, how refreshing, Lovie!" Pop exclaimed. He liked to call Mom that.

"Good golly, Mom, that hits the spot!" I added.

She smiled and glided back into the kitchen, saying, "I've got some nice cool melon slices for you boys, too. Just one minute."

Pop sat back in his favorite chair, but I was so sweaty I merely leaned forward. He noticed drops of sweat coming off my forehead and called to Mother saying, "Bring Augie a nice, cool washcloth, would you Dear?"

Turning to me he said, "You're working too hard these days, son. 'All work and no play,' as the saying goes. It's good to work hard, but in this heat, I don't know. Can't you get some time off and just go fishing?"

"Soon, Pop, soon. We've got about another month's worth in the Yards and then we'll probably be back at the docks in September. We'll have some time then since we've got temporary help at National and can switch off and on with those guys. It's all good."

"Is that right?" He sounded doubtful.

"Why, yes, Pop. You bet it's good. Why, in fact, tonight we're celebrating at the Black Garter, with dinner, music, and cold beer!"

"Ah, a bit of singing, perhaps?" He seemed upbeat at that.

"Yes, I'm certain Nicky will belt out one or two."

He smiled, and added, "A bit of dancing, maybe?"

"Yup, well, there will be some real ladies present, so I may take a turn at that."

"And a little poker afterwards, perhaps?" He got a wry smile on his face as he said this.

"Well, sure, Pop. That's what we do. I'm playing just a few hands, though, as I may still have a run to the docks to make before I can come home after closing time."

"See what I mean, son?" he concluded. "You work, work and work, and then finally when you get a chance to play, you work some more!"

"Ah, Pop. I learned it from you!"

"*Ach*, my son. Maybe I should have taken you boating more often, instead of having you help in the store after school every day. You'd relax more often."

"But where else would I learn how to sweep?" My sweeping was a family joke and always brought a smile from everybody. I just couldn't get the hang of it; I was a disaster.

Mom came in then with the melon slices and gave us each a nice China plate and small, spearing fork. She rested a bowl of cantaloupe slices between us on the small table and next handed me a cool wet washcloth she had draped over her forearm.

"Thanks, Mom!" I immediately mopped my face and neck, feeling instant relief.

"Enjoy, you two. There's even more where that came from."

"Thank you, Dear," Pop said, and speared a nice slice for himself as I guzzled some more tea. We sat there for a few minutes, quietly enjoying a refreshing break. Finally, he just leaned back and closed his eyes, and I picked up the plates, forks, and the bowls and went into the kitchen. Mom was at the sink, so I whistled a tune on my way in so as not to scare her when I came up with the china.

"Mom, may I give these to you to wash?"

"Sure, *Liebchen*, just put them right there on the sideboard. Did you have enough?"

"Oh yes, Mom. I had plenty, but maybe a little more iced tea — here are the rest of the ice chips."

She poured the tea and added the chips, and I pulled out a towel from the closet shelf, declaring, "I'm in a sorry state that only a nice cold bath will help." I began to make my way past her to the bathroom, where sits the claw foot tub.

"Augie, aren't you forgetting something?"

"Huh?"

She held the tea at arm's length and said, "Maybe your father is right – you are working too hard!"

I smiled, took the glass, and said, "I've got big shoes to fill, from the both of you."

She smiled in return, patting me on the back as I went to my well-needed bath. Like Nick always says, "Ya gotta keep 'em smiling."

32

The Hot Streak: 7/29/16, Saturday Night

"FULL HOUSE!" DECLARED NICK. "LOOKS like I did it again!"

"Yea, well, don't rub it in," said Lenny as he tossed his cards back into the pile. I had folded with a failed inside-straight and was down to my last seven bucks. Both Ollie and Nick were doing well, to the detriment of Karl, Lenny, and me. We were at the Black Garter again — Patrick Ryan's place — and it was nearly midnight. The place was crowded and still a bit noisy.

Vince Malloy was observing us from a barstool and went out front by himself a few times to talk with some of the patrons. He said it would be better if folks didn't think he was with us when he did these interviews. "If someone had a problem with you fellers," as he put it, "They wouldn't give me the time of day if I asked them, don't you think?"

Well, it made sense, so we just sort of kept at our game and let Vince handle things his own way. We figured other chaps may be forthcoming with tidbits on Mr. Pisser if they remembered the night he tried to pass the fake gold piece here and got thrown out into the street. Who would favor a chump like that over Patrick Ryan?

Ollie took the next hand with grace and a smile — and three aces. Lenny looked a bit off-kilter. I thought my two pair weren't strong enough and folded again. Nick had bid the hand up with just a pair of tens yet was unperturbed at losing the pot. Karl was nodding off and we stopped dealing him in a while back.

We had been playing Draw Poker for about two hours since the ladies had left together in a cab. Thankfully, a breeze had come up and was blowing in from the river through the open windows. That, and the ceiling fans above us, provided some relief from the stale, humid air that filled the place.

Vince came walking past our table and somehow said without moving his lips, "He's got himself a flat in Bayonne," and continued toward the Men's Room. I was wondering how he managed to talk that way when Lenny said, "Give me a minute lads, I hafta take a leak." Ollie dealt him out, giving cards to Nick, me, and himself. I had some curious cards: four spades — the eight, nine, ten, Jack, and a red three. Well, I tossed the three of hearts face down on the table and said, "One." Ollie picked up a couple new cards, and Nick asked for three, so he probably had a pair. I picked up my card and fitted it into the middle of the hand, even though it was the Queen of spades whose normal spot would be all the way on the right. I was excited but don't think it showed. They might think I was looking for a full house before they'd expect me to be hoping to fill a straight again, not after I had tossed my cards face-up in disgust a few hands earlier trying for an inside card. Yup, I had just filled an "open-end" straight, and it was a flush to boot! I only had seven bucks, so I'd have to play it carefully. Nicky led off with a dollar, which I matched, but Ollie raised it another two bucks. I thought I'd call at that, but Nicky upped it yet another dollar. Ollie raised it another two bucks. "Damn," I thought, at this rate I'll run out of money." Nicky saw those two bucks and raised it another dollar-fifty. "I'm in," I said, and pulled my last dollar bill out as I reached into my pockets for some quarters. Thankfully they didn't realize I was short and did not raise it any further. Ollie called and Nicky laid down a Full House of, "Kings over sixes." In his excitement, Ollie splayed out his, "Four sevens," which of course beat Nick's hand. I guess the two of them forgot I was playing, because when I laid out my "Straight flush," and raked in all the dough, they both exclaimed incredulously. It felt good. It felt really good. I had over twenty-one bucks again!

Lenny came back from the men's room and took his place, saying jovially, "Deal me in, boys, I feel a lot better after that!" As Nicky shuffled and started to deal out the next hand, Lenny gave us the scoop on what Vince told him back there.

"Yeah, well, Vince got one of the guys who knows Pisser to tell him a few things, like, where he's been working, and about the boarding-house he's been at the past two months. The guy's name is Kristoff all right, Michael Kristoff, and he's holed-up in a place in Bayonne."

"Bayonne?" I asked. "Where exactly?" I had friends who lived there.

"Avenue C and 23rd Street," he replied. "He's living with an aunt. It's on the corner."

Nicky chimed in then with, "Be nice of us to drop in an' pay him a visit, wouldn't it?"

Lenny said, "Nah, don't want to scare any old lady." He picked up his cards and continued, "I think it would be more fun to stop by his job on Monday and have a word or two with his foreman. If the boss is on the up and up like Vince says, he'd appreciate knowing he's got a crook on payroll. Works at Tidewater Oil. Give me two wouldja, Nick?"

Ollie reminded us, "From what Karl said, he's got some powerful friends. Maybe the boss is one of them? I'll take a card, please."

"Karl," Lenny asked from behind his cards, "what was it you said about these friends of his?"

We all looked at Karl and could see he was out for the count.

Lenny looked up at Karl, too, and stated, "We better see if Ryan has a room where Karl can sleep it off."

"What about my dropping the hooch off and loading up the other Indian?" I was anxious to get the new machine but added, "I'll take three cards."

Nick dropped an unwanted card in front of himself and proceeded to hand out the new ones as my question hung in the air. Vince Malloy walked past us and out the door without even casting a glance in our direction.

Lenny exhaled the smoke from his cigar, said, "I fold. Augie, we'll take care of Karl and maybe you can run over there and lock my Ford in the warehouse instead of unloading it yourself. It's parked right out front here, packed to the gills. Then ride the motorcycle home and bring it to the Yards on Monday. I'll have your car for the weekend instead. Sound like a plan? Karl wears those keys on his belt there."

Well, yea, it was a plan. A good plan. A great plan, as I'd get back on an Indian sooner than expected! I reached over and grabbed the ring of keys. Karl mumbled something that I couldn't figure out. We all laughed.

I managed to bid Nick and Ollie up again and pulled in a thirty-dollar pot that time, with three queens. I won the next hand, too, but had to leave without giving the guys a chance to win it back. Yup, I was on a streak. A real hot streak. But I had to get over to Black Tom and take care of business.

Saying good night to all, I made my way through the swinging doors. It felt muggy again, but then the breeze rattled the tree leaves a bit, so maybe it was breaking. A voice called my name from the shadows. It was Vince. He told me to watch my back.

33

The Smudge Pots: 7/30/16, Sunday, 12:45 A.M.

T HERE WAS NO ONE ON the road down by the docks. Oh, there were people about — drunks, prostitutes, a few sailors making their way out to the saloons — but there were no other vehicles, and it was a quiet ride over to Black Tom Wharf. The lights from the great City across the way illuminated the river and you could imagine the night life over there with folks carousing and having a grand old time. I'd be content simply to stow this Model T in Karl's warehouse and be off on the motorcycle. I'd take the long way home, too, and really enjoy myself tonight.

"When Molly gets back, I'll teach her to ride," I said aloud as I got on the road next to the Hudson. "And then we'll take both bikes out on a ride to forever."

I took the turn off the waterfront street onto the wharf itself and crossed a few sets of tracks with boards in the roadbed to form a ramp. It was important to drive slowly in the presence of so much cargo stowed right on the decking, for several reasons. One; you never know when something might topple if not stacked properly, and two; a lot of this stuff was explosive. I recalled the freight train with the red flags moving slowly onto Black Tom the last time I was here; it was broad daylight then and there was a lot going on. I remembered the dogs chasing my Model T and kept a wary eye out for them this time.

Several mosquitoes buzzed my ear and I slapped myself on the right side of the face. Karl's warehouse with the huge pile of kegs out front should be coming up soon.

Up ahead I saw sputtering tongues of flame on either side of the train tracks and a couple fellows I recognized who were guards on the night shift. I pulled up and applied the brakes, "Hey boys, it's me, August Landesmann."

"Whatcha say, Augie?" said the taller one, who I think was called Fred. His pal Harry extended his hand, and we shook.

"Where you headed, August?" Harry wanted to know.

"Over to Karl Eisener's place. I gotta drop off a load for him."

Fred pointed up to the left and said, "It's just up ahead, five or six hundred feet, maybe more. He's got a bunch of geese fenced in out front – you can't miss it." They both thought this was funny. I asked them if the smudge pots were safe with all these explosives around.

Harry shrugged, and said, "There's millions of friggin' mosquitoes eatin' us alive tonight. The pots help a bit and they're perfectly safe; we've used them for years. Long as we don't kick 'em over, eh Freddie?" Again, they laughed. These guys don't get to see many people on their shift, so you gotta play along. "Well," I said, "if anything happens, you'll be the first to know!" They got the biggest kick out of that.

I made my way up the wharf past a string of about two dozen box cars and soon saw the geese pens and Karl's warehouse up ahead. A massive barge had tied up to the dock across from it. As is my habit, I looked for the name on the bow. She was called the *Johnson 17*, and I recalled seeing her on the river before. I pulled the T up to Karl's front doors, climbed down, went over to the padlock and took out the key ring. The geese appeared to be fast asleep, and I could swear I heard one of them snoring. I tried five or six keys before getting the right one and the lock opened with a click. Pulling the doors wide open, I stepped inside. A small electric lamp was lit in the corner and in its light, I could see the motorcycle on its stand.

Ah, I thought, *there she is.*

I went over to the bike and immediately unscrewed the gas cap to peek inside. Yup, this machine was full up, so I wouldn't have to siphon fuel out of the Model T. I smiled and said out loud, "Looks like I'll be taking an enjoyable ride tonight after all."

Screwing the cap back on, I raised the kickstand and wheeled her out through the open doors and off to the side so I could drive the Ford in, lock her up, and get on my way. However, the "kick" wouldn't go down too easily and my foot slipped, scraping my ankle bone on the metal rod. As I looked up with a grimace of pain and a loud, "Ouch," I thought I saw movement in the shadows just the other side of the switching engine at the front of the freight train. Peering from behind some crates for a spell, I failed to detect any further motion and figured it was just a rat jumping down from his perch. We get lots of wharf rats, even though they don't store much food here on Black Tom. I'm sure they chew on cloth bags or whatever they can find. Heck, Karl's tobacco might be very tasty to a rat.

I managed to get the kickstand down and went back inside to move a chair out of the way to make room for the hooch wagon. I came out cautiously, looking from left to right, but saw no-one. Up into the T I climbed, put her into Forward gear, and let her roll slowly to a point not far inside the warehouse until I could figure out where Karl most likely would want it. *Yup,* I thought, *this may be in the way here; I better have a look.*

I let the engine idle and pulled the brake handle as I jumped down off the seat. Looking over the warehouse before me, I saw stacked barrels, crates, boxes, and oh so many burlap bags of tobacco. Off to the right was a bare space that looked good but there were a few kegs I'd have to move first. In the furthest corner, I could see where Karl had his furniture stored and recalled that conversation we had about his wife leaving him. I shook my head and was thinking, "Poor Karl," when the geese outside began making a racket. I turned toward the open doors to see what was going on when suddenly a dark figure jumped from behind a crate and swung something at me!

34

The Flashes:
7/30/16, 1:30 A.M.

I DON'T RECALL EVERYTHING GOING black, like people say, but black it was. I was out like a light and have no idea for how long, but think I remember coming out of it. Ever have a dreamless sleep you wake up from where you cannot move your arms or legs? That's just what I felt. My head was pounding, much worse than the biggest hangover I ever had. The room was spinning wildly; just like a good drunk or two I remember putting on. But this was worse spinning than ever before — more like reeling. There were moving lights before my eyes, of red, yellow, white, green, and pink. Pink! I heard a banging somewhere that intensified when I moved my head to the right. There was an odor of some good tobacco. Mmm, I could use a smoke. I realized I was lying on my stomach and on top of both my arms. I managed to pull my right arm out from underneath me and touched my forehead with it, for that's where the pounding was coming from. Squinting through the pain I could see my hand wet with something orange and sticky. No, it was red. It was red blood. Shit! What happened?

I rolled off my other arm and managed to sit up. There were wisps of smoke coming from over by the burlap bags, so that's what I smelled. The cloth on one had a red ring on the side of the bag, and the ring was expanding as I watched, smoking as it grew from a few inches to six, then eight, then *whoosh*, up it went in a burst of flame! There were several such fires now over in the tobacco pile, with the biggest of them on the far side away from me. Billows of smoke blossomed from it, up into the rafters.

I didn't think I could stand up yet but thought I had better get off my ass and do something while I still could, even with a banging head. There were fire extinguishers all around the docks; you just had to look a little to find one. Crawling toward the Ford, I grabbed hold of the metal bar at the rear. I pulled myself up onto one knee, then the next. My vision was blurry, and I concentrated on the open tailgate, *Funny*, I thought, *I didn't leave that open, and the canvas was closed tight.* I smelled White Lighting and could see a few shattered bottles on the floor of the ambulance. The booze seemed to clear my head a bit. Peering into the darkness, I saw four or five cloth bags of tobacco on the floor with a small yellow stick up on top of one. Just as I realized it was a pencil, it burst into flame, catching onto the burlap, and turning the surrounding booze puddle into a pillar of bright blue and yellow fire!

"Holy smoke!" (I realize now how silly that sounds, but up to that time it had always been my favorite expression). "Holy freakin' smoke!"

Somehow, I found myself standing fully up, paying no mind to the pain in my head, and I began backing away from the ball of fire inside the ambulance. Bottles of hooch began exploding inside the Ford, sending glass everywhere. I thought letting down the canvas flap and shutting the tailgate would be my best bet, so I went around the side and got them both closed, which should help contain the damage. White lightning jugs were going off inside like so many little bombs, and I had to get the T out of the warehouse. But first, the tobacco fire was spreading fast! Looking quickly for an extinguisher, I spied a large brass one by Karl's desk on the wall next to his telephone. I stumbled toward it and pulled it off the mount, turning the wheel open and pointing the nozzle in the direction of the tobacco bags. I approached warily and got a good stream going onto the burlap, aiming at the largest fire first. I knocked that one down pretty good and got good coverage on the smaller ones before running out of the chemicals inside the extinguisher. Dropping it, I went for a second one on the wall, grabbed it, and turned. I heard another bottle go off in the Ford, which by now showed fingers of flame searching out of the sides.

I attacked the pile of burlap once more, squirting fluid all over it and kicking bags onto the floor, stamping out the embers. The Model T was next. The canvas flap in the rear was burning from the bottom up; the wooden sides were glowing red and white like campfire wood. The heat was intense. Bottles continued to explode inside but maybe I could make a difference with the chemicals before it was too late. I let fly the stream and soaked down the canvas pretty good and as I was about to squirt down the insides through the flap, the stream trickled out completely. "Shit!" was all I could say. By now it was too late to look for more fire-fighting equipment; I had to get the burning Ford out of the building and onto a safe part of the wharf before it caused the whole warehouse to go up!

I went to the shed doors to open them wide, figuring whoever hit me on the noggin must have shut them. I pushed the right one to no avail. I shoved the left one with all my might and still couldn't budge them. The padlock! Damn, they must have locked me in here! I made my way to the ambulance as best I could and climbed in with difficulty as the seat was hot and smoldering. Releasing the brake, I put her in reverse and hit the gas, heading backwards at the damn doors, multiple hooch bottles banging off behind me!

The doors splintered outward as the powerful Ford engine did its job. The rear of the ambulance erupted in sparks and burning pieces of wood flew every-which-way as I gained my freedom. I slowed a bit so I didn't run into those box cars, steering over to a nice empty space where I figured the machine would burn safely. As I shut the engine off and hopped down, there was a massive detonation, and I dove to the planking for dear life!

I looked for the Ford and it was still there, continuing to burn slowly. Glancing down the wharf toward the way I came in, I noticed one of the loaded freight cars had gone up in flames — pieces of its wooden sides and roof were descending from the sky — a half mile away. "Wait a minute," I said aloud. "What's going on here?"

At that moment, a diesel fuel tank erupted, shaking the pier down toward the New York end with an extended tremor. Large tongues of fire reached up toward the stars as billowing clouds of black and grey smoke reflected the orange and red of the flames.

In quick succession two more box cars blew up between me and the mainland — to my right — followed by a small stack of black powder kegs that were stored in front of a shed not far to my left, knocking down its entire front wall, exposing cardboard boxes piled high inside. Flaming embers were falling from the sky as small fires began to catch onto rooftops, cargo, or some of the small tugs and lighters tied up alongside the wharf. I looked back at the Ford just in time to see the spreading flame reach the gas tank and tumbled inside the warehouse as the Model T herself went up in a fireball!

I cautiously peered around the doorway at the burning ambulance thinking, "Gee, Lenny is going to be pissed," when two night-watchmen ran down the *Johnson 17* gangplank across from me. I did not recognize either of them, but one saw me and hollered, "Get the hell off the wharf — she's gonna blow!" He pointed at the forward hold of the barge where flames had burst forth out of a structure near the bow. I had no idea what they had stored on the *Johnson*, but from the way these boys were running, I had better get gone too or I'd die like a rat in Karl's warehouse!

Just as I started to take off after them, I heard the furious honking of the caged-in geese behind me. "Awww, shit." What else could I say? Opening the pens, I watched the frightened fowl hurriedly waddle off toward the edge of the pier and dive into the Hudson, one after the other. I thought I may join 'em, too, because as I looked down the wharf toward the shore, all I could see was a horrible gauntlet of fire, punctuated by explosions both large and small. You could hear the crackle of small arms ammunition going off as it superheated, and the occasional rocket or artillery shell would fire off skyward and burst in a yellow star, raining down shrapnel. Chances of getting through that alive did not look good. They did not look good at all.

Greasy black smoke was wafting by me toward the shore making it difficult to see now, and I stumbled over a shattered barrel as I tried to get my bearings while hot cinders began to fall all around. Then I saw the Indian right where I left her — still on the kickstand.

"Thank God for the geese."

Up on the bike I jumped, bringing her forward off the stand. I gave her some gas and advanced the spark lever and kicked down. She started on the first try and I was off in a hurry, weaving back and forth between dangerous obstacles on the boards before me. I couldn't help but run over debris — it was all over the place.

I made my way down the row of boxcars with trepidation, as I could see the fire starting to spread to the adjacent cars from those that were alight. A dock dog emerged snarling, but the poor thing was singed, and he didn't even notice me as I rode on by him.

A pile of burning tires to my front created such a pall of smoke I had to slow down and curl to the right as I passed it, or I would surely crash into something. It's a good thing I did, too, because that was the instant when the next box car in line disintegrated with a thunderous roar. Luckily, avoiding the smoking tires put me behind a brick tool shack or I would have been caught in that fireball. More flaming boards descended from above as I took off again searching for a clear lane ahead. Problem was, there didn't seem to be any openings in front of me at all. What to do? I couldn't go back to get around the train — I'd have to find a way forward. I went slowly ahead.

In a moment, my prayers were answered – with my worst nightmare. There was a clear enough path alongside the three burning freight cars all right, the explosions having hurled most of their debris far and wide, but once past them the way was blocked by a large pile of what once was the corner of a box car. It was ablaze, naturally. However, a large plank lay on the edge of it at such an angle as to remind me of my taking flight over that curb in the meadows the other day. Hence, it invited escape. No, it screamed escape!

I was off like a shot. As I passed the first burning box car my hair frayed from the heat; the second one seared my face. By the time I passed the third I felt like my ass was on fire, and it may well have been, but I could only think of that big board ahead of me. I aimed that front tire straight up the plank and was airborne for real this time, rising over the burning pile of wood, flying through the black smoke, and coming back to earth with a jolt and a few bounces. Yet, I maintained control of the machine and she took me right out of that inferno!

A few firemen appeared at the shoreline at Communipaw with their horse-drawn pumper and were trying to unravel their hose as I flew by. Other men were running all over, hollering, screaming, and generally terrorized by the conflagration. "Get down!" they yelled. "Get back!" One large fellow hollered the unforgettable, "Get the fook outta here, lads!" This did the trick, for, as he ran behind a brick building, most of his mates followed him to shelter. I had no choice but to turn south toward Liberty Island, since the way straight through was blocked by a burning livery stable and the route north by a hook and ladder truck and other apparatus.

I weaved in and out of running men, only then noticing my left sleeve was burning above the elbow, so I reached over and patted it with my right hand to good effect. My shoulder smarted a bit, but I couldn't think about that for the moment. I got past the wharf buildings south of Black Tom and opened the throttle wide to put some space between me and that firestorm. Here a cattail swamp begins and nothing but railroad tracks crisscross this part of the shoreline, so I felt I had made it to safety. Looking at the wharf toward the *Johnson 17* barge I noticed the fire on board had moved amidships.

Karl's warehouse was now completely engulfed, and I was just about to comment on the waste of all that good tobacco when there was a bright flash followed by a loud *kaboom*! My eyes were almost rendered useless from the burning hot image on the retinas. Knowing the throttle well by now I nudged it down and began braking when suddenly there was an even greater flash of such heat and devastation that the world turned upside down! A blast wave like an invisible giant's hand grabbed me and the Indian, throwing us both up into the air and into the reeds. This tremendous eruption began with a giant scream but grew into a humongous roar as if everything was being thrust upward from the mouth of Vesuvius! I felt my leg snap as the bike tumbled over me, then a heavy whack to my head from the handlebar as she spun away.

I thought, *God...*, and felt a long, long rumble of thunder. Then everything went white.

35

The White Forest

THE SLUSH WAS UP TO my waist as I pulled myself out of the icy water. A few inches of snow lay on the ground; clean, white, and powdery. It moved away from me like confetti as I crawled out onto land. I shook my head; how did I end up in a puddle of slush? My jeans were becoming stiff with frost as I felt the water dripping off my legs. "Odd," I thought. "I'm not cold, and it's snowing."

Yes, it was snowing. Large flakes, too, like the kind you see at either the beginning or the end of a snowfall. It's the small flakes that really accumulate in blizzards, they say. Most of these flakes were the size of quarters, but there were some half-dollar sized ones, too, which I had never seen the like before. I wasn't dressed for this sort of thing, but thought, "With any luck it will blow over."

A mosquito buzzed my ear as I dragged myself up out of the wet snow unto the drier ground under a tree. Brushing a few inches of flakes away from the roots, I uncovered a pile of last year's leaves and buried my face in them, smelling the rich loam. The ground was shaking continuously, so maybe a storm was approaching. I've heard thunder during snowstorms and seen lightning as well. Ah, lightning. I wish I could have a swig of that Jersey hooch right now. I looked around but didn't see any jugs, just a lot of trees. I found myself in a dense forest of white birch with golden leaves. There were thousands of them, mostly straight and tall, but, as is found with birches, many were forked at the base into twos or even threes. There were some scrub white pines, too. The temperature began to drop.

Snow had fallen for hours, apparently, and the branches were all weighed down and dripping a bit. I stood up and shook it off my clothes. My right leg was very stiff but the left one was fine. "Must be from lying on the ice, I guess," I said aloud as I grabbed a stick and used it to help me walk until my leg loosened up. Looking at the descending flakes I thought, "This must be an early snowfall like back in '06, what with the leaves still on the trees. Odd about the mosquitos, though." I slapped my cheek and got one of the bastards. It was starting to get much colder.

The sky was lit again and again by flashes. It was sure to be a big storm all right. The ground shook, causing snow to fall off the trees. There was a nice smell of wood smoke coming from a thicket ahead, where a bright light shone between the trunks. "Someone must have lit a campfire," I muttered. I made my way cautiously through the trees, favoring my right leg. The stick I was using broke in two and I tossed it aside, grabbing onto the trees on either side of me for support. I began to shiver.

Coming into a clearing I saw a roaring bonfire before me. The flames were as tall as me and gave off intense heat. Yet, I felt a chill in my back. Except for the bare ground near the fire, all else was covered in white.

A man came into view pushing a wheelbarrow full of wood. He put it down gently and began tossing pieces onto the fire, causing sparks to jump upward. Turning to me he said, "Well, don't jes stand there, give me a hand, wouldja?"

"Huh?" I replied, teeth chattering.

"If y'all want some supper, ye best be helpin' tend the fire, is all."

"Well, sure. I'm famished." I made my way over to the man and pitched in, trusting the heat would help me. The wood was of all different sizes and shapes, most of it pine, but oak as well. Some had lettering stenciled on them as if on cargo boxes. There were nails sticking out the ends, too, so you had to be careful not to cut yourself.

It was weird — the more wood we tossed onto the fire, the more seemed to still be in the wheelbarrow. It was a bottomless pit. The fire grew. I was warming up again, at last.

"Gee," I ventured, "how long 'til we finish piling on this load of wood?"

"What?" He replied. "Y'all goin' someplace?"

"Ah, well, I'm not sure. I was going someplace, but I don't remember where."

"Don't fret none, young feller," he said. "We can chat about it later over some of this here duck I'm fixin'."

That sounded delightful to me, and I smiled at him. When I looked back into the wheelbarrow, it was suddenly empty.

"Thanks for the hand, son. Why dontcha'll take a set here by me and we can talk while the bird finishes charren' up. Greasy bird is the duck, eh?"

"Well, yea, I guess. We don't get duck much at home."

"Why's that, sonny?"

"Mom just doesn't like it, I think. Like you said, it's very greasy. Anyways, I'd love to try it; I'm starved."

With that he lifted the bird from the wooden spit at the edge of the burning pile and put it on an old, chipped China platter. He pulled a large knife from his belt and neatly halved the bird down the breastbone. Handing me the larger piece he wished me a "Bone appytite," and bit into his half.

"Thanks, Mister," was all I got out as I dug in like a wolf. It was great duck.

We sat there munching in silence and I began to feel better. Looking at the fire I could see another duck was spitted and the skin was beginning to pop with the searing heat.

"Hey, I didn't even see you put that second one on!" I exclaimed.

"That's because y'all was too busy scoffing down that there piece. Don't cha'll ever eat at home?"

"Well, yea, we do. I guess it's been a while since suppertime now that you mention it. I think we had pot roast, but I'm not sure about that. I'm not certain about anything, to tell you the truth. But this duck now, I'm sure I like it fine."

He poked at the second bird with a stick, and it flared up for a moment. Then he turned to me, stuck out his hand and said, "Now, where're my manners? Name's Tom McGlintock. What's yours?"

I took his hand and gave it a firm shake. "I'm August. August Landesmann."

"Pleased to meet you, Master August."

"Call me Augie," I said. "That's the nickname my friends use."

"Well, ok then, Augie. Then you'll have to forget McGlintock. My friends call me Black Tom, for obvious reasons." With that he took his hand back and I realized what he meant. I smiled, and he pulled the big knife out again and split the second duck in two. He then grabbed a large brown jug out of a box behind him and handed it to me saying, "Duck always goes better with moonshine. Try this here, but go easy on it, Augie."

Not being a stranger to hooch I lifted the jug and took a generous pull. It was White Lightning, all right, only this had a taste of apple to it.

"Hmm," I offered. "This here is some fancy 'shine. What do you call it?"

"I calls it Applejack. Some folks call it White Lightning. Don't matter much what cha'll call it, just so you knows where to get it!" At this he slapped his knee and about doubled over laughing. I laughed, too, as it was a funny sight to see this ol' feller having such a joy over hooch and a charred duck, sitting by a campfire in the snow. It was just totally amusing.

We sat there a few minutes eating in silence again and I realized his name was somehow familiar, but I couldn't quite place it. Nick always encouraged me to ask questions, saying, "Yer not learning anything unless you ask. Don't be shy, Augie."

With that in mind, I asked, "Where'd you get the name Tom?" No, that wasn't right.

He laughed again and said, "Don't you mean Black Tom?"

"Well, yeah. That's what I meant. Sounds familiar."

He picked up the jug again and said, "Folks used to call me that in the ol' days, is all. Used to be an island right-chere I lived on." He pointed through the trees. "They would call it Black Tom Island." He shook his head and said, "She's gone now."

He took a long pull on the jug and considered the fire.

"Things change," I mused as he handed me the jug.

"Yep. World keeps turnin', though."

"Amen."

"Praise God."

36

The Red Smoke

I OPENED MY EYES AND looked up at the stars in a black, somehow shimmering, sky. The Big Dipper was visible through the cattails, blowing in the breeze above me. Red-lit smoke drifted by and soon obliterated the constellation.

I said aloud, "Yep. World keeps turnin', though." I then moved my right leg to get up and passed out when it exploded in pain.

37

The Papers:
Monday, 7/31/16

L ENNY GOT DOWN FROM HIS Ford and joined the group saying, "What ya got there, Nick, the *Newark News?*" He tried to take it out of Nick's mitt, but Nicky pulled it back and said, "Let *me,* would ya?"

Nick, Peter, Ollie, and Vince Malloy were gathered near Ollie's shed out in the open air, discussing the catastrophe and what they had just been through yesterday at the river. It was Monday morning, and smoke was drifting west over the meadowlands from some of the still smoldering demolished structures at the docks.

Nick took a swig from a coffee thermos, put it on a table, and resumed reading page one with his finger:

$25,000,000 Loss due to Explosion of Ammunition and Munitions Destroyed Were Awaiting Shipment to Allies and Were Stored on Black Tom Island Off Jersey City.

New York, July 30. Property loss estimated at $25,000,000 was caused early today by a series of terrific explosions of ammunition awaiting shipment to the entente allies and stored on Black Tom Island, a small strip of land jutting into New York Bay off Jersey City.

The loss of life still was problematical tonight. It will not be determined definitely until there has been opportunity to check up the workmen employed on the island and on boats....

Lenny interjected, "Still no word from Augie, huh?"

They all shook their heads, looked down, or said, "Nah, nothin'."

"Have you all given your names to Boss Schuyler?" He asked.

They answered in the affirmative. All the dock and rail yard workers that could be found had already signed various lists that were being passed around; these were then typed up and copies sent to the yardmasters, dock supervisors, Jersey City Police Department, the various railroad organizations, and so on. A separate list of missing workers was also being passed around but was getting smaller by the hour as men checked in or were found in hospitals. There were about thirty names still on it; August Landesmann was among them.

Nick sipped his coffee and continued:

.... Number of deaths will probably exceed 50, but it was said that owing to the extent of the wreckage, it might be several days before the exact figures could be obtained.

Cause Not Yet Determined

The cause of the disaster had not been determined tonight. Officials of the National Storage Company and the Lehigh Valley Railway, which also suffered heavily through loss of property, declared that reports to them showed a fire started shortly after 1 o'clock this morning on a barge belonging to an independent towing company that had been moored alongside a dock used by the railroad used to transfer ammunition shipments from trains to vessels in the harbor. The barge, it was said, was there without authority either of the railroad or the storage company. The officials refused to disclose the name of the independent towing company, saying they were investigating, "to ascertain whether the barge purposely had been set on fire as the result of a plot."

The body of an unidentified man was recovered from the water near the Lehigh Valley pier. A child in Jersey City, according to the police, died from shock after the first explosion.

Many men told stories of having been blown hundreds of feet over land and water.

Most of the sixty or more injured taken to Jersey City hospitals were struck by shrapnel, falling glass or debris. Nearly all were in the railroad yards or on craft moored near the island. Included among them are a few women and children whose homes were on barges.

Statue of Liberty Shaken

Every window in the pedestal of the Stature of Liberty on Bedloe's Island, opposite Black Tom, was broken, and the main door made of iron and weighing almost a ton was blown off its hinges. The statue itself however was not damaged except from the rain of shrapnel which bespattered it.

Although the plant which furnished power for Bedloe's Island was shaken....

Lenny interrupted again, asking, "Anybody check the Morgue?"

Vince affirmed, "Yes, I did, but August wasn't there. Hospitals, too."

"Good work, Vince," replied Len. "I hated to ask it, but I'm glad you took care of it. I don't suppose his Ford showed up either?"

"Not that I could determine in all that wreckage," Vince said. "I asked around if anyone had seen him or his ambulance. But there was too much going on yesterday to really get a chance to find all the guards who were on duty, never mind interview them. I did stop by his parents, though, and they had no word either. I told them there was so much chaos at the docks, with every able-bodied man pitching in yesterday, people sleeping in makeshift tents and all, that they must be patient — we'll keep them posted."

"Damn, I never even thought about stopping by the house."

"Len, don't kick yourself." Pete patted his brother on the shoulder, saying, "We barely had any sleep since this happened and have been busting our asses searching through all that debris. We're all exhausted but we're still going back 'til we drop. You, especially."

Vince added, "He's right, Len. You're all a sight after all that heavy lifting. Leave the inquiries to me — that's what we detectives do best; consider any angles. I had hoped to find the Hooch wagon out in front of his house and the boy fast asleep. There was also the chance he had telephoned them from some other part of town, or from his girl's house, Molly, wasn't it?"

"Yea, Molly," Lenny answered. "Oh, that poor gal if he's gone. But no way she'd know anything — she's gone off on vacation in Pennsylvania. He shook his head, but suddenly looked up all perky, and blurted, "Hey, what you said about the Ford makes me think — what if he got it to the warehouse and made the switch for the Indian?"

"Yes, what about that?" This from Ollie, who thrust his fist in the air as he exclaimed, "Ask around if anyone saw a motorcycle on the Wharf the other night!"

Vince bit his lip, looked pensive and said, "Great idea. I never thought of that. Let me get going. Can one of you fellers take me to the river in one of these cars? Time's a-wasting."

Lenny clapped him on the shoulder and said, "Let's get moving," and the two of them were off.

Peter almost went with them but thought it over and said, "We'll wait fifteen more minutes for my boys to get here to help, if they're not here by then I'll write 'em a note and stick it on the door so we can get going."

Nick tossed his paper on the table, sat down, and took a big gulp of his cold coffee.

Ollie then took a folded newspaper from his back pocket and began reading it aloud:

The Jersey Journal:
Big munitions explosion at Black Tom; 50 believed dead;
21 hurt in city hospital; damage 75,000,000

> *Fire at national docks set off big shells and shrapnel and then came two terrific explosions of dynamite which rocked the country for 25 miles around; showers of glass from wrecked windows in homes, churches, stores, and public buildings littered the streets here, New York, Brooklyn, Staten Island, and points even more distant; Not one of dead recovered so far; one man blown nearly to Liberty Island survives and swims ashore; damage many times greater than last big explosion at Communipaw . . .*

Ollie stopped reading and said, "Look at that, gentlemen; one paper says twenty-five million in damages, the other says seventy-five million. It sure makes you wonder if they even have a grasp on the facts yet, whether the cost in dollars or the human toll."

Nick joined in and said, "Indeed you're right, Ollie. Yet while both stories mention the number of dead at fifty, only time and tide will tell."

"Yar, literally, too, where concerns the tide," said the Swede. "They'll begin to wash up and need to be gathered in."

Boss Schuyler approached then carrying a bottle of Bushmills and several glasses, despite the hour. He sat down on the bench and motioned Pete to fill the glasses while he opened yet another newspaper. He said, "Boys, this is a terrible day for us, to be sure, and let's be thankful there are not more of you missing. I'm sure August will turn up soon, let's hope alive and well. Let's have a drink to him, fellows."

"Hear, hear!" They all raised their glasses and drank.

The boss then continued, "An engineer came through from Hyde Park about an hour back and slowed the loco as he passed me. Tossed me the, *Kingston Freeman,* tied up with string and said he was pulling a work train to salvage more of that wheat we saw yesterday. I just finished reading about the tragedy when I looked up and saw you guys talking. Listen to this:

Kingston Daily Freeman New York 1916-07-31

On the Jersey shore lay all that remained of many lighters after they had been eaten by flames. When they caught fire and threatened other shipping nearby they were set loose to burn up.

It is alleged there were many violations of the federal law in the manner of storing ammunition at Black Tom Island and the way they were handled there. U.S. District Attorney Davis is said to have secured the help of a number of the best men in the government secret service to investigate these violations. The result of their inquiry may result in action by the department of justice.

The Jersey City police assert there were many tons of dynamite in the warehouse on the island. This is the most powerful and destructive explosion known in this country. In commenting on the arrests made in connection with the case, Chief of Police Frank Monahan of Jersey City said today: "These men were subordinates. They did what they had to. We shall try to reach the men really responsible." That the loss of life was miraculously small compared with what might be expected from such tremendous explosions was asserted by the Jersey City authorities. A number of firemen from that city probably owe their lives to the fact that their hose buckled. They had gone to the point where the kink was when the first explosion occurred, leaving only two men at the nozzle. These two were blown fifty feet.

The fire is still burning in part of the wreckage today. Firemen said that a week will pass before the flames will burn themselves out. Every few minutes the blaze reaches one of the many unexploded 3-inch shells that are scattered about and a sharp report follows. For the most part the shrapnel flies into the air.

The scene of the explosion is like a bit of the western front in France. About twenty-eight acres have been gouged out to a depth of thirty to forty feet and water from the bay is making a lake of the hole. Whatever stood on the ground there was blown into atoms. Twisted pieces of steel — and not many of them — remain to suggest what happened.

Of the 25 storage houses which a few hours ago stretched a mile along Black Tom's Island and the filled-in ground that connected it with the mainland only four and a half are left. One great concrete grain elevator stands also, but its interior is ruined and there is doubt if the walls can be used again.

There is a likelihood, in the opinion of firemen and officials, that all the dead will never be accounted for. The explosion that destroyed the cars and buildings and excavated the acres of land, without doubt blew some workmen to bits.

The bodies of such as were blown into the bay will appear again in a few days.

The Jersey City police have drawn a line about the approaches to the scene of the explosion through which no one can pass without giving a good account of himself. A score of policemen remained at the scene under Lieutenant Shugrue all night and this morning their places were taken by others under Inspector Lennan.

The salvage of millions of dollars' worth of merchandise began early when C. E. Jacobs, general supervisor of the department of bridges and buildings of the Lehigh Valley railroad, arrived with three work trains and five hundred laborers. He first looked after $2,000,000 worth of wheat, which remained in barges beside the ruined grain elevator.

His forces will be increased by 500 more men within a few hours.

He said that in the destroyed warehouses $5,000,000 worth of Havana tobacco consigned to Germany was stored. This tobacco was to have been shipped abroad as soon as war conditions would permit.

Boss Schuyler stopped there and removed his specs, filled his glass once more and said, "I want you men to get back there and see what you can do. Everything else here can be put on hold. Most of it can't be unloaded at the docks now anyway; we're going to have to send some of this freight down to Elizabeth tomorrow to get it on its way to France. I'll work out the schedule and we'll get on it first thing tomorrow. Get going lads."

With that he picked up the bottle and wandered back to his office.

"I heard that they thought they had the guys who did it. What's that he said about the men were subordinates?" Pete wanted to know.

Nicky shook his head, saying, "That's malarkey. They were blaming a few of the guards because they had some smudge pots lit for the mosquitoes. Everybody does that; we've never had any problem."

"Yar," Ollie joined in. "Smudge pots on one end of Black Tom would not explain the fuel tanks at the opposite end going up in a fireball. That's sounded strange to me as well."

"Yea," Nick agreed. "And that bit about the government secret service looking into those violations, cheesh, you'll find violations all over the place on the docks. We do it ourselves!"

Pete laughed at that, saying, "Lenny's got the books covered with our Fords and supplies, but I hope they don't sniff out the White Lightning!"

"Oh, they've got their hands full, and then some, from Black Tom, so I don't think we've got to worry." said Ollie. "What's really got them concerned is that *Johnson* barge – she was loaded with 100,000 pounds of TNT and over 400 cases of blasting caps. Without papers for that lot, she really had no right to be there, and they'll nail that captain for sure."

"They think he's dead."

"What, Nick?"

"I heard the captain never left the barge," Nick replied. "He's gone to smithereens, I expect."

Ollie shook his head, saying, "I imagine he was awaiting a tug to get underway. Probably never felt a thing."

Pete finished his drink, standing as he did so, and suggested, "Well, speaking about getting underway, we'd better 'weigh anchor' ourselves. How about we take three of the Fords in case we need to give some of the men rides back into town?"

38

The Black Swamp: Monday, 7/31/16

LENNY DROPPED VINCE OFF AT the foot of Communipaw and continued to the National Docks office farther south, hoping to get updates on the lists of employees there. He said he'd swing back to pick him up, "In about twenty minutes." The docks were a mess; shattered glass and splintered wood lay everywhere. The smell of charred beams and burnt creosote were heavy in the air. Smoke was rising from piles of debris, and men were carrying items seemingly every-which-way. The air was still and hot, and many workers were shirtless and sweating profusely. Steam was escaping from burnt timbers jutting haphazardly into the river. Flotsam lay all over the surface of the Hudson, some of it identifiable, most of it not. A few cargo ships lay at anchor farther off in the bay, but smaller craft were carefully picking their way through the larger obstacles.

Black Tom itself, originally a grassy, hardscrabble island connected to the mainland by landfill, was now reduced to a huge crater of a couple dozen acres slowly filling in with water from New York Bay. Spectators were lining the river edge watching the activity, pointing, and speculating amongst themselves.

Vince sauntered over to a knot of policemen gathered behind wooden barricades. Two of the cops gave him a curious once-over and blocked his way as he approached. He folded back his lapel and showed them his Pinkerton badge, said, "Morning, fellers," and walked on over to an officer with gold braid on his cap. The man looked up to see what this latest interruption was but launched into a broad smile as Vince Malloy said, "Well, Frankie Monahan, as I live and breathe!"

Frank exclaimed, "Vince! Of all people!" and the men embraced. The policemen gathered around smiled at the sight of the Jersey City Chief of Police getting a bear hug from the stranger with the Pinkerton badge but taking him as a brother-in-arms, went about their business and resumed their conversations as if Vince had not appeared.

"How long has it been, buddy?"

"Oh, I'd say about seventeen years."

"Kettle Hill, wasn't it, or that damned valley?"

"It was Kettle, all right, after that counterattack. You Parker's guys fired the Gatling's down from the heights and busted it up. We met in the middle taking those prisoners, what few of them were left."

"Yes, that was some fight," said Chief Monahan, "but it was the three days in San Juan getting drunk together I remember most!"

Vince added, "I sort of remember that naked gal on the horse the most, unless I'm making that up!"

"Oh no, that was real, come to think of it. Never got her name, though."

"We ought to do it again soon, Frankie, once things begin to fall into place around here, eh?"

"You bet, Vince," he replied, laughing. "OK then, let me guess, you're looking into this disaster for the agency?"

Vince answered, "Well, I'm retired now but still doing things locally for the firm. In this case, I'm working with the railroad and am trying to track down one of its missing men; name of August Landesmann."

"Don't know him, bud. That's a new one to me. To be honest, we're looking at quite a few fellows with German names. Any reason to suspect this one?"

"Oh no, not at all, Frank. August is a friend and a man I can vouch for. We think he was on the wharf shortly before the main explosions but may have gotten out on a motorcycle. I need to talk to the guards who were on duty that night. Mind if I ask around?"

"Go anywhere you like, Vince, but let me get one of the boys over here first." The Chief put his hand up to the side of his mouth and hollered a command over the noisy throng, "Shugrue, get over here, wouldja?"

A tall, thin man with black curly hair and a dapper blue uniform with polished brass buttons and a Sam Browne belt approached and saluted.

"Yes, Chief?"

"Lieutenant, this is Vince Malloy. He's with the Pinkertons, but he's also an old friend of mine. He needs to talk to that bunch of guards we've got rounded up in the diner. Vince, this is Lieutenant Shugrue. He'll show you around."

"Thanks, Frank. I appreciate it. Hey, I should have asked, did you lose any men in this event?"

"Yea, well, we've got Patrolman Doherty in the hospital listed as critical; suffered some severe blows to the head during the explosions. Poor lad doesn't look like he'll make it. Plus, we've got five men banged up a bit, but they'll be back on duty in another day or two. Then the Lehigh Valley folks lost their Chief Leyden, but you must already know about him."

Vince nodded his head slowly, saying, "Yes, in fact I knew him well; sad loss."

The lieutenant offered, "A half-dozen civilians are confirmed dead, too, and the barge captain. Plus, an untold number may be missing. Yet, it could have been much worse."

"And that's a fact, Robert," agreed the Chief. Shugrue beamed at his commander's use of his given name.

There was a commotion behind them then, with someone calling, "Oh Chief, Chief Monahan!"

Vince peered over his shoulder, then turned back and took his old comrade's hand, saying, "All right then, Frank. I'll catch up with you later."

The Chief nodded and then turned to greet a man in a dark suit and top hat accompanied by a lady of some advanced age.

The lieutenant extended his hand, saying, "Sir, shall we go see the guards now?"

"Name's Vince, lieutenant," he replied, giving a firm handshake. "First thing, has anyone mentioned seeing a man on a motorcycle in the area that night?"

"Ah, the man on fire."

"What's that?"

Shugrue pointed down Communipaw and said, "Two of the guards mentioned seeing a man on a motorcycle tearing down the blazing wharf through the explosions. Said he was on fire himself! Riding like the devil, he was."

"Well, I'll be damned," Vince rubbed his chin and looked where the officer pointed. "It's got to be him! Did they say which way he was going?"

The lieutenant pulled out his notebook and flipped through to the last page of notations and read, "South, he made a left here and headed south toward the swamps below us. Nobody knows what became of him."

"Well, let's get on down there, Robert. The guards can wait. Can you spare a few men?"

"You can have two patrolmen, sir, but I'm responsible for the rest of this detail and have a lot to handle right here. Best I can do."

Shugrue called two men over and was giving them instructions when Lenny arrived at the river's edge and hit the *ah-oogah* horn. Vince had the two officers climb in the rear of the ambulance as he explained their mission. He joined Lenny up front and pointed the way south. Len opened the throttle slowly and began the difficult maneuvering around people, debris, horse carts, and firehoses. A few minutes later they cleared the main area of the wreckage and picked up some speed, yet it was still necessary to be cautious. The Ford bounced over boards, bricks, and broken glass laying about. Soon they made it to the end of the cobblestones and onto a dirt road snaking its way along the riverbank through saltwater ponds edged with cattails, railroad tracks, piles of coal, and groups of white birch or sumac trees. Vince ordered a halt and climbed out of the car to get a look at the blackened earth before them. He called to the officers to join him as he searched for fresh tire tracks in the soil. He could see the dual tracks of a truck that had passed recently; the rain in the ruts put them a few days old, when there had been a storm. Quite a few horses had clomped by, too. But hey! Here was a solo track with a tread of diamonds that had to be a motorbike (and not a bicycle), since there was enough weight on the machine to press almost an inch into the soft loam. No rainwater appeared in it anywhere, so it was a recent print.

"Men, I'll follow this track; you go to the right and left of this path and see if you can't find anything similar coming onto this trail. If so, call out. Len, follow me slowly."

Vince hunched over slightly and began walking at a good clip, since there was an unmistakable track to read. When it disappeared in a pile of cinders that locomotives had dumped, he merely hastened across the coal dust until the tread pattern reappeared beyond it. He carried on this way until Lenny gave a shout while braking to a stop, yelling, "Hey, will ya look at that!"

Vince looked over at what Lenny was pointing to and saw a strange sight: two possums were balanced on something off to the right ahead, sticking out of a salt marsh. The grass and weeds leading up to the pool were burned to a crisp; only the cattails and reeds rising out of the water were still living, although somewhat wilted, bent, or broken. A small island lay in the middle of the water, festooned with a group of white birch trees; several of them were split into multiple trunks.

"What the hell?" said Vince, who hastened his pace and left the path for the pond's edge. Lenny hopped down and ran over to join him. The two men gazed at the varmints, who suddenly got uncomfortable with their presence and froze in position.

"That's a motorcycle wheel," stated Lenny, as he began walking into the swamp water.

Vince called to the patrolmen "Over here, fellers, we think we're close!" Then added, "Be careful, Len, she might be deep."

Lenny didn't care; he went up to his waist, stumbled once and sank to his chin, but arose dripping and continued to the jutting wheel. No longer feigning death, the possums bared their teeth and began hissing, arching their backs. Vince fired a pistol shot into the air and the animals dove into the water to escape. Lenny grabbed ahold of the wheel and shifted it to the right. He pushed the floating duckweed away and felt around below the water and exclaimed, "It's an Indian, all right. Front wheel. I can feel the handlebars and the headlight. The paint on the wheel forks is olive drab." He felt around with his feet. "I don't feel anybody stuck underneath it. He's got to be around here someplace!"

The two patrol officers arrived, and Vince directed them to search the environs surrounding the pool. Then he told Len "I'm headed over to that island."

Wading into the water he thought Len replied, "Things change."

"What, Len?"

"I didn't say anything."

Shaking his head, he continued to the small spit of land in the middle of the pond and heard the word, "Amen."

Rushing ahead through the water he peered among the birch trunks and saw a muddy pair of blue-overall clad legs sticking out among the reeds. "Lenny! Lenny! I found him!"

Lenny lunged through the water in a race to the small island, but Vince was already at the body lying there, probing, listening and finally yelling out in excitement, "He's alive! He's alive!"

39

The Cleaning Lady:
Friday, 8/4/16

I WAS ALIVE ALL RIGHT, but I wasn't going to be doing much moving around for a while on my own two feet, what with the cast on my right leg. "Fracture," the doctor said, "in both the tibia and fibula." They gave me some codeine the first few days to ease the pain but pulled me off it this morning because I must start walking with crutches. As for my head still throbbing, he said it was a moderate concussion that will settle down in a week to ten days if I get a lot of rest. Well, I ain't going anywhere anytime soon, so what the hell, I'll rest up. I didn't feel much like eating, which got everyone concerned. Plus, I was getting dizzy when I tried to read the paper. I didn't tell anybody that or they'd keep me here longer.

One day Doc Johnson brought in a special doctor from Vienna who now works across the river in New York City. He is supposed to be tops in head injuries. This fellow examined me, all the while saying, "Tut, tut, tut."

Curious, I asked him, "Tut what, Doc?"

"Oh, nothing. I just like to say that; it gets the patients anxious."

"Anxious?" I thought that was weird, so I added, "Do you mean, like, worried?"

He smiled and answered while scratching his back heavily with his fingernails, "No, I'm not worried."

"Excuse me?" I wondered, and had to ask, "Not worried about what?" I thought it was a fair question, considering one of us was getting confused.

He took a pocket comb out and, opening his top two shirt buttons, he loosened his tie and reached down the back of his shirt, scratching vigorously with the comb. Sated, he put the comb back into his pocket, looked me dead-on and replied, "There, does that feel better?"

Was this guy nuts? Or was it me? I asked him flat out, "Doctor, is there something wrong with me?"

"Well, *ja*," he said. "You have two contusions on your forehead, one small, one large. The bigger one was from the motorcycle handlebar striking the hard, boney surface of your skull just above your left eye. The other was a bit higher up, on the same side, and is not as bad. However, if that handlebar hit you a half inch lower, you would have lost the sight in one eye; maybe both."

"What?" I exclaimed, and added, "Holy shit!" That was as serious as it gets.

"*Ja*," replied the doctor from Vienna, nodding his head, "shit."

Then he got quite serious, and said, "You will have to take it easy to prevent dizziness. Rest is the most important thing right now, but it's also vital that you start eating the way you did before the explosion. It's natural for the body to suppress hunger after trauma, and you've been through a lot the past few days. The brain will swell from blows like you've gotten, which explains the pain you're feeling. A flow of nutrients can help things improve. Having no appetite is no excuse for not giving fuel to your engine."

"OK," I put up my hands and responded. "I'll eat, I'll eat." Then I asked, "Will it help the pain in my head?"

The doctor shook his own head, saying, "It won't make the pain go away quickly, I'm afraid. But, once you do start sleeping well, you'll find it settles down a bit, quite a bit. The key thing to remember," he went on, "is to do your best not to get hit in the head by anything further. If you keep getting injured to this extent, you may become susceptible to blackouts, for longer and longer periods, and may even suffer from brain damage, which is *ir-reversible*!"

I nodded, deep in thought; it's not every day you learn you may become dumber than you are right now. Finally, I had enough, and asked, "Doc, how do we deal with this terrible hangover I've got?"

"Ah," he smiled. "Take two aspirin with meals, and rest."

I did so when he left and washed 'em down with a flask of White Lightning Nicky gave me.

I'd also gotten some 1st degree burns on my left shoulder and back, but they weren't so bad once they got them cleaned and plastered up. I recall my sleeve was on fire and I was reaching over to pat it out as I escaped the pier. Evidently, winding up in the brackish water put it out and cooled my skin both.

From what the boys told me, I had been out cold for about a day and a half. I could remember riding the Indian off the wharf, through the explosions and all, but then it fizzles out. I get glimpses of snow and a campfire, of all things. Must be something I remember from when I was young, you know? I was surprised to hear that the Indian's saddle bags were ablaze through the ride; the cleaning rags and chemicals inside them having caught fire. This gave some folks the impression I was a human rocket! Imagine that?

Later, I found myself sitting in a wheelchair looking out the window at the Hudson River from the Hoboken side, smoking a cigarette and reading the Jersey Journal. It turned out one of the cops died the day before, fellow name of Doherty. Only twenty-eight years old, damn. Makes you wonder, it does. I mean, I was lucky getting off that wharf when I did. Had that barge gone up when I was still at Karl's warehouse? I hated to think of it. I guess I would have been blown to "Kingdom come," as they say. Hmmm, like in that prayer, "Thy Kingdom come, Thy will be done." I guess it wasn't God's will that I suddenly disappear like that after all.

I lit another cigarette and pondered the immortal question: Why was I here? I could have been snuffed out like a candle. Well, maybe not a candle — sometimes they smolder a bit when you try to put them out and can even relight themselves. Not like Doherty, the poor soul. He lingered a few days — but he's gone. His flame extinguished. Why him and not me? Why the barge captain, or Chief Leyden from the railroad, but not a dumb guy who let a bunch of geese out of their cages just as the barge was about to blow?

It would have been more like flicking off an electric light switch. On, off, on, off. Alive, dead. And I wouldn't even know it happened, it would have been that quick. I'd never get to say good-bye to anyone, never get to thank Mom and Pop for every little thing, never get to tell Molly that I love her. Love her? Where did that come from? I love her. I guess I did!

She had no idea I was here and that was fine. She'd be back from the mountains in a few days and Lenny would bring her by to see me. They must have seen the papers by now, even in the Poconos. I wished she were here right now talking with me and holding my hand. I'd tell her how I feel. What she means to me.

Why was I still here then? Mom always liked to say, "Everything happens for a reason." But what kind of world did we live in where something like this catastrophe could happen? I hung my head and simply thought it over. Hmmm. Well, there was a great war raging, that's why. Yea, that's a reason. But what kind of reason could there be for me to still be alive but that ten-month-old baby I just read about could be thrown from its crib by the same explosion and break her neck?

I shook my head and reached for another cigarette. Damn, the last one? I crumpled the empty pack and tossed it into the pail but held off on lighting the butt for a spell. Staring out across the river at the city on the opposite side, I made a mental note to ask one of the boys to get me some more smokes. Then I laughed, and thought, *Hah, too bad about all Karl's tobacco, huh?* I could use some of that right now.

I thought back to the tobacco fires in the warehouse I had squirted down with the extinguishers. The flames, the smoke, getting hit on the head — it was all a jumble. There were shells going off on that dock, with some of them flying up into the air and exploding in star-shapes. There was a lot of rifle ammunition firing off from the heat, too. It now occurred to me what was causing all that zip-zipping sound after I escaped the burning warehouse — had to be bullets flying all about. I could have been killed! Well, I wasn't. But I could have been hurt! Well, I was, yet I was alive. I was alive.

If it all happens for a reason, I guess I was going to find out why one day.

Was it because I was supposed to marry Molly, raise a family, work the docks, and live a long life? If so, maybe I had enough flames and explosions for one lifetime. Could it be that volunteering to drive an ambulance over there just seemed like a good thing to do at the time? Perhaps working at the French ports would be a better usage of my talents instead?

Nah, that was Lenny-type work. I wouldn't want to do that. Maybe I should just keep working here, forget the volunteering nonsense.

Yeah, but that was chickenshit. How could I do that if Molly was going to France to treat the wounded and sick? "Bye, dear girl, and have a care. I'll load these ships here and help keep the world safe for democracy!" Yeah, right.

It could be that whatever the reason, it might have something to do with driving an ambulance over there. Everything pointed to it. I just wasn't sure, is all. Mom and Pop might have some thoughts on it. I wished I could talk it over with Pop alone, because I felt funny bringing it up in front of Mom, who never liked my idea of volunteering. I was glad I didn't talk about it when they were just here. I had better plan that for next time they visited because it had to come out.

Well, this might be the last smoke for a while, but I'd held up long enough. I struck a wooden match on my cast, lit the cigarette, and took a long drag.

I thought again of my parents. It was great to see them. They both hugged me, and brought a whole bowl of fruit, some chocolate, and a couple boxes of crackers. Mom couldn't stop crying; Pop looked relieved. I'll never know what went through their minds when I was missing. I guess I'd have to raise a kid myself one day and start going through all that grief they hand you to get some sort of idea. I calmed her down by pointing out that, "It could have been worse, like that poor barge captain, or those two policemen." She nodded and sniffled a bit into a hanky. She's looking forward to me being home a few days and I'll straighten her out.

Earlier, Vince brought the good news that Mr. Pisser was locked up. He stopped by this morning with an Inspector named Lennan from Jersey City and Captain Rigney of the Bayonne P.D. and told me the details of the arrest: The night of the explosions, Kristoff's landlady heard him moaning in his room. She's a distant relative, so she had no problem going into the room to check on him. She goes in there and he's sitting on the bed, on the side of the bed, running his fingers through his dirty hair, all the while saying, "What I do? What I do?" So, this lady, Mrs. Rushnak, talks it over with her daughter and they remember the guy coming home late most nights, sometimes smelling like fuel, or having soot stains on his hands or clothes. They go to the cops and he gets picked right up, just like that. When they interrogated him, he talked about some accomplices. They're not through with him by a long shot, and I couldn't be happier.

Vince had me tell the cops how Pisser pulled a gun on me that night he stole the Ford. Oh, I filled them in all right, and thought, "I hope they nail his ass to the wharf."

Ollie stopped in the day before and we shared a few nice Jersey Tomatoes that he grew in the garden next to his shed. We ate 'em like apples and I got juice all over my hospital night shirt. He was telling me how they tracked me down in the burnt swamp and how there were those possums that helped point the way. "Remember our talk in the Yards that evening? We talked at length of nature and agreed that sparing the life of even such a creature may have an impact one day? Well, I'm not saying one of these was the same possum, but you must admit, there could be some force at work here!"

I agreed that there was something weird there, but hey, the Jersey Meadows is like one big, living being. She was merely taking care of one of her own.

He went on to tell me how they retrieved the water-logged Indian and how he was going to approach taking her apart to see what he could do about cleaning her up. "Without some replacement parts, I'm not sure I can ever get her up to speed like before."

"That's ok with me," I let him know. I didn't much feel like riding one of those anymore. I'd stick to four wheels from now on.

"Don't tell me you're through riding motorcycles after one small mishap?"

"Mishap?" I replied. "Are we talking about the same fellow here?"

"Well, my good man, if one falls off a horse he really ought to climb right back up, right? Did your father not ever tell you that? It's all part of our growth as humans."

"Ollie," I stated sternly, "from what I recall, my growth as a human was nearly ended on that thing!" *He was right, though — Pop often said that to me about falling off a horse.*

Since he looked upset at that retort, I relented, saying, "But, to please you, I will climb back up on her if and only if you get her working good as new."

There, I thought I'd got him, as I was pretty sure that even Ollie Olson's magic had its limits. From the way he smiled at that, nodded affirmatively, and continued that big grin of his as he left the room, I began to have second thoughts.

I stubbed out my cigarette and, finished with the paper, folded it up and tossed it into the pail by the lamp table as I rolled myself past. It missed and fell on the tile floor, coming apart in sections. "Damn," I muttered, halted, and made a clumsy attempt to turn around by manipulating just the left wheel with my hand, conscious of my right leg sticking straight outward.

"I get, mister," came a woman's voice from across the room. As I turned to see its owner, I was startled by a white-haired lady with a mop and bucket in her hands walking my way. This was strange because I could have sworn I had been alone. Yet, you could see she had been there for a while, quietly mopping the tile floor on the other side of the room. She put the pail down and leaned the mop against the wall, then went and picked up the paper for me.

"Sorry, I meant to throw it away, but missed." I wasn't quite myself yet, it would appear.

"Oh, yes, yes. I trow-in," she said as she folded it up and tossed in it the basket.

"Thank you, Ma'am." I managed. "I didn't want to leave it on the floor and trip someone."

"Is good, is better. People fallen down all time and get broken, like you. You had fallen down?"

"Oh, I fell down all right. Fell off a motorcycle and yup, I got broken." She sounded Polish. "*Dzięki* (pronounced *Jenn-koo-yeh*)," I added, which is "Thanks" in Polish.

"No *Polpolska*," she replied. "*Ash Lituvisk.*"

"Ah," I understood. "Lithuanian, how nice." We had all sorts of folks living in the neighborhood. The Lithvaks got along with the Polocks who got along with the Micks who got along with the Krauts and Yidds, who got along with the I-ties and Frogs who, well, you get the picture. We had a regular polyglot of expressions at our fingertips, along with lots of good food from all the European countries, the music, the dances. I lived in a great neighborhood.

"You, German make it?"

"Yes, but we came to America twenty years ago. I don't remember much from when I was little. Mom and Pop still speak it at home, but I don't, unless they include me in their discussion."

"Well, you should speaky. No, you forget it, no forget it. Is good speaky English and old country."

"Why, yes, I suppose you're right. Well, I only speak it when Pop or Mom talk to me, but not anywhere else. With this war on, who knows? Maybe I should not speak it anymore at all. This war is bad."

"Yes, war is no good. No good. Too many die. French bad, German bad, English bad, Russkie bad. Nobody good in this war. America good. America not in war, yes?"

"No, America is not in the war, but we will be soon, I think."

"If America in war, America only good one in war. Only America good."

This was interesting. I had to ask her. "Why do you think only America would be good if we got into this war?"

"What?"

I rephrased it: "If America in war, why only America good one in war?"

"Oh, because America good people. All of us good people. We no fight and taken cows. We not fight and taken houses. We helps peoples. I work in church. We given food to peoples. We given clothes to peoples. All America is good, no?"

I had to smile, and said, "Well, many Americans are good. We are a good country. We do help people and you're right; we don't attack and take cows or houses from people. I guess if we do go to war, we will try to be good."

"Yes, mister. If America is in war, we will be good for peoples."

This was helping me feel better already. I was smiling, anyway. I had to ask her name.

She answered, "My name Hebruka Masotovich, but please my name, call me Bobci."

"Yes, Bobci, I will. And my name is August Landesmann. Please call me August."

"August! Is a good name. Thank you, August. I go now, I mop."

"All right, Bobci. It was nice to meet you and thank you for talking to me."

She left her mop to go dump the bucket and get more water, I guess. She gave me a little wave.

Now that I had a chance to discuss the war situation with a fellow citizen who shared my views about America and our place in the world, my mind was made up. If I went to war, I would be good. I would be good for peoples. I would drive an ambulance.

I smiled to myself and wheeled the chair back to my room for some well-deserved rest.

~*FIN*~

About the Author

B ORN AND RAISED IN HUDSON COUNTY, NJ, Rich worked the past twenty-two years for the City of New York, just two blocks from the WTC site. He watched the resurrection of the neighborhood, making friends of all stripes while doing his own small part. The father of three great kids, he spends weekends in the Pocono Mountains of PA with Patty, his wonderful wife of forty-eight years.

www.hellgatepress.com